Venus Blue

Venus Blue

A NOVEL

Gustaf Sobin

LITTLE, BROWN AND COMPANY
BOSTON   TORONTO   LONDON

I WISH TO EXPRESS MY DEEPEST GRATITUDE
TO HARRIS SOBIN, PETER ANSIN, AND MICHAEL IGNATIEFF
FOR THEIR CONTINUOUS SUPPORT AND ENCOURAGEMENT.
G. S.

FIRST U. S. EDITION

THE CHARACTERS AND EVENTS IN THIS BOOK ARE FICTITIOUS.
ANY SIMILARITY TO REAL PERSONS, LIVING OR DEAD, IS
COINCIDENTAL AND NOT INTENDED BY THE AUTHOR.

Library of Congress Cataloging-in-Publication Data

Sobin, Gustaf.
    Venus Blue : a novel / Gustaf Sobin. — 1st U.S. ed.
        p.   cm.
    ISBN 0-316-80255-7
    I. Title.
PS3569.037V46   1992
813'.54—dc20   91-3284

10 9 8 7 6 5 4 3 2 1

RRD VA

PRINTED IN THE UNITED STATES OF AMERICA

In loving memory of my mother,
Rena Pearl

PART ONE
(Stefan Hollander, 1989)

THIS IS MILLICENT'S STORY, then, rather than mine. It's mine only to the extent that I've preserved what she'd written — jotted down, anxiously — in a tall, black, box-calf journal exactly half a century earlier. I've preserved and, where I could, elaborated on that erratic narrative she'd compiled, amassed out of so many bits and pieces, out of every scrap of hearsay, every unverified, unverifiable rumor that touched upon the presence of that elusive and apparently unqualifiable creature, Molly Lamanna. For Molly, it would seem, was always "elsewhere." She was always beyond, or behind, or either side of anything that might possibly be said about her. In Millicent's eyes, she was the essence of myth itself, a modern icon of sorts who'd continually vanish from the very blaze — "the burning, spike-headed aureole" — that she so unwittingly generated. One might even say that the less substantiated Molly became, the higher, the fiercer that blaze grew. And, in turn, the more consumed, or — in the language of the times — hallucinated Millicent became.

Millicent recorded this "blaze," this fever, assiduously. Her journal, in fact, might be read as an attempt to control or, at least, contour her own feelings with a kind of breathless verbiage; to shape, through any available image, any scavenged detail, the edgelessness of her own predicament. An earring would do. Or a description of one of Molly's thick, tortoise-shell combs, studded with a burst of blue rhinestones and stuck, at what Millicent might call "a savage angle," into Molly's high, piled, and now coroneted hair. This, at least, according to Millicent, could be described. This, at least, could be *said*.

Or occasionally she'd glean a phrase, a quote, some cherished utterance of the vanished icon herself. These, immediately, took on all the properties, densities of artifact. They'd emanated out of conversations (heard and overheard), or interviews, or — increasingly — out of those very earliest feature articles in magazines such as *Modern Screen* and *Photoplay* devoted to Molly's "rapidly rising star." Hadn't she been quoted, for instance, as saying: "I'm not altogether certain that being in Hollywood isn't exactly like being anywhere else. I haven't yet noticed differences, *essential* differences, that is."

Or, when asked by an interviewer what she most sought in life, hadn't she replied — without hesitation — "exits."

This, then, was the kind of ephemera that Millicent fed on. These were her morsels, her tidbits. Yet, meager as they might appear, they provided her with the running, albeit sporadic, substance of her journal. They were, ultimately, what Millicent "possessed." They represented everything about Molly she'd managed to gather, and hold, and shore, in a tight menagerie of images, against the sustained and wordless immensity of her own unfettered adulation.

Early on, Millicent's husband, Sidney (perhaps foreseeing a "situation" that Millicent already considered foregone, even irreparable), had said, as if in passing, that the whole aura, the whole mystery surrounding Molly — what she cast about her as nonchalantly as a perfume, or dragged behind like some exhausted stole — all of it "would vanish, volatilize, with one single, well-written paragraph." And that Millicent, better than anyone, could write that paragraph. That even with a single, perfectly observant, penetrating remark, Millicent could clear the air. Could bring Molly out of that vapid mist she seemed to thrive on, and into some kind of perspective. That Millicent could "shape" Molly: could press, mold her — on language alone — into something palpable, plausible, true.

Then, changing the subject as simply, imperceptibly, as he'd broached it, one might imagine Sidney, now, talking about the day's takes at the Studio, or the problems of "fabricating palms" for an upcoming extravaganza. Or closer, more immediate, one might picture him tending to his wife in any number of small, solicitous ways. Hadn't he said — and repeatedly — that he was happiest in moments like that: mixing her some tall, tropical concoction, or massaging the long, slender tendons — the "pampered wings" — of Millicent's shoulders.

"*One single, well-written paragraph,*" Millicent repeated, entered into her journal on almost certainly that very same day. "*As if,*" she went on, "*there were words for that rush, that flutter, that immensity. As if one could verbalize on light itself, could twist it into so many sharp, incisive syllables.*"

Then, probably in a quick, impetuous scribble, and in a paragraph of its own (as brief, punctual, as a cloudburst), she'd added: "*Reduce her to a phrase? If only I could.*"

This, then, is Millicent's story: what Millicent wrote about Molly in 1939, and kept — covetously — in the tall, black, box-calf journal. The journal, however, went on to lead a curious and somewhat autonomous existence of its own. A number of years later, in 1959, acting on some still obscure motive, Millicent decided to publish its entire contents in a very private, very limited edition. She must have quite deliberately chosen to print twenty-five copies, that being the minimum number necessary for securing a copyright. As a title, Millicent had the initials M.L. printed on both the title page and — foil-stamped — on the binding's blue spine. The book itself, hand set in Bembo and run off on thick Fabriano stock, was printed by a small vanity press on the outskirts of Santa Barbara. On the same day as its publication (the same day, that is, the commissioned work was delivered and, upon delivery, paid for in cash), two of the twenty-five copies, along with the necessary applications, were duly shipped, registered mail, to the Library of Congress. Then, slightly over a month later, and on the very morning Millicent received, in return, her Certificate of Copyright, she invited her private secretary, a Miss N.T., into her living room. There, with the secretary serving as witness, she proceeded to burn — in an open fireplace — not only the original handwritten pages of her journal, but all except one of the twenty-three printed copies still in her possession. Nothing was said, not a word. And no reason was given. No reason needed to be given. Miss N.T.'s function, clearly enough, was exclusively ocular.

Remained, then, the three copies: one in Millicent's possession and two at the Library of Congress. These — the Library's copies — scarcely a month after having been registered, classified, and ranged on their appropriate shelf, as might be expected — predicted, even — vanished. No one would doubt, today, that this wasn't Millicent's doing, that one of the Studio's innumerable agents hadn't simply lifted the two slender volumes and hand delivered them, a day later and on the opposite coast, to their author. Nor would anyone doubt that the two copies, in the witnessing presence of Miss N.T., didn't suffer the same obliterating fate as their predecessors. A few curls of smoke, catching in a Santa Ana, and the copies were gone, absolved in the dry, ambulant, late-summer light.

Remained, now, the last and unique copy, the copy-elect, the one for which all others had been deliberately sacrificed. This was the one, clearly, that mattered, the copy patently intended (and still legally protected) for the sake of a single, exclusively privileged reader. Because Millicent, it seemed, was putting "her affairs in order," preparing her estate (from her own considerable holdings down to her least scarf and platinum stickpin) against what could still be called "all eventuality." A cancer, diagnosed half a year earlier, had begun spreading its pale, pestilent fire — a bit quicker with each week — throughout her lower intestines, and Millicent was laboring, but without desperation, to stay on the far side of that particular interval which, with each day, could only diminish, contract. Few, aside from those treating her, knew of her condition, and Sidney, whom she'd been separated from for a number of years now, had no idea whatsoever. One can only imagine him, in such circumstances, rushing to his wife, whatever differences they may have had. He, however, wasn't informed. Millicent preferred managing things in a kind of refined silence of her own. She went about her affairs each day with a cool, unruffled dispatch, clearing, clarifying, eliminating and, most especially, designating. For when she died in the summer of 1960, alone and in a large apartment facing the sea, nothing whatsoever remained in her name except for the contents of a flat safe-deposit box in a large, downtown Los Angeles bank.

A month after her death, in the presence of her attorneys, the bank seals were broken, and the box opened. The box contained, aside from a bit of jewelry and a copy of her will, a quite sizeable fortune in government and municipal certificates (assets, for the most part, she'd brought to her marriage so many years earlier), and, of course, the single remaining copy, bound in flamboyant sapphire, of her journal, *M.L.*

The entire estate (the journal, thus, included) was left in the trusteeship of Millicent's Los Angeles lawyers for the sole benefit of her own rightful heir: a certain Luis deSaumerez. His address, as indicated in the will ("care of General Delivery, Main Post Office, Tallahassee, Florida"), did little to dispel the suspicions that immediately gathered — like so many shadows — about the quick, piston-like sibilations of the beneficiary's name. No one, in fact, had ever heard of Luis deSaumerez, and those closest to Millicent were the first to express a kind of suspended incredulity. Then, too, there were those quick to interpret, to offer their own gratuitous assumptions. Gossip, for at least several months, was — as they say — "rampant." Most of the stories, naturally enough, suggested some kind of erotic liaison, a "late flowering" in Millicent's life, even though everything inherent in her character — a certain puritanical rigor, and a marked penchant for solitude — indicated otherwise. Much of the gossip, certainly, was fueled by the name alone, by everything "Luis deSaumerez" suggested of crescent moons and maracas, of glass dance floors and gardenias floating on the placid surface of fingerbowls. The rumors, by extension, grew more and more explicit. Every kind of "arrangement" was evoked, as were so many nights and so many long, torrid weekends at "such and such places" along the coast, and all in exchange for a slender envelope or a dangling pair of mint, glistening car keys.

The rumors, though, as rumors will, began to subside, dissipate, after a certain number of months, victims themselves, perhaps, of their own fabulations. Other rumors — in a second wave of whispers, muted attributions — considerably more intricate, complex, and certainly more plausible, replaced them. But, being less sensational, they foundered, in turn, all the quicker. They seemed to dissolve, *ipso facto*, into the very air in which, a few weeks earlier, they'd been so eagerly — even triumphantly — released.

Finally, with time, nothing outwardly remained of the whole episode except for a few, loose, still floating threads: the remnants, no doubt, of a once rabid mystification. Quietly, though, and infallibly, Millicent's trust fund continued to function. On the fifth day of each month, month after month, year after year, a check (an elongated jade rectangle with three of its four edges as finely serrated as a minute, high-frequency oscillation) was sent to whatever General Delivery address Luis deSaumerez had last happened to indicate. The addresses, it would seem, kept changing. From Tallahassee (after four years) to Panama City (for three); then, just as slowly, across Alabama, Mississippi, Louisiana, Texas and the Southwest, deSaumerez — it would appear — was locked into a slow, relentless odyssey westward. Then, too, not only did his own addresses keep changing, and continuously, but early on, in 1964, that of the lawyers did, as well. Millicent's law firm, after so many years of respected, respectable practice, closed and passed on its entire clientele to a new, heterogeneous organization which, almost immediately, acquired a somewhat ruthless reputation for its immensely subtle — and immensely successful — deformation of basic statute.

None of this, however, kept the checks (the monthly "distributions") from coming, month after month; nor, year after year, Luis deSaumerez (presumably with the one copy of Millicent's journal somewhere among his trundled belongings) from his slow, tellurian migration, westward.

* * *

I should add, at this point, that almost all of the foregoing material has been drawn from the archives of the Studio where Sidney (Millicent's husband) was once an associate producer. The archives, sometimes referred to as "the bone heap," not only contain the entire history of fifty years of Studio production, but anything touching upon those who — even vaguely, inadvertently — contributed to that production. Nothing, it's said, ever escapes the bone heap, not even the slightest shred of seemingly inconsequential material. So that, along with all the documents one might readily expect (all the treatments and proposals, all the scripts in various states of completion, revision, or utter abandonment, all the glossies and inventories and heated, hour-by-hour, interoffice memos), along with all of this comes an entire world, an underworld, a cryptic substratum composed of pure minutiae. Here, nothing's too small. Here, having passed down a narrow staircase and through a long, neon-lit corridor, its white file-boxes crammed, ceiling to floor, with tightly packed bundles of blue, twice-folded legal briefs, with contracts both broken and fulfilled, with the now scarcely invaded oblivion in which sleep the titles and disclaimers upon which the entire power of the Studio once rested, one comes at last to the ledgers, the account books of unit managers, the canceled checks and stubs and balance sheets. One comes, that is, to the tiniest units of trivia, to the bone heap's finest grindings. Here, meticulously recorded, are the day-to-day dolings, the tight trickles of cash, the scrupulously overseen, twice-audited outlays that might be measured (but elsewhere) against the Studio's fabulous, fabulously growing annual receipts.

Here, in fact, resides everything one might possibly need to reconstitute — even a half-century later — the daily lives of particular actors or actresses, both in their professional activities and — by an astute reading of their files, marked "strictly confidential" — their personal lives, as well. One simply needed to receive permission, a visitor's pass. Once within (or, more exactly, once under, for one didn't enter the archives: one delved, one plummeted), it wasn't so much an act of scholarship that was called for, as that, precisely, of an exhumation.

It was here, naturally enough, that I'd first come with my small, budding collection of memorabilia. I was, as they say, "specializing," collecting everything I could on the life and work of that very actress who was still, so many years after her death, referred to at the archives as "Miss Lamanna." This, in itself, was a significant tribute, a title of sorts, what collectors would call an "evidence." I'd telephoned the archives (it was sometime last September) and requested an appointment. After several secretarial "screenings," I was connected with the Curator, the Dis, the Pluto of those regions, a certain Mr. Jasper May. His tone, over the telephone, was tart, condescending, predicatory.

"I only authenticate at lunchtime," he snapped, "and even then only by rendezvous. Shall we say twelve-fifteen, Wednesday? You're perfectly prompt, I assume?" His question, clearly enough, was rhetorical: it called for no answer.

"Furthermore," he went on in a steady, imperturbable staccato, "I should forewarn you, I don't deal in artifacts. I don't speculate. I don't appraise, either, do you understand? I certify. I say 'yes' or 'no' as to the authenticity of the article in question. The article, of course, must have originated here, in our Studio. It makes no sense, I mean, presenting me with 'doodads' from Columbia, or Universal, or wherever else. We only authenticate what's ours." As he spoke, his words evoked images of those errant dignitaries, papal delegates, charged with the verification of holy relics, moving from crypt to crypt, chapel to oratory, across the entire surface of the

evangelized world. Weren't they (and long before Hollywood, before California, before America itself) invested with
the selfsame power to identify, authenticate, to tag or untag,
as the case may be, a particular splinter, or thread, or the
black knuckle of an alleged saint, the bone itself as if floating
in the windows of a gold reliquary's high, hammered shafts?

The analogies, of course, were many, and not altogether
fortuitous. Wasn't the rush of present-day collectors for anything belonging to, or reflecting, or touching upon the
radiance of their elected and — almost inevitably — extin-
guished "stars" only the modern vulgate for those earlier, ho-
lier acquisitions? Those cups? Those severed skulls? Those
femurs slick as water and gone — with age — a lacquered,
nicotine yellow? Wasn't the modern rose, plucked out of black
satin, or — quivering with light — the "mystic metal" of
some aluminum button (the unwelded scrap of a wrecked rac-
ing car), weren't these our cherished counterparts? Our con-
temporary equivalents? Weren't they exactly what we'd
chosen, driven as we are by some vestigial impulse to produce — and relentlessly — more vestige? To make, out of so
much cast-off matter, so many derelict accessories, the very
tokens of a late — and fading — mystery?

Jasper May's knowledge, or should I say "memory," was
encyclopedic. His mind seemed to move like an uninterrupted
tape, a living inventory in which every treasure in his custody
was meticulously noted. His somewhat supercilious manner
gave way — and quickly enough — the very moment he recognized me as a genuine votary, an adept of those exact same
chimeras — with their vaporous blacks, silvers and myriad
grays — as he himself. His hands moved rapidly as he spoke.
They'd dart, exultant, to an affirmation, swoon to a doubt,
collapse in perplexity. His bow tie, with its four floppy petals,
rose and fell, mimicking his every gesture like a tiny, cajoling

dwarf. I watched him now as he made his way through the small pile of glossies I'd brought, all allegedly of the ambivalent Miss Lamanna. Most of them showed her in all her heavy-haired splendor at various nightspots, or "taking the pose" at a seaside pier, or decked out in flying togs, scarf blowing from the open cockpit of a floatplane. Slipping one picture under another, smooth as playing cards, his hands moving almost as fast, now, as his glance, Jasper May could vouch, finally, for the authenticity of — perhaps — only one of them. And even that one was subject to doubt.

"Pure Hollywood," he sighed, and with him the florid dwarf at his collar, the facetious midget, as if contracted, deflated. "You see," he continued, "the instant a star emerges in these parts, you get its duplicate, its double, its dark echo. You might call it a kind of counter-star," and with this his arm stretched sideways into nothing, really, but its own fluorescent shadow. I caught the quick, pinched glitter of a cuff link.

"Exactly like the universe, don't you see," he continued, "with its negative spaces and all that. A replica, but in darkness. In utter obscurity.

"Well, within a month of the time Miss Lamanna had signed her first, twelve-month contract with the Studio, *she* appeared. Her 'other.' Or should I say: she materialized, conjured up out of heaven knows where. Central Casting, perhaps. Or, more likely, out of some beauty salon ('parlor,' she'd call it) in Spokane or Duluth. Or even likelier yet, some backwater luncheonette with a backwater newsstand just big enough to handle a magazine like *Photoplay*. And there, just then, in the September 1938 issue, I believe, she'd discover a large, glamorous spread — photos, interview and all — of that very person who'd become, maybe that very instant, the model, the prototype for her every borrowed gesture, the mannequin for her own, floating, indeterminate identity.

"Granted, there were certain basic similarities. Vivien Voigt, for that was her name, had the same facial proportions: that perfect, perfectly raised oval with its high forehead, its brows like the spread wings of a long, languorous Y or a Greek upsilon that joined invisibly over the nose, then traced a fine line downward into an exquisite pair of scarcely flaring nostrils. What a face, or, should I say: what faces. And yes, the eyes, if not the exact expression: the eyes, themselves, gray, immensely gray, and tapering either side to two, slightly pendant, slightly dolorous points. In that, one must admit, both these ladies were nearly identical."

"But look, look closer." And here, Jasper May leaned over one of the photographs and, with a lead pencil, pointed to Vivien Voigt's cheeks, first one, then the other. The picture, catching the reflection of an overhanging lamp, flashed — for an instant — like tin. "Look carefully," he said, and pointed to a tiny dimple, a minuscule crease, half-buried in each of those lustrous cheeks. It would be a first distinguishing feature, a subtle mark that would forever differentiate Vivien Voigt from Molly Lamanna, no matter what efforts the former might resort to. "And here, over here, as well." The tip of Jasper May's pencil moved smoothly over the gray, opalescent landscape of the photograph to reach Vivien Voigt's chin. Here, he pointed to a slight cleft, a nearly indiscernible "fault" in the lay of her features. This tiny, ineffaceable sign, this, as well, would separate the two women; would preserve, with a few scarcely discernible traits, their separate, physical identities.

There remained, however, an even more obscure and certainly more intriguing point of differentiation. Jasper May, clearly enough, was saving it for last. For high on Vivien Voigt's right cheek floated — like a mysterious punctuation — an exquisitely situated birthmark, a dark, irradiant star. "Here," explained the omniscient Jasper May, "here, the young lady made a serious, very serious, mistake. She'd had the birthmark burnt in artificially, exactly the same size and in the same place as that in the *Photoplay* pictures of Miss Lamanna. How could she have known that those particular photographs by Sam Haskill were taken (and this was one of Sam Haskill's professional secrets) in a floor-to-ceiling mirror? That Haskill often posed his female figures gazing into the eyes of the most absorbing, transcendent of subjects: that of themselves? How *could* she know? How could she possibly have been aware of this when she had that tiny nevus burnt into her all-too-ambitious flesh? That she was copying an inverted image? A kind of white negative? That her star had just been branded, but on the wrong side?"

"But Molly — Miss Lamanna — what was *her* attitude?" I asked, irritated by my own intrusion, by the necessity to intrude. "How did she take to the arrival of that mock double, that sham twin, coming — as you put it — out of some backwater, and landing in the midst of all this glitter?"

"Oh, she loved it," Jasper May exuded, letting the slick photographs fan across the glass surface of his table, then leaning back into the lavender recesses of his armchair. "First of all, she must have felt terrifically flattered having a 'stand-in' already, an 'understudy,' and she scarcely more than a starlet herself. Can you imagine it, at age twenty-four, twenty-five? Having a salaried look-alike? And she certainly loved (as much as she loved anything, that is) appearing in public with Vivien Voigt, going to parties together, or the beach; loved being puzzled over, being the subject — or is it the object — of a reversible identity.

"She, who had so very little use for herself, who remembered, or cared to remember, so little, must have taken an intense pleasure letting someone else be Molly Lamanna, even for the length of a quickly forgotten reception, or soirée. She seemed, in fact, to derive as much pleasure getting 'lost' in the anonymity of her understudy as the understudy did in being 'found,' 'recognized,' and 'invested' with all the notoriety of the true icon herself.

"So, she cultivated Vivien Voigt. Or, to be more accurate, she let herself be cultivated, exploited, deliberately used by that all-too-eager predator. She let her wear her clothes, and whatever jewelry she possessed, gave her the keys to her car, her apartment, whatever Vivien Voigt desired. Let her become, in fact, a kind of life-size projection. A *Doppelgänger* in the flesh. I'm quite certain she would have let Vivien Voigt drink the full length of her reflection off a wardrobe mirror, if she could have. Would have let her drain her identity, entire. And that," Jasper May remarked, "is exactly the charm and interest of these photographs," as he picked up several of the eight-by-tens I'd collected, a victim myself — half a century later — of that "reversible identity," of Molly Lamanna's casually organized masquerades. For Molly wasn't to be "collected" altogether that easily. Even at this distance, at this late date, she still perplexed, troubled, laid a kind of labyrinth in the way of anyone who'd approach her, who'd attempt to touch her existence, or the rumors that constituted — for the most part — that existence. Of anyone, that is, who got "too close."

"There are articles and interviews, of course, and passages from quite a number of biographies." And here, Jasper May proved to be immeasurably generous with his knowledge, his recorder-like memory, his punctilious hold over the archival bone heap. "But," he went on, "she entirely escapes us, and quite unlike anybody else. She escapes us not so much from what she *didn't* leave (in the way of memories, memoirs, all the so-called surviving evidence), as from what she *did*. All

that mask, those mock appearances and feigned realities, all
that deliberate, deliberately trumped-up fiction that — under
the least scrutiny — simply dissolves. Clearly, she used whatever disguises, whatever ruses were available to preserve her
own privacy. But even more, and more meaningfully, Miss
Lamanna employed every conceivable subterfuge, I'm convinced, for the sake of making her escape — her own meticulously prepared flight, outward — all the more effective. She
took the very best of herself with her, and left — left what?
Luminous peelings. An exquisite shell.

"Still, still," he continued, "we haven't abandoned all hope.
We never do, really. For eventually every bit of evidence
comes our way. All the dark, jealously guarded secrets of our
most glittering figures, all, all of it, I can assure you, ends up
in our files; comes to a close, eventually, in these carefully
ventilated catacombs. Even," he went on, "that somewhat
mythical journal of Millicent Rappaport's. What Mrs. Rappaport wrote about Miss Lamanna so many years back and
that no one, yet, has seen, aside perhaps from her invisible
heir. Everyone, however, speaks of that journal as such a treasure, a gold mine of information, an ultimate sourcebook on
the period in general, and on Miss Lamanna in particular. It
will wend its way (everything does) into these cellars, these
humidified crypts," Jasper May promised. "Of that, I'm perfectly certain."

And so, for the very first time, I heard of Millicent's journal, of its existence, of the book that would be the source and
pretext for this present work, its very innards. But that afternoon, the mere mention of the journal struck me (if it struck
at all) as some entirely minor reference to some utterly
obscure memorabilia. I wasn't in the least intrigued. That
day, in fact, I was entirely preoccupied with Jasper May's
authentications. I'd brought along with me, aside from the

photographs, a few penny postcards, signed "Molly Lamanna" (all of which Mr. May deemed, without hesitation, counterfeit); a raspberry red necktie she was reputed to have worn in her second film, *A Glance Away* (which the Curator regarded as more than dubious); and finally a medium-size, heart-shaped mirror that had also appeared in that very same film. In one of its few memorable moments, Molly is seen as if swimming into the mirror, her face and hair filling the hand-carved heart in what could only be called, in itself, a "cameo appearance." This piece, at least, Jasper May esteemed "undoubtedly genuine." It had been expressly ordered by the Studio in January 1939. A local silversmith (his invoice and all the related correspondence were duly consulted) had carved, out of a silver plaque, the dark hollow of a heart. He'd then inserted, just under this hollow, in a pair of carefully prepared furrows, the thin sheet of a mirror, of a shimmering, heart-shaped reflection. This, this "artifact," received the Studio's "tags" with Jasper May's signature — his blessings — neatly affixed.

In leaving, I was given a quick glance at the newly installed wardrobe collection. Again, it was the good work of the Curator himself: his suggestions, his designs, his execution. None of the Studio's historic costumes remained now on clothes-hangers. The whole collection had been laid flat in specially conceived drawers, long as coffins and narrow as attaché cases. The drawers rolled open with the pale roar of exhausted thunder; rolled closed with a sharp, irrecusable click.

Here, I was given a very rapid peek at one of Molly Lamanna's evening dresses, a costume gown designed for her third film by Travis Banton. Fully beaded, it must have clung, once, as tight as fish scales, and slithered — in a languorous half-twist — from a shirred knot on Molly's left shoulder to her very toes. I imagined, at her toes, a pinched pair of emerald pumps. I imagined, too, the rasp — the dense, metallic rustle — the entire gown must have made as she moved. The costume itself, Jasper May pointed out, had suffered "all the indignities of time." Hanging as it had for so many years — decades, even — on a clothes-hanger, some of the weighty beads, with their knitted fixings, had shredded free from their thin chiffon base. I asked myself, though, whether this gradual degradation wasn't in fact another one of Molly Lamanna's many posthumous devices, one of a variety of means she might have employed for effacing her traces, eradicating every sign of her passage, leaving us — as she had — with so dramatically little.

Before I left, I ran the palm of my hand over that shimmering mass, catching, as I did, the thin clicking of its glass cylinders. Limply, the beads rolled over, like so many stranded seashells, caught now in an intertidal wash, and subject to the whim of the curious, or simply that of the happenstantial.

"IT'S QUITE UP TO YOU, SIR," the voice replied, "but I must have your answer now, immediately." The tone of the voice was too suave, too studied, to be entirely its own. It had, at some point, held itself up to the voices of the eminently successful, and adjusted itself accordingly. It sounded more like a stockbroker's or an investment banker's than that of a dealer in rare books, manuscripts, and what he himself qualified as "all kinds of literary desiderata." He'd telephoned from Miami a few moments earlier, and introduced himself as a "Mr. M. M. Sallow, Antiquarian." He went on to tell me that he'd "happened to hear" from some fellow dealer in San Diego that I might "possibly be interested" or know someone who might "possibly wish to acquire" a copy, "the unique copy, what's more," of Millicent Rappaport's hand-printed, hand-bound journal, *M.L.* The volume, he claimed, had "just happened" to fall into his hands a few days earlier. He didn't say how.

He, or should I say "his voice" (for he was no more than that, a voice), described the volume with its sapphire-blue binding and its heavy, buff-white paper as a work in pristine condition. He then remarked, somewhat puzzled himself, "It's as if no one had ever bothered to read it." Then, with only the slightest hint — innuendo — of licentiousness, he added,

"It's quite something to read, too, I can assure you." The thought of M. M. Sallow fingering through those pages and invading, indiscriminately, what I could only imagine as the immensely private account of Millicent's immensely private love for Molly Lamanna, left me considerably more offended than I might have expected. I was quite clearly "involved."

Sallow, of course, was asking an outrageous amount for the journal, but — I must admit — I was all too ready to accept. I wanted, at any cost, to protect Millicent's "confessional" and, in a vicarious way, Millicent herself from the hands of such "antiquarians." I knew, of course, that I'd be purchasing a book that, if not stolen, had at least been coerced, pried loose, even extorted from its rightful owner, the mysterious Luis deSaumerez. But collectors are voracious characters, and I'm certainly no exception. I not only wanted to "protect" Millicent, I wanted most of all to enter into some magnified, day-by-day vision of Molly herself. I wanted to *see* her, at last. See her said, evoked. For there was something about Molly's presence upon the screen — a certain vacuity of the spirit — that enticed, intrigued. It drew with the same involuting fatality as an offshore "low" — on absence alone, that is. For it wasn't Molly herself, but a certain lacuna, a zero at her very center, something missing in her heart of hearts, that invited entry.

It was this, then, that first attracted me. An inveterate collector myself, with a shamefully high income (I'm a lung specialist in a region heavily publicized as a haven for the afflicted), I'd begun accumulating "articles," "items," "artifacts" on Molly Lamanna a bit more than a year ago. It all started, as passions usually do, somewhat offhandedly. One night, on a Late Late Show, I found myself following — with a certain, distracted fascination — the movements of an ever-so-slightly plump, diaphanously veiled slave girl. It was Molly, of course;

she was playing in her very first film, a vapid, fifty-minute B-production from late 1938. Later that night, though, and probably toward dawn, she reappeared — wonderfully manifest — in a dream I was having. Not even in the film had she appeared so vivid, so perfectly focused. Now, no longer barebellied but somewhat severely dressed in a gray worsted suit, she was purchasing a string of train tickets, a paper accordion, really, of pleated sections. Each section represented a portion, a leg, of the voyage to be taken. It was, clearly enough, to be a long voyage, indeed. I stood directly behind her in line, catching — in quick whiffs — the smell of her hair. It smelled of beaches in midsummer. It smelled of sand burning and suntan lotions. I might have followed the way her hair came tumbling down in heavy curls across her shoulders, fanning — dark bronze — over the check fabric of her tailored jacket, but at that very instant a particular sound drew — even magnetized — every bit of my attention. It came in a flat, mechanical succession of coughs and sputters. It was obviously enough that of an airplane, its single engine being teased, prompted, trapped into ignition. The train station in my dream had turned into a small, rural airport. Molly's voyage, I now saw, wasn't to be bound by earth, but by air. Just then, the cylinders of the invisible plane suddenly caught, the engine turned over, and the "cough" gathered into the tremolo of a high, unsputtering idle.

I would discover (but how much later) to what extent this dream, in fact, was pure omen. Molly-at-the-gates, Molly-departing, Molly-aloft: all the basic elements of her myth were already in place. With my dream, her departure (one might say) was already "prepared."

In the following few weeks I managed to track down videocassettes of all five of Molly Lamanna's films. These would constitute, of course, the basis of my budding collection.

Then, after the films themselves, would come a sundry array of tokens, souvenirs, the holograph postcards that Jasper May would dismiss, a half-year later, as so much counterfeit. But Molly, at least, was collectible. Since she was an essentially minor actress in a golden age of cinema, much of the miscellany pertaining to her work and her person was still, on occasion, available. A brooch, for instance, might suddenly appear on the market, and, authenticated or not, be plucked like a speckled junonia off its beach. Or, on the very same day, a pair of Molly's gloves might come and go, swept up by one of her fervents. Because now, even a canceled check or some tattered pilot's license could be converted, instantaneously, into pure fetish. The age, it seemed, was begging for its own past. Was rooting about wherever for the ballast of some memory, some set of images, charged, ponderous enough to check its own irresistible drift into mythlessness. A rapacity of sorts for any object bearing even the slightest deposit of some previous luster had entirely overcome us as our own millennium thinned, imperceptibly, to a close.

"The sum of which," Sallow insisted, his voice smooth as watered silk, "must be paid in cash, in worn, well-circulated, hundred-dollar bills."

"Agreed," I heard myself saying. Heard my voice echoing down the long, empty corridor of the telephone's mouthpiece.

"No traces, either. Nothing that anyone can eventually audit. We're entering into a traceless time, Dr. Hollander. No invoices, no checks, no accountings. It's liquid transactions, and liquid only, don't you agree?"

The unctuosity of his voice, the neatly linked succession of his words, caught, suddenly, on the crackling static of a poor cross-country connection. Now, as he entered into the final modalities of the exchange, our meeting set for the very next morning at Tucson International Airport, I heard the word "International" shatter into five disparate syllables. I could only picture, at that exact moment, our communication being disrupted by some vast, towering electric storm, dragging its black anvil eastward. I imagined it, for no particular reason, moving over the last, already undulant cotton fields of northern Alabama, the shaggy plants splattered abruptly now by the first raindrops, and flashing — like so many erratic pulsebeats — an erratic acid-white. It almost seemed as if the storm itself, by some arcane arrangement, were in M. M. Sallow's personal service. Over the telephone it codified or, more exactly, obfuscated everything Sallow had to say; broke it (but for the sake of what subterfuge?) into a series of quick, decomposed segments.

I didn't so much hear the word "lavatory" as surmise, gather, divine it. What with the middle of the word missing, like a gutted vocable, I asked Sallow to repeat himself. But he didn't hear me, or — more likely — didn't choose to. I strained to catch, if not the next words, at least a few, isolated, indissoluble syllables. Judging by the static's frequency, the storm had grown, intensified. I wondered, at that instant, whether the Carolinas, in turn, hadn't gone under, the deep plowings of the fallow tobacco fields doubly dark now beneath the slip of that gray, incessant pelting.

Then, in a wash of brief, truncated segments, I interpreted (decoded, in a sense) the following: ". . . enter . . . turn, then . . . ," then something else as if hissed through the now nearly uninterrupted static. Then, "booth, the . . . third . . . on the . . . left . . ."

The remainder of Sallow's instructions reached me like a message that had been expressly ground, pounded into an ever finer, more minute, linguistic surf. Its final particles seemed to sparkle, now, like so many tiny bits of stray salvage.

". . . you in . . . the . . . sec . . . nd . . . re . . .
"emb . . . er in . . . c . . . ash in . . . e-
"qual . . . b . . .
"un . . .
"dles . . . of . . . hun . . .

"dreds . . . onnnn . . . ly . . ." And then: ". . . au-
tion," or at least something that sounded like "caution" but
corroded, flaked, pulverized into so much less than its sono-
rous parts. Then:

". . . or-
"row . . . at . . .
". . . en . . ." and then: ". . . d . . . ont," then ". . .
d . . . ont" again, and then nothing: nothing but the sound
of an oncoming wall of electrical discharge that grew to an
insupportable level, then burst. Burst silent, noiseless. The
communication, if one could call it such, was as if cut, severed, terminated. The line went — momentously — blank.

That night, on the evening weather report, a "bright,
cloudless, sunny sky" was recorded for the third consecutive
day "clear across our fair land." And "more, much more of the
same" was predicted for the long weekend ahead. There'd
been, then, no lightning, no electric storm, anywhere. The
announcer's voice, like his forecast, was radiant. He spoke
with the fanatic assurance of those who had censored every
form of misfortune from their idiom. He didn't so much pre-
dict fair weather as proffer it like some kind of natural condition, part of the nation's destiny to bask, untroubled, under
a solid monochrome of unremittent blue. Certainly clouds,
dust storms, even tornadoes, might exist, but only as states of
exception, as anomaly. What's more, their points of origin
were inevitably alien, obscure, suspect, and their sole intent,
in crossing our borders, was that of undermining the otherwise
unruffled heavens of a republic, divinely appointed.

"Hundreds. Remember, in equal bundles of hundreds." Sallow's instructions kept entering, over and over, into my thoughts. They'd become, finally, incised. I telephoned my bank just before closing time and arranged that the exact sum be prepared, in cash, for nine o'clock the next morning.

I never saw him. I saw his shoe, however. I saw it as it slid the parcel sideways beneath the metallic, gunmetal gray partition. Then, an instant later, I saw it a second time as it recuperated (with the very tip of its pointed toe) my three heavily stuffed manila brown bank envelopes. It retracted them, one envelope at a time, with all the methodology of an insect or a night-hunting reptile, and the exquisite precision of some consummate tap dancer. Sallow never spoke more than my name, and I, in confirmation, never more than his. Each of us, invisible to the other, dealt out of our adjoining booths, cells, out of those casual and now nearly traditional venues of dealers, pushers, peddlers in drugs or small-arms transactions. Between us, no thicker than a cardboard stage prop, rose the partition with its full repertory of barbs and conceits, offers and demands. Here and there, across its surface, sprouted the outlines of a somewhat florid vulva, or a phallus, powered — it would seem — by the obstruction of every other natural force imaginable, into a member of phantasmagoric proportions, and bearing, as sole legend, nothing more than the seven, quickly scribbled digits — the alchemical combination — of some local (and probably, by now, disconnected) telephone.

I could just detect Sallow's whispers. He was counting his cash. The sound of the hushed numbers floated — but scarcely — over the continuously flushed and running waters. While Sallow counted, I snapped the tightly knotted parcel loose with a penknife, and undid its wrappings. The narrow

blue of the book's spine shimmered against the wrapping's surrounding brown. The entire cover, now, seemed to ripple the
full length of its tautly stretched sapphire binding. Upon the
binding lay the tiny paste-on label, the foil-stamped *M.L.* Altogether, I found the volume somewhat slenderer than I'd expected, and a good deal more lavish. Within, the broad
typeface lay as if deeply embedded inside its thick, creamy
stock. The words themselves seemed to be sleeping therein,
voluptuously enveloped. They certainly weren't the kind of
words, phrases, supplications, that would wish to be awakened, that would wish to be stirred, once again, into those
immensities, those jagged expanses out of which they'd first,
so desperately, emerged.

I found the dedication inscribed on the opening page. It
was handwritten in a set of high, graceful, swiftly executed
loops. *"For you, Luis,"* it read. *"This is your book even more than it's
mine. My love forever, Millicent."* Having read this, I couldn't resist
asking M. M. Sallow whether he'd ever met Luis deSaumerez;
whether he had, at least, some notion, some vague inkling,
even some semi-informed guess as to the man's identity. As I
asked, a "last call" for a Northwest flight for Atlanta was announced, that very moment, over the public address system.
This was immediately followed by another announcement for
yet another departure, a Continental flight for Houston, "now
boarding at Gate Twenty-seven." Then, once again, the sound
of rushing water resumed, with all its monotonous insistence,
and, once again, I asked M. M. Sallow what he knew about
Luis deSaumerez.

The water kept rushing, but over its hissing cataract I could
no longer discern the float of numbers, the steady litany of
Sallow's swift, implacable accounting. Quite clearly, he'd
gone, vanished, no doubt, into one of the several airplanes
that, that very instant, were being boarded.

I folded the journal back into its wrappings, and carried it out of the men's "rest room," through the lobby, and down into the overwhelming radiance of a high, dustless, Sonoran Desert sky. The day, suddenly, had gone white.

Then, turning my car northward and heading for the Santa Catalina foothills, I began to realize that Millicent's journal — and, within it, that intimate, that devout portrait of Molly Lamanna — was now, at least momentarily, entirely mine.

"YESTERDAY, SOMETHING HAPPENED," it began. *"Something utterly new, else, something entirely other . . ."* And thus, with those two lines, Millicent's journal opens. I would happily have continued, let myself be drawn into the rush of her words — her ellipses — with all the precipitation of someone entering a new country, a fresh element, or simply undergoing a sudden but decisive realignment of the heart. But, unfortunately, a string of telephone messages, all identical and all demanding an "immediate response," was awaiting me on my return. "Something happened," I heard myself say, heard Millicent say, her words reverberating, inextricably, through mine. A law firm in Los Angeles by the name of Bliss, Plinsky and Lee (these were the successors to Millicent's attorneys, I was soon to learn) had been trying to reach me at my office for the past half-hour. It was Mr. Plinsky himself who'd been calling every five minutes on the fifth, and my normally glib, imperturbable receptionist was, for once, suitably impressed.

Her messages, or rather his, Mr. Plinsky's, lay like so many box-shaped butterflies, unfluttering and speckled (at first citron, then pink), across the glass-smooth surface of my desk. "You'll see," she said. "He's totally ferocious."

And ferocious he was. I had no more than a minute to

glance through the first, heavy, hand-pulled pages of Millicent's journal, scavenging — as fast as I could — one phrase
after another. *"It's the eyes,"* Millicent had written. *". . . that
gaze, the enormity of Molly's regard, one notices first . . . floating as
it does in the mirror's quick, silvery updrafts. . . . Look, look at it. . . .
Look how it barely flickers, now, among the reflected backs of so many
stiff, star-hearted lilies . . . incommensurable. . . ."*

Then, on the following page: *". . . gazing. But gazing at
what, exactly? . . . Not, certainly, at any of us . . . some* bibelot,
*perhaps. . . . Or . . . some distant, still imaginary cloud bank . . .
some far-out turbulence that only she, as yet, could discern . . .*

". . . only she . . . interpret."

That was as far as I got. The telephone buzzed dully in
the outer office and then, a full octave lower, in mine. I closed
the journal, slid it once again into its brown paper wrappings,
and answered. It was Plinsky, of course. His voice sounded
hard, hard pressed, that of a man who'd come to measure (and
most certainly invoice) his every instant. His words weren't
so much uttered as expelled. A high, thin, mechanical wheeze
(which I diagnosed immediately as advanced emphysema) ac-
companied his each breath like some stray, insubordinate
wind instrument.

I should have foreseen Plinsky's call, I now realized. I
should have known. I was only beginning to sense, if not
intuit, the moves and manipulations inherent in the somewhat
broken geography — all crags and chasms — that I'd ventured into. But then, I was only at the outset of this modern-
day *terra incognita*, and — I must admit — a bit guileless as to
its true complexities.

Here, briefly, was what Plinsky had to say:

— We have substantial evidence that you've recently —
very recently, perhaps within the last month — come into
possession of Millicent Rappaport's private, privately printed

journal, dated — if we're not mistaken — nineteen fifty-nine. Is this correct?

— Well, is it? We're asking you, in short, for your assistance. Your corroboration.

— Yes, that's right, your corroboration. No, we're not accusing you. We simply want to see the whole matter brought to light and the property returned to its rightful owners, that's all.

— What? What's that?

— No, absolutely not. And furthermore, it's *you*, we feel, who owes us an answer, Dr. Hollander. It's *you*, we're quite convinced, who are concealing, deliberately or not, stolen property. You're aware, aren't you, of the liability you're running? Of the possible consequences? Of the warrant that could be issued against you at any given moment?

— Who? (This, followed by a long silence.) What about Luis deSaumerez?

— What does Luis deSaumerez have to do with what we're discussing?

— That's absurd. You're talking about a man who vanished years ago. About someone the State of California has long since declared legally deceased.

— What? What exactly are you implying?

— What?

— Why, that's perfectly fallacious. If you must know, this property is neither Luis deSaumerez's (how could it be, he's dead), nor yours. You have no legal claim to it. As co-trustees to the deSaumerez estate, and in default of any other heir, natural or otherwise, we have become its unique beneficiary. As such, this property belongs to us, is exclusively ours and no one else's. *No one's*, do you understand? For two years, now, we've been trying to trace it. And during those two years we've suspected the wrong man, run an investigation on this particular individual. And during all that time, this same good citizen . . . yes, that's right, he's a bookdealer . . . an antiquarian . . . yes, yes, from Atlanta, Georgia, that's correct . . . this same good citizen has spent a considerable amount of time and gone to considerable expense tracking down those that are truly responsible, and clearing, in the process, any charges that might possibly be brought against his own good name. Yes, that's right, exonerating himself. Not that we're insinuating that you had anything to do with the original extraction from our offices. We're not accusing you of anything, Doctor, except of detaining stolen property. And we're giving you a period of grace — let's call it twenty-four hours, no more — to return this property to its rightful owners. To wit, ourselves.

While Plinsky talked, I interpolated. I filled in, wherever I could, the frequent blanks. This much, at least, was certain: M. M. Sallow, within an hour of the time I'd purchased Millicent Rappaport's journal, had telephoned Plinsky and, in sorts, denounced me: given him my name, address, phone number. He'd done so, of course, to rid himself of that somewhat nefarious halo he'd no doubt come to accumulate, the vapors of his own tenebrous reputation. But how, in fact, had Sallow come upon the journal in the first place? Had he simply stolen it — "extracted" it — from a law office in Los Angeles two years ago? And why, if he had, had he waited this long to unload it, be rid of it? And how had Bliss, Plinsky and Lee become the beneficiaries of an estate that they had only been designated to supervise? And lastly, who in fact was that most mysterious creature of all, Luis deSaumerez? Had he really vanished? Was he truly dead? And what, in the first place, had been his relationship to Millicent Rappaport, a relationship so meaningful that she had left everything — down to her last chattel and holding — to a pure nominative? To the ghost of a pure nominative? She had endowed a shadow, it would seem, with her considerable fortune.

I needed time. I knew that Plinsky's call would be followed by others, that whoever owned Millicent's journal would, in fact, be the moving target now for any amount of personal cunning, avidity, machination.

First, I had my receptionist cancel all my appointments for the remainder of the day. Happily, the pollen rate was down, and the number of patients in the past week had considerably thinned. None, in any case (I checked this carefully), needed immediate attention. I then drove home (I have a house literally in the shadow of the Santa Catalina Mountains) and, upon arriving, left a message on my answering machine to the effect that I wouldn't be available before seven, that evening. I now had the remainder of the afternoon in which to read Millicent Rappaport's journal; to begin, perhaps, unfathoming some of the mysteries both surrounding and contained within it.

I settled into a white, slowly deflating armchair in my living room, the very room in which all my collections, it would seem, have come to rest. On either side of the armchair stood one of a matching pair of tall glass display cases. Each contained a near perfect pre-Columbian *olla*, one of those great, red-on-buff storage jars that the Hohokam — the Vanished People — had crafted over a millennium ago. The work of that people — that lost culture — had obsessed me for a number of years now. Wasn't it, in fact, a kind of vanity on the part of so many collectors to be obsessed by the vanished, the extinct? To covet the relics of the otherwise obliterated? To become guardians of so much sifted residue, monopolists over the very little that still remained: those scarce, scarcely surviving artifacts? Wasn't Millicent's journal, in fact, a supreme example of exactly that? A kind of glittering salvage, a

verbal hoard, dredged up out of the ambient dark? And —
what's more — something still menaced, at every instant, by
those obscure forces, acting upon their own, obscure direc-
tives, that would readily drag the work — the words — back
under?

I opened it. Its sapphire covers reflected in long, squirting
crystals — transparent needles — across the glass display
cases. The reflections stretched and dissolved, reappeared —
quivering — against the burnt, earthen jars. *"For you, Luis. This
is your book even more than it's mine. My love forever, Millicent."*

And thus I began.

PART TWO
(Millicent Rappaport, 1939)

YESTERDAY, something happened. Something utterly new, else, something entirely other . . . Things happen, happen continually, of course. Happen without our asking, our solicitations. And yet, even here, leading what most people would consider a very active and thoroughly enviable life, even now, approaching forty-five, I'm haunted by an existence in which, quite possibly, nothing has happened. What, I wonder, ever does? What can I actually say has actually *occurred* in my life? Has truly mattered? Twelve years, perhaps, of a more or less consistent marriage? A string of short stories, innumerable scripts and three somewhat slender novels (each, a *succès d'estime*, though scarcely more)? At forty-five, one turns. Takes stock. Counts each and every accomplishment, blessing, fortuity, on the tips of one's fingers, and still ends up staring into the shallow palm of an empty and altogether too anxious hand.

Yesterday, "yesterday," I write. And already, it's today. Already, as I write this, I've opened my journal, spread its first two pages flat with the palm of my hand. And already, I must admit, I'm somewhat amazed at how unabashed I feel in my need — call it lust — to record each glint of yesterday's encounter, each recollected instant. To fill these pages, and densely, with every thread, every whisper and innuendo. To cram them with those small, incandescent details that only the already enthralled, occasionally, can evoke. But evoke out of what, exactly? Out of the hazard of a few moments' chance encounter? Out of even less, in fact? From that tiny span in which virtually nothing was said, nothing (for that matter) was implied or suggested, but where, for the first time, something, I felt, might actually have happened?

What, though? And why am I so astonished to discover, this morning, that whatever it was that happened has left me with something incalculably less, rather than more. Brought me to such a state of inner diminishment that I find myself holding on to the sudden polysyllable of her name as if on to some magic property, some impromptu rite by which the sounds themselves could be teased — like a tiny fish bone — through the teeth. Could be pulled — reverently — from the lips as a singular and absolute antidote against one's own dispersion. One's own dissolution.

As if a name, and only a name, could protect one from the very presence — that annihilating force — that it designates.

We're here. We've been here, in Manhattan, for five days now, staying in this overly furnished suite the Studio maintains at the Sherry Netherland. The flowers, however, the vases of buff-white lilies scattered throughout, are entirely my doing. So, too, was the reception Sidney and I gave last night for an entire cast that's been on location in the area, as well as for Studio personnel and a few, very few, select friends. We were expecting, among the latter, Robert Taylor, but Robert called just as the reception began, and excused himself. I, for one, was particularly disappointed, as Robert's a dear, and a dear friend, and someone who never fails to stir a totally unstirred and unsuspected part in my nature. Something hidden, securely hidden within each of us, simply echoes, corresponds. In that sleek, streamlined elegance of his, I could only imagine a hidden grain of — what? — of pure, unfailing receptivity, perhaps. Of some otherwise immaculately disguised second nature, an androgyny of sorts, a profound warmth in the midst of all that suave and shapely and marvelously jointed metal.

I especially wanted to speak with Robert about an upcoming production in which he's been assigned the male lead. I've been asked to doctor the screenplay to this particular production, to vivify it, give it — as they say — "some life." As it stands, it's an abysmal piece of work. Poor Robert throughout plays a stereotype Mogul emperor moving slowly but ineluctably toward Samarkand. Within something less than two hours and twenty minutes, he and his legions are called upon to bring under heel the entire Islamic Empire. The whole spectacle, beginning to end, is a single, seamless, unrelenting cliché. In fact, when Sidney and I return to Hollywood next week, I'll have to rummage about in this cliché, and give it whatever relief, contour, verisimilitude I can. I was hoping, last night, to chat with Robert about certain aspects of characterization, and garner a few hints, suggestions. Between what he knows about acting, and I about script repair, we might have begun, at least, making some preliminary improvements. Instead, there I was at my own reception, thinking about Robert, missing Robert, and — at the same time — nattering inanely with Dorothy McGuire about one vapid subject after another, when — in the vestibule mirror — I first caught sight of someone whose name I didn't yet know was Molly Lamanna. Or, to be more precise, I first caught sight of something I didn't yet know was Molly Lamanna's glorious head of hair. It swarmed like so much kelp still caught in the writhing of its own currents. As if alive, it spread its full, unbraided length over the shoulders and sleeves of a gray —

slate gray — satin blouse. The blouse, in turn, rippled like a taut, shimmering liquid of its own. It was neatly tucked into a rather high-waisted pair of wide white flannel trousers that hung in two ruthlessly sharp, uninterrupted creases, eclipsing, at their flared base, all but the tiniest protruding points of a black, juvenescent pair of pinched patent-leather pumps.

Who exactly was this creature? Hadn't Sidney promised us a surprise? Told us that there'd be someone at the reception whom none of us had yet met? Who'd just signed her first twelve-month contract with the Studio? Wasn't this, in fact, the "bush pilot" they'd discovered quite by chance on the edge of a dirt airstrip somewhere in the heart of the Mojave? An "orphan adrift," a "gorgeous vagabond," as Sidney had put it. Wasn't this, indeed, her?

While I tried to follow her movements (more often than not in the inter-reflecting mirrors of our large but infallibly introspective rooms), Dorothy launched onto the subject of zodiacal signs and ascendants. I vaguely caught something about Sagittarians. "Especially now," she insisted, "at this particular moment, what with Venus and Jupiter in conjunction. It simply couldn't — couldn't — be less auspicious." While I heard the word "auspicious" on one register, I distinctly saw, on another, this young woman (whose name I still didn't know) sink a somewhat infantile finger into her whisky glass and stir it with disarming insouciance. I could only imagine, from where I stood, her slender finger magnified to a near fatness by the glass itself, and the roll of that oily liquor over the dully colliding, dully clicking ice cubes. I wanted to move closer. From that very first instant, yesterday, I wanted to "see" her. Get as close as I could. Learn what she smelled of, her soaps, talcs. Find words — names — for her every feature. Gather everything I could, every scrap, every straw that — by some miracle — might have escaped her all-too-consuming incandescence.

For, from that very first instant, yesterday, there was something evidently so fugitive, so attractive in its fugacity, that anything that might be said about her could already be considered a victory of sorts over that drift, that broken articulation she seemed to move in, that slow, inner deflection that took her not simply from room to room (as at that very instant) but, seemingly, from vacancy to vacancy. "An orphan adrift," as Sidney, always judicious, had put it. Instinctively one wanted to save her, keep her, preserve her — most especially — from herself. Coddle her against that vast abstraction that she seemed so fatally magnetized to.

"Child," I whispered. The word had arisen of itself, unexpectedly. And like no other word, it seemed to qualify everything that the situation had only vaguely, if sensuously, suggested.

"Child, child," I whispered, and heard the word vanish, evaporate, in the very span of its own saying.

The living room, meanwhile, had filled with small, intense clusters of actors and actresses, of the whole gamut of those even peripherally associated with the Industry. The clusters as they moved, as they gradually exchanged places — positions — reminded me somewhat of Dorothy's zodiacal arrangements. They shone, turned, rotated with both the luster and the sluggishness of stars, affecting one another as they did with the effluence of so much smoke and scent and glitter. With all the idle circulation of so much idle, disembodied sound. They, too, had their signs, were obedient to their own orbits. One could only wonder, though, in those charmed circles, whether anyone had any notion of the "real world" beyond. Whether anyone here ever read a newspaper, for instance, or simply glanced at a headline. Had any idea of the atrocities committed in Abyssinia or the latest rumors arising out of Central Europe; had heard, for example, about the somewhat obscure displacements of the Wehrmacht in the past few weeks. Here, within these circles, these clusters, everything still remains rigorously normal, unruffled. The world isn't something one questions. The whole Hollywood set still behaves as if it were divinely protected by the very fictions (the density of those fictions) that it, itself, had perpetrated. Here, the heavens, fictive or not, continue to rotate, and loftily so, oblivious of the ground beneath us that, day after day, is quite clearly being dug, tunneled, undermined by an implacable mystique of its own.

Dorothy was still enumerating the attributes of Capricorn when Sidney joined us. His timing, as ever, was impeccable. "Yes, yes, that's the one," he told me, pouring us two fresh glasses of champagne. "That's Molly Lamanna, the girl we discovered flying the day's takes down from our desert location. She'd return from LA the very next morning with the developed rushes. That's her, exactly." Sidney gestured to a waiter for a tray of iced hors d'oeuvres. "Molly Lamanna, you'll see for yourselves. The results of her first screen test are astonishing." Molly, at that very moment, was standing no more than ten feet away. Her sudden proximity, I found, was strangely intimidating. She was talking to no one, and staring at nothing in particular except, perhaps, the extent of her own detachment. She didn't, however, seem in the least bit uncomfortable. In fact, she was smiling.

It's the eyes, I noted, even more than the bewildering mass of her hair, that draws one's attention. It's that gaze, the enormity of Molly's *regard*, one notices first. An infant's, an infant madonna's, really, floating as it does in the mirror's quick, silvery updrafts. Gray, ascendant, and ballasted by nothing, apparently, if not some slight, belated curiosity, the gaze — momentarily — seems to turn, look back, linger. Seems to glance (but at what?) out of a space so utterly remote, so irredeemably immense. I say a madonna's. But it's more detached, bereft, abandoned than that; more the exquisite "orphan" that Sidney had depicted. Or that of a soul in some deep state of perdition. Look, look at it, I kept saying to myself. Look how it barely flickers, now, among the reflected backs of so many stiff, star-hearted lilies. How easily one could lose oneself — would want to lose oneself — in something as lost, as incommensurable as that.

Eddy Duchin, at that very moment, was playing Cole Porter on the suite's baby grand. While a few stray bars of "Night and Day" reached me, carried as if on the back of so much chatter and clattering glassware, I let myself lean, ever so gently, against Sidney's shoulder. That's the one, I wanted to tell him. That's what I've wanted, what I've always wanted. What you, sweet man, who would have given me anything, hadn't given. Couldn't give. "Wait, wait," you told me, as you'd leaned over (was it already twelve years ago?). "Wait," you'd said, as you held me pinned in that fixed, reverential expression of yours. "Wait," while you doted on the silk droplet buttons of my nightgown, on the bracelets you wouldn't let me remove, "Wait, wait," you'd muttered, your voice going weak, enfeebled by what you saw, while what you saw lay its full, heated length, and waited. Kept waiting.

"Child," I said — still say — as my sole response. "Child," I whisper to no one now except, perhaps, that hollow, those white, worthless viscera I bear as others bear memory, or knowledge, or some singular ambition.

"Child, child," I say, keep saying.

And, at the very same instant, saw Molly Lamanna pluck, with a kind of savage delicacy, at a bit of crabmeat, or lobster.

Saw her lower it, between her bare fingers, into her glittering
teeth. Saw her chin rise, ever so slightly, as she swallowed.
Then (in that same miniature sequence, that film perfectly
framed by a low, rounded arch that led from one room to the
next) I watched her turn, move off, enter into some light
exchange with a bartender, then break into a sudden laughter
that left me, like nothing else, as if rent, torn by that ripple
of tiny pleasure from which I had just, that very instant, been
eternally excluded.

A moment later, she'd moved. She'd stationed herself, almost petulantly, on the far side of that same room. With
a single white-flannel knee plunged into the scarlet cushion
of a somewhat squat, baroque settee, she began — once
again — glancing, looking about, or, simply, gazing. But
gazing at what, exactly? At walls? Pictures? Not, certainly, at
any of us. I couldn't imagine Molly Lamanna being drawn
toward anything essentially human. To some *bibelot*, perhaps.
To some seemingly inane object that might miraculously have
held her attention long enough, or provided her with some
small, psychic anchorage, some tiny, albeit ephemeral sense
of her own existence.

Or, perhaps, she was gazing entirely outward, away, into
some abstraction, some distant, still imaginary cloud bank
she'd fabricated out of her own obscure ruminations. (For
hadn't Sidney told us that she's an aviator, an aviatrix? That
nights she often vanishes, pilots her own airplane? Makes solo
excursions in whichever direction her whim happens to take
her?) Perhaps, too, those spaces that she flew through had
become so embedded, so inscribed in her own mind, that part
of her, at least, now inhabited those very dimensions. Lived
them, dreamt them, even — perhaps — prefigured them.
That at that very instant she might have been gazing into

some far-out turbulence that only she, as yet, could discern, determine.

That already she might be "seeing things" simply from so much familiarity with that emptiest of elements; "things" that only she, so far, could interpret.

Then, no more than an instant later, I turned and found that she had gone. She'd abandoned that squat, baroque settee as abruptly as a seabird, startled from its reef, and had left nothing as a trace but an already vanishing indentation — a dimple, really — in the cushion's deep scarlet.

I broke free from Dorothy and Sidney and the little circle that had grown around us, and rushed into the entranceway. In doing so, I nearly knocked into Molly Lamanna herself. She'd vanished just long enough to fetch her overcoat, a gray Persian lamb "half-length," and was now lifting her hair high over its collar, letting her hair quite literally pour, pour and fan over the coat's full, fully padded, die-straight shoulders. I noted, with a particular fascination, how the open curls of her hair caught on the tauter ones of the lamb's wool; how they formed together, like some Renaissance drypoint, a paradigm of tight, interlocking orbits, a small but sumptuous cosmogony of their own.

"Here," I said, or rather heard myself say before I even realized that I'd said it. "Here." And I handed her, before I even realized it, the small, pendulous, blue-sequinned opera bag I was carrying.

She hesitated an instant, and then very slowly, circumspectly, received it like some kind of anatomical curiosity. She cupped it rather cautiously in the hollow of both hands as if she were holding an organ, or a gland, or the mummified remains of a once-venerated testicle. Then, carrying it now — like so much living evidence — over to the table lamp, she silently inspected the bag with a pure and utterly detached fascination. Within the strict circle of the lamplight, the light from the beaded sequins flared outward. And, as it did, I saw Molly's face, suddenly sequinned itself, in the purse's slowly rotating reflections. Her face was as if webbed in blue, in a fluttering network of cool, cerulean fires. Here and there a dart, a barb, a blue arrow, would detach and attempt to wedge itself into one of her features, catch in a curl or insert itself surreptitiously behind the carnal bud of an unrung earlobe. But the whole spectacle, the whole artifice of this tiny, gyrating planetarium, came to an end, suddenly, as Molly laid the beaded bag down onto the table and, with an expression that was both perfectly engaging and thoroughly indifferent, looked back.

"Black," she said, with the very faintest of smiles. The smile wavered, equivocated for an instant, then addressed itself in all its allure not exactly at me but through me. I could only imagine its damp, compressed density evaporating, almost immediately, in some netherworld of its own, far, far behind me.

"Black," she repeated, and then, very slowly, almost laboriously, added: "and white. White, too. As much white as black. And occasionally, very occasionally, I'll mix both — sometimes — with something gray."

Then, glancing down at the small beaded bag as if it were so much spilled lacquer or wasted glaze, she added, in that slow, deliberate, almost infantile manner of hers, "But never blue."

" . . . never blue" echoed silently through me, as Molly Lamanna turned, and, exquisite orphan that she is, unschooled in even the most basic amenities, in the simplest "sorrys" and "thank-yous" and "good-byes" on which the rest of the world operates, headed toward the door. As a bellboy swung the door open, I watched the heavy, triangular bulk of her hair as if drown, deep bronze, in the darker lights of the hotel corridor. Then, as if she'd never been, she left, was gone, had vanished.

January 12th. We're back. We returned yesterday, and just as soon as I'd bathed and brushed out my hair, I went about the house, touching — from table to table — my beloved jades, my collection of stout, bald-headed figurines. Once again, I was setting my small world in order. Once again, I was announcing my return to those mute, mineral witnesses with their thin-lidded gazes. (Wasn't it they, though — the silent ones — that greeted me, rather than the opposite? That told me I'd truly returned? Weren't they responding to the touch of my fingertips with something so much deeper, guardians as they were, the green-rooted deities, once, of place? Of residence? Perhaps of reality itself?)

Outside, the sea wind was still blowing. It's been blowing, now, according to the gardeners, for a full week, battering our tall hedges of hibiscus, knocking the long-tongued petals loose from their flared blossoms. I managed, nonetheless, to rescue a ragged armful, and brought them in, their flamboyant reds gone now a rather cosmetic pink from the accumulated deposits of so much sea spray. As I arranged the flowers in a loose, somewhat fluffy round, I caught myself saying that, no matter what, I intended to keep this journal *alive.* That anything touching upon Molly Lamanna, no matter how trivial or secondhand, would be included. Would be cherished within.

Nothing, after all, could be considered too small when dealing with someone apparently as elusive, ill defined, as she. For Molly's not a household deity — a Kuan Yin — that's certain. She doesn't root. If anything, she disperses, scatters, and would probably leave anyone she encountered with that same disquieting sense of having just suffered a somewhat obscure and now totally unlocatable loss. Didn't I, the day after we'd met, a bit absurdly, run through all the belongings in my handbag, wondering what it was that was missing? My license? Car keys? My hammered gold cigarette case? My Du Bois brooch? Nothing, of course, had been lost: nothing, that is, except some entirely intangible quality, some innate sense of my own belonging, that dark center whose cartilage had just — stealthily — been torn.

I went on, however, pulling out car keys, earrings, compacts, for quite some time. Everything was there but myself.

January 13th. A journal. A journal's, at least, somewhere one can go. A cache of sorts. A refuge. A room within the very room one lives in. An intimacy. A place where one can finally lay out one's most inadmissible secrets, unroll them like so much coveted brocade. Can spread, exhibit, flaunt them in all their pettiness and splendor to that enlarged privacy of the page; can air them — at long last — in a light of their own.

Molly. Molly in light. Of all words, her name, suddenly, is easily the most luminous. The lightest and fullest. How wonderfully round it is to roll those two syllables about in my mouth. Like ripe olives. Or loosely, over the tongue, like the salty, somewhat resilient phlegm of an oyster.

There, there's my entry for the day: rolling the two syllables of her name over my tongue "like the salty, somewhat resilient phlegm of an oyster."

January 15th. As offhandedly as possible, I asked the parking attendant at the Studio what kind of car Miss Lamanna drives. "A battered, dark green Plymouth sedan," I was told. He

added, however, that she sometimes took the bus, and arrived
from the bus stop on foot. Or, what surprised me even more,
she'd occasionally hitch a ride and appear on the lot with
whatever stranger had happened to spot her, her thumb out
and her clothes probably flapping in that little, early morning
breeze that precedes — and perhaps even invites — the first
bustle of activity in this city that fabricates — often, all too
shabbily — the nation's dreams.

The attendant then added (somewhat puzzled himself) that
whenever Miss Lamanna hitched a ride or arrived on foot, her
stand-in, Miss Voigt, would pull up around noon, "fresh as a
daisy," at the wheel of the battered Plymouth sedan. "Like
two drops of water," he remarked. "You just can't tell one of
those ladies from another. Except," he observed, and clearly
the nature of his information gave him the license as well as
the courage to lean over and, in a half-whisper, disclose: "except by the look in their eyes. Because Miss Lamanna's not
looking at anything, really. Not at anything or anyone. I saw
her walk clear past a full-length mirror, once, and not even
give herself a glance. That's rare in these parts."

This, then, is the day's "scrap." Not nothing, but nearly.
One gathers what one can.

January 18th. I plunged into the rewrite of *Mongol Moon* this
morning. Clearly, there'll be little time in the next three weeks
to muse and daydream about Molly Lamanna; the work, at
hand, will keep me busy enough. I must convert a rigorously
linear narrative, dealing as it does with the invasion of
Genghis Khan's armies across Uzbekistan, and the siege they
laid before the walled city of Samarkand, into something vi-
able and entertaining. As written, nothing really occurs in the
script aside from so many banalized scenes of rape, pillage
and mass devastation. Add to that the totally stereotyped

kidnapping of an Islamic princess who, of course, has strayed too far, on horseback, from the city gates. She serves as both political hostage and emotional pawn in this utterly hapless narrative. But not even she, and the implausible love that she bears for Khan, can keep the indomitable warrior from his work. Samarkand, in this hundred-and-twenty-page cliché, shall burn to its last cinder.

Here, basically, is what I've decided to do. I shall insert a series of well-timed flashbacks, each like an illuminated moment in Genghis Khan's memory, recalling a single suppressed episode in his adolescence: a first love, a love cloistered in a walled garden full of flowers and pendulous with fruit. The memory of this love, in all its fragility, will be the one tempering force in Khan's heart. Before the barbarity he's about to perpetrate, it will serve as the only civilized, civilizing constraint, at least potentially. The image of the garden and the girl inside the garden — both repeated and, in brief episodes, elaborated — will cause him to hesitate, reconsider. The captured princess, in turn, so reminiscent of Khan's lost love, might be booty enough, might (if properly treated) serve as his heart's plunder, and bring him to lower his siege, break the encirclement of Samarkand, saving in the process both the princess and her city, and granting him, at long last, some kind of peace with himself. Yes, Khan will have found peace finally, even in the midst of a world he has largely set fire to.

Obviously, I'll have to cheat with history — with recorded fact — and take whatever liberties the story demands. Also, I'll be running the risk of converting one totally sentimental scenario into another. Caution, restraint, and total fidelity to the exact workings of the heart, throughout, must be scrupulously observed, and considerably more so than in the usual Hollywood rewrite. For the garden that I'm introducing, here, must be perfect. The image of a garden, after all, in all its implications, can still — properly evoked, and mythically invested — check the stampeding of barbarian hordes, of those high, sporadic dust clouds that trail across the desert skies like so many unraveled turbans. But the garden, first, must be faultless. Damp, and damp with the promise of endless felicities, the garden must be redolent of the highest — albeit the most hidden — of human realities.

January 23rd. Over breakfast, I discussed the proposed script changes with Sidney. He found all of them excellent, "exactly what we've needed from the very beginning." He then asked me if I had anyone in mind for the new role I'd introduced, that of the girl in the garden. Was Sidney, I wonder, second-guessing me? Was his mind running, as it often does, not only inside mine, but slightly ahead of it, as well? Or was it simply an instinct, a flair he has for foreseeing my wishes long before I've even formulated them myself?

"Yes, of course," he said in reply. "Molly Lamanna would be ideal. I'll check with casting, see what's on her schedule for the next few months. Whether she's available or not."

Molly, I mused. Molly as "the girl in the garden." Molly among the ripe pomegranates, her ankles caught in a thick white carpet of burst asphodels. "Ideal, ideal."

January 27th. On the way to my masseur, I caught sight of a battered, dark green Plymouth sedan at the corner of La Cienega and Santa Monica boulevards. Was it *hers*? The bells rang, the lights changed, and all I saw was the elbow of a white sleeve and the thick cables of so much long, curly hair streaming past the unrolled window, as the car surged forward, ran neatly through its gears, and headed toward what I could only imagine as some empty, early-morning beach with the ocean breaking in slow, gunmetal gray rollers, just beyond.

Five minutes later, I was at Abdul Izmar's. His unfailing discretion and exquisite comportment have made his address among women the most coveted, some say, in all Hollywood. Having him massage my neck, shoulder and back muscles, each Wednesday, is one of life's greater pleasures. Abdul, in his blindness, has transferred his sight entirely to his finger-tips. His thumbs seem to stare — somewhat fixedly — into the small of my back, or gaze deeply into my shoulder blades, while his other fingers glance, dart, sometimes even wink across the surface of my flesh. Abdul's the perfect magician.

"There, just there?" he'll ask.

"Just there," I'll respond, and feel one of those tiny vaga-bond knots in my back suddenly vanish, worked loose by a rapid set of infallible manipulations.

While Abdul works (pressing, spreading, pummeling), voices seem to drift, meander into the dark, heavily draped room. There's Madame Izmar, of course, humming as she pre-pares mint tea in the kitchen alongside, or talking with neigh-bors, or relatives, or some client who, anxious from an excess of idle time, has arrived far in advance. Voices, always voices. They seem to hover about the crowded parlor like the threads that run — shot — through the room's dark hangings. Like the voices the threads, the arabesques that they form, seem to suggest so much more than they reveal. They twist sin-uously through their fabrics — vanishing, reemerging — with all the vaporous consistency of some partially overheard whisper.

It's here, however, in this heavy labyrinthian space, piously guarded not only by the hangings but by the dense phalanx of their shadows, that, unclothed — yes, finally unclothed — my own thoughts come clearest. It's as if they had been urged forth out of so much obscurity by the constant prodding, pressure, insistence of Abdul's dense fingertips. By the rhythmic kneading of his palms. Touched (at last), the body (at last) releases its little bevy of words. The words swim free.

It's here that whole paragraphs, the outlines of entire chapters, have been given me, in single, unbroken sequences. It's here, each Wednesday, I come to unravel my plots, determine forthcoming passages, elaborate conclusions. This Wednesday, however, what was given — released, one might say — by Abdul's deft manipulations happened to be exactly what I could never write. Or, rather, could never publish. Happened to be, once again, the ineffaceable memory of that unmentionable evening, twelve years earlier: the night of our aborted nuptials.

"Wait, wait," he'd said. And while he said it, hadn't I caught the glimmer and heard the mechanical collapsing-into-place of a tripod, halfway across that lengthy bedroom. Wasn't this followed by the sound of lesser, lighter tripods being set into position, these — certainly — for the elevated spotlights that would pin me, within a few moments, to the first of how many fixed images, swathed to the ankles in a single wave of pearl gray satin. Desire frozen within the metallic foaming of so much arrested fabric.

For Sidney wasn't a man, I'd learn, but an eye, an optic, an entire set of ocular proclivities. The greater those proclivities grew, the more exclusively visual they became, not only in his mind but in his heart as well. He wasn't, I'd learn, a husband, but a votary, a devotee of whomever he had imagined me as, freshly arrived on the West Coast twelve, thirteen, fourteen years earlier. "Goddess," he'd call me, and loved, worshipped me not as a woman (any more than he was a man) but as a totally mystified image, as the inviolate, inviolable creature of a pure occultation.

"Wait, wait," and while I waited, propped on one elbow with my head and hair flung backward exactly as he'd instructed, arranged, composed me — the mannequin of his adulations — I felt the light from the free-swinging boom flood across my cheekbones, laying those surfaces flat for the sake of what lusters? What mysteries? Hollowing, accentuating, modeling me into the image of utter unavailability while I lay there, more available with each passing moment, my eyes swung upward, my gaze fixed on the fat, decorous cherubim, the *putti* that, puff-cheeked, studded the ceiling's rose red cornices. "Now," I murmured to no one, except, perhaps, those plump intercessors. "Now," I said, supplicant to whatever dissolved orders, ontologies, they'd once obeyed, while, in the same moment, I heard the massive, eight-by-ten portrait camera being wheeled within arm's reach, and Sidney — gently, so gently — begging me to keep my lips moist ("sparkling," he'd called it), while adjusting the angle of my new pear-shaped emerald earrings to catch the exact glint, the "star-points," in one meticulous portrait after another. Passive, unquestioning, I assisted in what, years later, I'd recognize as the embalming of my own image. As its mortification.

"Sidney," I called out.

"An instant more, my beloved. Just an instant more." And while I lay there, waiting, he went on guiding my gaze with his upheld fingers, lifting it to one side, then another, teasing me into every conceivable aspect of feigned seductiveness. Of glamorous abandon. "There, just there. Like that," he'd say excitedly. "There, that's perfect, Milly. Just there."

That night, as I lay there, as I moved through my poses, one after another, I felt, or rather sensed, for the very first time, the shadow. It was no bigger, that night, than some tiny, incipient tumor. Than a wart growing obscurely on the flank of some tissue. Not the mass, the vast growth that, year after year, it would come to be. Only the whisper of a shadow, then; the thin, nearly indiscernible hiss of its whisper, nothing more. But from that very night onward, I was pregnant. Pregnant with shadow. I'd been impregnated by shadow for the sake of bearing, suckling, rearing shadow. Shadow, and nothing more.

I must have fallen asleep, my naked arms around the pillow, and my blonde hair, I can only imagine, arranged like a bright coil across it. I awoke in that position much later, alone in that large bed. The room was dark. From the headlights of an occasional passing car coming down Cold Canyon Drive I could make out the skeletal outlines of the tall, metallic tripods. They'd flicker an instant — as if shivering — then vanish. Once, I even managed to spot one of the chipped plaster *putti*, perched in its rose red cornice. It lit up slowly, I remember, caught in the arc of some passing headlights. The angel, momentarily, appeared trapped, lassoed, in that slow, scanning luminosity. Its mouth, I remember, was red. Was agape.

January 29th. This morning, I must admit, was something of a miracle. I'd gone to the beach for the air, for that heavy sea spume that's still blowing landward, and has such a cleansing effect on both the spirit and on every pore of one's skin. Wrapped in its transparent mask, it leaves one feeling perfectly radiant. That's exactly how I felt, this morning. How I'd wish to feel, always.

I'd walked down the beach from Santa Monica Canyon, and had nearly reached the pier (a ghostly wood outcropping in that half-gray, half-gold curtain of moving humidity) when, from a certain distance, I spotted them. They looked, from where I walked, exactly like twins. Long-haired, loose-limbed and dressed in identical, ruffle-trimmed swimsuits, they were frolicking with a huge, inflated beachball, tossing it back and forth as if there were only one of them, and that one were playing in a mirror.

They let the wind take the light, candy-striped ball just far enough downwind to float free of them, but sufficiently near, nonetheless, to catch, if each were quick, nimble, calculating enough to pluck it — weightless — out of the living air. They were having great fun and laughing, taking a kind of daredevil joy at the risk of losing the ball, each time, to either one of those blue elements. They were teasing, cajoling those elements and, at the same time, deliberately excluding them as well. For theirs, essentially, was a *jeu à deux*. It was a game, a ritual even, that they were acting out in midair. They were toying with their own echo, their own reciprocal, inter-changeable identities. From where I stood, they formed (caught, as they were, between ocean and air) a tiny, utterly captivating vignette of seemingly mythological proportions.

I could have gone on watching them forever. I loved lis-tening for the moment when, silent, they'd quit the soft shoals of white, powdery sand and strike the damp, compacted slick of the shoreline. There, their feet would slap the dampness with the hard, incisive beat of young, gamboling mammals. They'd spin, turn about, move downwind once again, their long, sinewy thighs pumping rhythmically with so much wild, pure, guileless exertion. They moved as one, keeping a fixed interval, a constant distance in continuous displacement.

"Molly, Molly," one of them cried out.

"Molly," she cried. And from where I stood I could hear the last syllable literally torn, shredded from the first in a long, protracted "*eee* . . ." that was then dragged into the thick marine mist like some small verbal sacrifice. Some morsel for a sea god, or simply a reluctant offering to the heavy, complicitous elements that, all morning long, surrounded us.

I couldn't stay. I could neither go on watching them, nor find the pretext, the perfectly natural, offhand excuse for walking up and addressing them. I hadn't, I must admit, the nerve. Molly had already grown too large in my heart, too vivid in my imagination, to be treated as casually as the circumstance demanded. And, as for myself, I'd become altogether too transparent. I would have given my "game" away too readily; of that, I'm certain.

As I was about to walk on, I noticed, lying on the sand in a scattered cluster, two pairs of cork-soled beach sandals and, alongside, a somewhat faded pair of once-colorful beach robes. They lay there, limp, abandoned, as if they'd just that morning been washed ashore. Without a second thought, without realizing what I was doing until I'd done it, impulsively, almost mechanically, I reached down and ran my hand — hesitating, at first — across the still plush terry-cloth interior of the first robe I'd come upon. As I did, I watched my ringed fingers fan upwards and out. I repeated this movement. I repeated it several times, each time slower, letting the fork of my fingers comb the tufted pile of the fabric, then withdraw, contract once again into the single, slender draft of my branched hand. I had never seen my hand so attractive. I had never seen my hand so beautiful. I, who paid little — too little — attention to myself, who lacquered my fingernails each week as impatiently, distractedly as one could, suddenly found myself utterly fascinated by that svelte member in all its deft, sensuous operations. I watched it fan and contract, wonderfully intricate, like the webbed apparatus of some delicate marsh bird. Like one of nature's most elaborate devices.

Then, abruptly, it stopped. Went still. Lay as if magnetized, now, to the very robe it had so thoroughly invested. Lay fixed. Transfixed. Mesmerized.

A moment later I'd watch them from the pier through one of those chubby, penny-a-peek telescopes that line the promenade, either side, like the light artillery of the voyeur or simply that of the casually curious. Was I learning from too much example? The two young women were still frolicking, splashing, running along the shoreline, except that now they had left their beachball together with their other belongings. Left it, that is, with their sandals and robes, in exactly the same place as I'd stood only a few moments earlier.

Through the telescope, they appeared enormous. Heavily magnified, their hair seemed to slash like ropes about their bobbing heads, to gag their mouths or, occasionally, to mask their eyes in a flat, lateral curtain of shimmering filaments. They were shouting joyously, their teeth flashing like so many beads of sea foam, but what with the pounding of the surf I could only guess at their words, their taunts. Far beyond them, but rendered immense — immensely close — by the telescope, lay Malibu and the last reaches of the Santa Monica Mountains, rippling deep cobalt under the already high, mid-morning sun. As they ran, as if grazing the mountains behind, I'd catch shoulders, ankles, a bit of flowing hair through the telescope's minuscule eyepiece. Then, suddenly, I'd lose them, see nothing but blue: but blue air, or rock, or ocean. But a loop of burning gold where the surf had just broken, or an eyelet of white for an occasional, wind-struck umbrella. When, once again, I'd pick up their quick, moving frames, slick with sunlight and splashed water, I'd find myself, at last, exhaling. For how long, I wondered, had I held my breath?

How long had their romping bodies broken free from my sight, and lost themselves in so much wind and rock, in the vacuous haul of so much ocean?

They were back, now, and walking, and well fixed within the narrow angle of my vision. I followed their movement along the beach with all the avidity of an ornithologist glimpsing, for the very first time, a species he'd spent a large part of his life studying, tracing, tracking down now to its very last and highly precarious habitat. How very beautiful the two of them were.

I might have gone on watching for hours and hours if, at a given moment, one of the two young women — magnified at least double by the telescope — hadn't suddenly stopped, and, letting her mate — a bit oblivious — walk on alone, turned directly toward the telescope itself. Just as suddenly, she lifted a tall, lanky, athletic arm, and gave me a wide, sweeping wave. At first, a bit absurdly, I thought she might be waving at the telescope. I thought she might be performing one of those endless, endlessly eccentric beach spectacles so common to this area. One of those small, self-advertising performances that are still an integral part of the world in and about Hollywood. But, of course, she was waving at me, not at that machine I'd been feeding pennies to for the past fifteen minutes. She waved once, maybe twice, and then — with a quick jog — caught up with her "sister," her "twin," her own sleek, shimmering reflection. Together, and identical, they headed off.

This evening, immediately after dinner (somewhere, that is, around nine o'clock), she telephoned. Sidney and I had just sat down to a game of backgammon when the houseboy announced that I had a call on my studio telephone, upstairs.

"I hope I'm not disturbing you," the young woman said, and then introduced herself. She sounded somewhat breathless.

"No, of course not," I replied. "But is there something —"

"Well, yes," she interjected. "You see, I'd so very much like to speak with you." And here, suddenly, she hesitated. It was as if her voice, at that very instant, had been replaced by her breath, and her breath, as if in compensation, had accelerated. Had rushed, just audible, into that very silence she had created out of so many unspoken sounds.

"It's about your novel," she said, at last. "I'm simply enchanted by your novel." She pronounced the word "nah-vill" with a very distinct Boston accent.

"Actually," I replied, "there are three novels, altogether. I've written three of them over the past few years. None of them, I must admit, has made much of an impression on the public. I'm just a bit curious to know, actually, which of those three you're referring to."

I heard her breath quicken once again, and could only picture, at that very instant, the coral tip of a starlet's perfectly manicured index finger being pinned, trapped, by two equally perfect incisors. It might well have been (I went on imagining) some tiny device she'd perfected in childhood to keep her already nervous, precipitant nature at least partially in check.

"Maybe," I suggested, "it was my last book, the one about India."

"That's it," she immediately replied. "The one about India, that's exactly the one. It was just wonderful."

"The book with the bright yellow dust jacket," I added.

"Bright yellow," she responded. "That's it. That's just the one. From the first page to the last, I just couldn't put it down."

"I'm delighted," I replied. "I'm perfectly delighted you enjoyed it so. Now," I asked, as casually, as gently as I could, "what can I do for you?"

I'd never, of course, written a single word about India, let alone an entire book, and all three of my novels had blue-and-gray wrappers and black bindings. Over the black bindings lay a discreet scattering of dark gold florettes.

"I wonder if . . ." and here, the young woman's voice seemed composed, now, of as much oxygen — respiration — as speech. "I wonder if we could meet somewhere, maybe. I'd like to meet somewhere and talk to you about your wonderful novel. Your wonderful novel about India."

Her voice, turbid, anxious, equivocating, had so little to do with the extreme simplicity of that body I'd seen only a few hours earlier, exulting in the surf. The body — I should say "bodies" because there were two of them, and they were identical — had moved with all the spontaneity of whim and the confidence of instinct. Nothing about her physical bearing spoke of anything but speed and grace and that sensuous dispensing of energy that belongs only to the young and the genuinely guileless.

I suggested that we meet downtown: as far, that is, from Santa Monica and the crowd that Sidney and I frequent as possible. As far as I could get, that is, from even the slightest chance of any public exposure, whatsoever. A small, somewhat swank cocktail lounge on lower Wilshire Boulevard came to mind. It's called the Zebra Room. Inside, that frisky, cantankerous beast is represented in every conceivable manner. There are zebra-stripe doormats, carpets, bar stools, while overhead whole herds can be seen galloping across an elegant set of wall murals like so many wild, ecstatic horses. Even the tables and cocktail piano there are trimmed in neat, confluent panels of exotic zebra wood. And yes, the napkins, the napkins themselves bear those thick, sinuous, brown and white stripes like so much undulating contour on a heavy, cartographic relief.

It seemed the ideal place. Aside from being light, airy, and totally *mode*, it possesses, for a cocktail lounge, that rarest of qualities: it's thoroughly disengaging. It doesn't corner or commit: one can walk out as easily, unobtrusively, as walk in. Furthermore, being deliberately frivolous in its décor, it seems more a place for uttering hints, suggestions, muted proposals, than flat statements. One goes to the Zebra Room more to whisper than to speak. More to conspire than contract.

When I suggested four-thirty, Thursday, she agreed before I'd even finished saying it. She seemed to snap at the assignation like a scavenger at some tiny strip of freshly slaughtered meat. Her breathing, I noted, went suddenly regular, and the tone of her voice — as if appeased, placated, now — repeated the time and place of the rendezvous with an air both flat and perfunctory.

"I'll be bringing you something," she added, in that newly acquired intonation, that neutrality of hers. "Something I'm quite certain you'll like."

Then, as a coda, an addendum, a final gush from that nearly arrested source, she added, in a quick whisper: "Thursday," and hung up.

February 3rd. I haven't told Sidney. Haven't felt the need to. It's not a secret, of course, and yet it's nothing I'd wish to speak of. Not yet, at least. Not until something significant enough actually happens. Meaningful enough. Like what, though, I ask myself, with the sun streaming, this very instant, through my studio windows, and the top of my pen touching the very tip of my chin, the sunstruck page of the journal staring — almost aggressively — upward. Like what, Millicent? Like what?

February 4th. Either I was a few minutes early, or she a few minutes late, but no more. She paused at the entrance, a parcel under one arm, just long enough to spot me at the corner table I'd reserved that noon, and long enough, too, to stun me with her astonishing resemblance to Molly Lamanna. As she stood there, full shouldered, in a gray, tailored suit, her hair rolling like so much oily, uncontainable surf over at least five or six slack, matching strands of pearl before coming to rest, finally, on either side of a deep, plunging, ivory-white V neck, there was no one in the normally discreet Zebra Room who didn't pause to look. I even caught a momentary ripple of silence, no more than a split second's, as it swept over the lounge and, just as quickly, reabsorbed itself within the continuum of so much animated chatter.

"Here, this is for you," she said, as if by way of introducing herself. She handed me the bundle. "I think it might be something you'll appreciate."

She had walked up to the table with such perfect self-assurance, such a loose, relaxed but unmistakably professional gait (one narrow foot stepping precisely, infallibly, in front of the other), that I realized we wouldn't be wasting any time whatsoever on small talk. I took the bundle, and laid it on the sofa alongside me. I knew exactly what it contained.

"It's terribly kind of you," I said.

"I like being kind," she replied without the least hesitation, then added, somewhat circumspectly, "whenever I can be, that is."

We ordered drinks. While we waited, I noticed that each time she crossed or uncrossed her rather long, polished legs,

I'd get a thin but cloying whiff of Shalimar. What with its sweet, somewhat clerical, byzantine aroma, I've always associated Shalimar with intrigue, with a furtive world of immensely subtle transactions and covert procedures. It's not a scent I appreciate.

"Miss Voigt," I began.

"Vivien," she corrected.

"You see, Vivien . . ."

"There," she said, "that's better . . ."

"You see, I've just begun writing a novel," I continued, a bit astonished, I must admit, by my own inventiveness. "I started it — the outline, at least — just a few weeks ago. I'm still in the process of constructing the plot," I went on, "of finding, that is, the kind of circumstances I'll need to develop an exciting narrative. Then, to bring it, eventually, to some kind of satisfactory resolution."

"How fascinating," Vivien Voigt said, somewhat flatly. She clearly hadn't believed a word I'd said.

"In fact," I continued, "I'm gathering characters right now for my story. It's a bit like in films," I heard myself lie. "You know, like in casting. Looking for exactly the right person to fill each particular role."

"How utterly fascinating," Vivien Voigt said, even flatter than before.

"To tell you the truth, I've had my eye on Miss Lamanna for several weeks now. That's why you saw me watching her so intently — didn't you — on the beach the other day. I'd already picked her out as a kind of model for one of the key characters I'm trying to portray." As I said this, as I went on elaborating what was clearly a shallow dissimulation of my own growing ardor, it struck me that what I'd just said — had just said to Vivien Voigt before I'd even hinted, suggested such a thing to myself: announced out loud to a stranger what I hadn't even whispered to anyone (or anything) within reach of my own hearing — wasn't a lie at all, wasn't a ploy or falsification, but in fact a truth I'd been keeping — quite assiduously — from myself. I *would* be writing a novel about Molly Lamanna, I now realized. I probably, in some semiconscious way, had already begun. This wasn't, obviously, the cause of my fascination. But it could quite easily become the effect, the result of so much lavished attention. A new novel, in fact, or a script, a screenplay, might be the one thing I could ever hope to redeem from such an impossible predicament. Might be its one salvaged flower.

"So," I continued, "if my fiction writing interests you altogether as much as you say, you could, in fact, be very useful. Very useful, indeed."

"I suppose," she replied, "we're all looking for something, aren't we. You're looking, you say, for a female character for your novel. And I'm looking — quite frankly — for a job. Yes, a job. A screen test. For a real chance in the movies. That," she said, staring straight across, "makes us kind of equals, doesn't it."

I noted that, unlike Molly, Vivien Voigt had a slight cleft to her chin and, whenever she smiled, a pair of narrow dimples. Her eyes, though, weren't lovely like Molly's. They were as gray, as immense, as pendant at their very extremities as hers, but they lacked absence, that strange, displaced, inconsolable quality that made Molly's eyes mysterious — even metaphysical — and Vivien's virtually common.

"Well," she said, somewhat offhandedly, "who starts?"

"Go ahead," I replied, lighting a cigarette. "I came here, after all, to listen. To hear what you have to say."

I caught, that very same instant, another whiff of Shalimar.

She'd swung her legs very slightly sideways, and bent her head — her hair slipping forward — to sip a Tom Collins from a tall, frosted, acid green tumbler.

"All right," she said, leaning back and shaking her hair out in the very same moment. "I'll start. Mind if I borrow one of your cigarettes?

"You see," she began, taking a long draw, "we've only been living together in the same apartment for about four or five months now. And the first thing I can tell you about Molly Lamanna, quite frankly, is how little I know. How little — for that matter — anyone knows. How little maybe even Molly herself knows. I mean, she's still rising up out of that amnesia, you understand." The word "amnesia" stopped me short. "Yes, you see, whatever it was that happened left her like in a cloud. She has no recall. She can't remember a single thing from before. *Something* happened, that's certain, but she can't remember what. Can't even remember where, or when, or who she was, or whom she was with. All she remembers is being repatriated — she calls it that, 're-patriated' — because she must have been abroad, probably in Europe, in France, when it happened. And it must have been pretty terrible, you know. Too terrible to re-member.

"So, the first thing she can recall — and even that's pretty vague — is the office of some federal agency in New York City. There, they gave her what they call the basic necessi-ties. Just enough to start life all over again, such as a name (because she'd lost even that), identity papers, and the loan of just enough money to pay for her hospitalization and a few days' living expenses. Because it seems that she was at least three weeks coming out of a kind of coma — a 'cloud,' she calls it — at a city hospital on Staten Island. So, she accepted the money, but instead of paying her hospital bill, she took a taxi right out to Floyd Bennett Field that very same day, and went flying.

"Because — maybe you already know this — Molly Lamanna is simply crazy about flying. Simply wild about it. 'Where are you going, today, Molly?' I'll ask her.

"'Going up, that's where,' she'll answer, and toss off one of those saucy little smiles of hers. 'Way up.'

"'Can I borrow your silver lamé gown?' I'll ask her, or for some other such thing.

"'You can borrow any blessed thing you like. Just take it, understand? Don't ask. Just take, take anything.' She'll say things like that. It's as if she's in a rush to get rid of her own belongings. Be done with possessions, commitments, obligations, anything that might keep her, as she'd say, 'grounded.' How many times have I caught her throwing clothes, papers, whole bedspreads out the apartment window. 'I suppose,' she'll say, after the tantrum's over, 'that that's my favorite thing, getting rid of other things.' I remember her saying that, once; remember her saying exactly that."

Vivien Voigt, Molly Lamanna's double, her near perfect twin, and — I was beginning to realize — her pure opposite, as well, took another long sip of her Tom Collins, then leaned back and smiled, rather lazily, across the low, zebra-wood table.

"Is this the kind of thing that you wanted to hear?" she asked.

"If it's true," I told her.

"It's not exciting enough not to be true," she said, then fitted the nail of her index finger, its very tip, between two sharp incisors, exactly as I'd imagined her doing over the telephone. I watched her as if grind the nail delicately, almost delectably. Saw it as it pivoted in the clamp of those two imperceptibly rotating teeth.

"I hear she goes out flying at night," I suggested. "That she takes whatever airplane she can, and flies it clear until morning."

Vivien Voigt removed the tip of her long, elegant finger from that tiny, enamel vise she employed with such deftness. In the same instant came the same scarcely audible rush of breath, of breathing, that I'd heard over the telephone, several days earlier. Clearly, her index served as a kind of "stop" to those momentary, barely contained assaults of sheer anticipation.

"I could tell you things. I could tell you lots of things," she said. Even her breath, now, was full of suggestiveness.

"Please, please go on," I asked.

"I could tell you, for instance, about the company she keeps, and all the strange little ways she goes about doing this thing and that, every day. How she ties her hair up, and does her eyes, if that's the kind of thing, for example, you're interested in. But first," she said, her gaze leveled and fixed intently upon mine, "first, why don't you tell me?"

"Tell you? Tell you what?"

"What you're really after," she replied, with the vaguest of smiles spreading, now, across her lips. "Why you're so terribly interested in hearing so many trivialities about someone you don't even know. Or scarcely."

"I've been perfectly explicit, Miss Voigt. I've told you, I'm gathering material for my next novel. Do I need to repeat myself?"

"I suppose," she replied, "I'm not altogether certain that I believe you, that's all." As she said this, her smile floated to the very corners of her lips. "But then, I don't *need* to believe you, do I."

"How do you mean that, exactly?"

"I mean, all I have to do is the talking, the telling. And all you have to do is the bidding. Isn't that what it's all about?"

"Bidding? Bidding for what?"

"Why, bidding for me," she said with absolute nonchalance. "You know, I'm not always going to be Molly Lamanna's stand-in. I have a career of my own. I mean, I could become anyone I choose. I'm a free person, after all. I could become an ash blonde at the drop of a hat if I so decided," she said, running a hand through her hair. "I could go Nordic, go Latin, do dancing or sing. All I need," she said, her breath at last catching up with her words, "is someone like yourself to do my bidding. Someone like yourself," she added, "to whisper the right word to the right person, if you know what I mean."

"But I *don't* know what you mean, Miss Voigt."

"Vivien . . ."

"I simply don't —"

"Then," she interjected, "maybe you should ask someone who *does*. Maybe you should ask your husband, for instance. Ask him. He'll tell you what I'm talking about."

"My husband?"

"Ask him about that south-of-the-border musical, that extravaganza they're in the process of casting, right now. There's an opening. A part. A small supporting role that I want, want badly. A little word, a whisper, a tiny nudge coming from you, Millicent, would do the trick."

"Why don't you simply ask him yourself?" I answered, angered by her sudden familiarity. Of course, it was a ridiculous retort on my part, reacting to her crassness with pure pique rather than formulating some measured response of my own. Vivien Voigt, in any case, could have no possible access to my husband, or, for that matter, to anyone of Sidney's rank.

The closest she could possibly reach, in terms of Studio ech-elon, would be Dick Liddington, the Assistant Casting Direc-tor, and, even then, she'd have to confront a whole set of obstacles.

"But I *have*," Vivien Voigt responded. "I *have* spoken to your husband. Several times, personally," she said, lingering on the word "personally" a bit longer than she might. "Several times, I've asked him, and each time he's said that he'd speak with you. 'I'll speak with my wife, Millicent,' he's said, as if it were your decision, not his. That it was up to you, not him."

I didn't answer. For the moment, I didn't need to answer. I toyed with the tall, black-and-white-striped swizzle stick, letting it set the ice cubes in my tumbler into so many taut, inter-knocking orbits. I listened to the cubes click as they touched, and, at the same moment, marveled at the incredibly suave, intricate workings of my husband's mind. Dear Sidney. My sweet, complicitous man, you'd engineered this encounter from the very first, hadn't you. You'd never said a word to me because you didn't even need to. Didn't wish to cause me, perhaps, some slight, undue embarrassment. Didn't see any need, furthermore, to be explicit. You simply put the idea very quietly into Vivien Voigt's mind, like a drop in her ear ("I'll speak with my wife, Millicent"), and let it happen of itself. Knew it would happen, that it would have to happen, that Vivien Voigt was ambitious, voracious and cunning enough to create the opportunity, the pretext, the "Indian novel in the bright yellow dust jacket" or some such outra-geous contrivance to contact me, and — as informant — of-fer up her considerable services in exchange for my "bidding." For my so-called influence at the Studio.

As for me, I'd given her, quite unwittingly, more than the perfect pretext. And she'd seized upon it immediately. Yes, the other morning at the beach, seeing me touch, caress the faded, terry-cloth beach robe, she'd been given a power of sorts, what might be called "a right of invasion." It was certainly well beyond anything Vivien Voigt, in all her voracity, could have ever expected.

"I'll do whatever I can," I promised her.

"I couldn't ask for anything more," she replied, her wide smile, once again, returning. "And, please, call me any time. I'm available most hours of the day. If there's anything you want, anything you wish to ask . . ."

"There's one thing," I said, surprised again by the sudden emergence, on my part, of some carefully suppressed curiosity. "Does Miss Lamanna use the same scent as yourself?"

"Shalimar?" She laughed a bit too loudly, and shook her head. "Good heavens, no. She doesn't use a thing except baby lotion or talc, or olive oil when she's having her body pummeled — massaged to death, as she calls it. No, she doesn't use anything, anything at all." I heard her laughter trail to a sigh, and the sigh as if oscillate, quaver, chopped as it were into a tiny sequence of brief exhalations.

"You won't forget?"

"No," I said, "I never forget." The nail of her index finger was once again primly stationed between her two glistening incisors. Once again, Vivien Voigt was smiling.

I waited until Wilshire Boulevard began its slow, gradual descent toward the Pacific Ocean before pulling over alongside an empty lot and opening the parcel: Miss Voigt's soft, proffered bundle. As soon as I'd undone it, I drew the beach robe free of its wrappings, and pressed it — like a cool towel — over my entire face. Redolent of the sweet, oily unguents with which it's imbued, olive and bay and orange blossom, it was, I immediately recognized, *hers*. I kept it pressed against my face for the longest moment, and inhaled. Kept inhaling.

February 21st. I'm slipping, and know it. Every day, now, I'm letting go of some small part of myself, some tiny habit or scarcely acknowledged custom, some minor, moral tenet I've held to so instinctively that only now — violated — do I fully realize what I'd once, quite naturally, espoused. Where am I? What's happening with each passing week to that image, that idea of myself I'd so carefully nurtured, sustained, protected? Even my jade figurines — their green gazes — seem filled with reproach. Bit by bit, I'm falling, letting go. And, it would seem, the more I care the less it matters. I'm falling because I've chosen to. I'm letting myself be drawn each day, each week, into the ever-widening circle of an utterly solitary, utterly sterile fascination. I'm drawn as the addicted are drawn — incurably. Or the narcissistic — but toward an entirely vacant mirror. What's worse, there is nothing I can hope for, nothing I can expect or even — expecting — articulate. I've been drawn into the inexpressible. I've been drawn with the heart's weight, downward. And there's nothing I can do about it because there's nothing that I'd wish to do. I'm falling out of pure volition.

February 22nd. I worked on my rewrite of *Mongol Moon*, this afternoon, but distractedly. Sidney reminded me that the finished script must be ready for production in three weeks' time. How will I ever find the concentration? The sustained focus? The thread?

Furthermore, Sidney told me that Molly won't be available for the role of the girl in the garden. Once again, I take note, she has slipped away. Quite inadvertently, she has escaped us. Without caring one way or another (and why should she?), oblivious of her movements, of the effect of her movements upon others, once again, I take note, she has entered — with that perfect, perfectly insouciant predilection of hers — a space apart. An "elsewhere." A separate world of her own. Apparently, she's been leased to another studio for the next few months, and will be playing a kind of Jungle Jane in a set of three B-production remakes. One couldn't do worse. And yet, it would seem, she doesn't mind, doesn't care in the least. When *does* she care? What, if she did, would she care for? It's common knowledge around the Studio that she's working for money, and money alone. She's hoping to save enough by the end of the year to purchase her own airplane. A seaplane, at that.

No one in Hollywood cares less about her career than Molly Lamanna. About what the critics say, or the public. No one I've ever known, in fact, cares less about herself, altogether. She remains so open, so vulnerable, so exposed. "Protect her," I beg Sidney. "Whenever you can, protect her," I beg him.

February 23rd. As of dawn, this morning, my first white peonies are in flower. Strange what one says — whispers — to one flower and not to another. I say things to my peonies I'd never confide, for example, to my gaudy camellias, or the low, squirting circles of my cyclamen.

Peonies, my flower-confessor. "Protect her," I say, keep saying, to no one, now, but the flushed corollas of these near-earthless blossoms. "Protect those, too, who love her," I add, "who would keep her from that emptiness she seems to feed on. Feed on so avidly. Yes," I say, before burying my face in the deep, dew-studded blossoms, "those, too. Protect them."

*   *   *

February 27th. I've become, it seems, the *habituée* of an airfield. This began several days ago, prompted no doubt by my conversation with Vivien Voigt. Just after, I placed a series of phone calls to various pilots, stuntmen, flight advisers, all of whom had worked for the Studio at one time or another, and remained more than willing to answer, no matter how trivial, our smallest request. One favor in Hollywood always begets another. I lied, of course: I called Molly "my niece," and told them that I was desperately worried about her flying habits (which, in fact, I truly am), and would greatly appreciate being kept informed of her take-offs and landings, and — whenever possible — her every destination. "Nothing could be simpler, ma'am," a voice, mindless as it was cheerful, responded. "I'll get in touch with Flight Control. They'll keep you posted directly." And so, a rather complex, even compromising situation was resolved with something as effortless as a local sea breeze. I gave the young man the unlisted telephone number of my studio, upstairs. "My studio," I say, as if entering into a litany. It's there, in that spaciousness, that I not only work but sleep, but dream, daydream, and draw from my vaguest, most amorphous impressions my first, incipient phrases. It's there, in fact, cloistered in sunlight, with my jam jar of pencils and my private telephone line, that I truly come free and start creating. Or, at least, attempt to.

And so, a few days later, it began. The control tower at Glendale's Grand Central Air Terminal telephoned me at four in the morning and advised me, as "per instructions," that a Miss Lamanna had just signed out a Beechcraft "Staggerwing" 17S from the Plosser Flying School for a scheduled duration of three hours. Her destination hadn't been indicated, but her estimated arrival time was set for seven-twenty, that morning.

And so, as I say, it began. Toward three or four in the

morning, perhaps two or three times a week, I'd be advised of Molly's departures. I'd go on lying there in bed, half asleep, still hoping somehow to find her beneath the heavy, troughed quilting of some sustained dream, rather than plucked, as she was, abducted — her own exquisite captive — into those thin, ever-thinning altitudes that by that hour, certainly, she'd already attained. Bit by bit, I'd awaken to those spaces, to those gradually expanding distances. I'd begin visualizing Molly as she probably was at that very moment, wrapped in the raised collar of a heavy leather flight jacket, her massive hair tucked taut under and into a thin, scalp-tight aviator's casque. I'd imagine her tapping each dial on the instrument panel, from time to time, with the tip of a gloved finger. Now in my mind (call it my heart) I'd trace her flight northward, flying under a full moon and following the lovely Californian coast, with all its capes and inlets, its surf breaking black and brushed silver, now, in slow, successive bars, phosphorescent curlers that, from that altitude, would unroll with all the inertia, the relentless lassitude, of some mythical procession.

Or, inversely, I'd imagine Molly flying moonless. I'd flown moonless often enough with my brothers, years ago, to know what aviators will do under certain conditions, what little thrills they'll invent for themselves in the midst of the night. So I'd imagine Molly bringing her aircraft down against a flat stratum of cumulus, for instance, and — flicking her landing lights on — seemingly "bounce" the belly of her plane against the vaporous bed of the cloud bank. This, of course, could go on almost indefinitely. It was fabulous fun. One would skim across the flat surface of the clouds, letting the whole airplane skip like a smooth pebble across so much pond water, the "floor" of the clouds not only lit but as if flooded by the brilliance of those low, fanned, overlapping lights. Those nocturnal marauders.

I could remain in bed, restlessly, only for so long. What was it, though, that pulled me up? That dressed me in slacks and a heavy cardigan as quickly, furtively, as it could? That asked for nothing in itself, really, but some distant glimpse, some gleaned ray from that glorious fugitive? Some trace from the traceless? I found myself unlocking the garage doors, rolling my Talbot out as quietly as possible, then heading, at three or four or five in the morning, morning after morning, toward Glendale and the Grand Central Air Terminal. I'd take Santa Monica Boulevard, empty now except for an occasional ice truck, through the somnolent suburbs of Beverly Hills and West Hollywood, the streets usually slick at this time of year from brief showers that pasted the pavements with so many star-pronged reflections. I'd turn north on Western and, on reaching Los Feliz, sumptuously landscaped, catch — if I were lucky — the smell of bougainvillaea rising up under the high, shaggy, overhanging eucalyptus. I loved stopping for traffic lights in places like that. Even the lights themselves seemed scented. From Los Feliz on, it went quickly. I'd cross the Los Angeles River and head north on the San Fernando Road with its all-night aluminum diners, either side, and — one after another — those hopelessly rickety, wood-framed farm trucks coming down from out of the hills ahead, and loaded, overloaded, with citrus. Then, within minutes, I'd be there.

I'd park (as I've just parked, only moments ago) along the dark dirt embankment of Sonora Avenue. I was now situated at the very tip of the runway, at its northwest extremity, facing the immensely long, gradually receding V of its sparkling lights. White and a rich, ruby red, the lights converged — merged — at the opposite extremity in a throbbing battery of indeterminate rose.

So, here I am. I've left my car motor running, and my

heater on. Fortunately, too, I've brought along a wool shawl, and have wrapped myself, twice over, in its deep navy. I'm writing these very words, this very minute, on a clipboard propped against my steering wheel and lit by a small overhead lamp. Sitting here, now, an eye on the runway, I find myself in these totally estranged circumstances astonished by the pressure that certain words, certain phrases, in themselves, will exert. How — even here — they long to settle, to alight upon the page, be brought, finally, to a kind of quietus. Out of all the incoherent riot that's arisen from my heart these past weeks, how they, of themselves, beg for measure, interval, grace, stillness.

Curious, too, in regard to words, how Sidney, infinitely tactful, solicitous as ever, had mentioned Molly — Molly's myth — over a light lunch we'd been having. How he felt that the mystery surrounding her, that whole, nebulous aura she casts about as nonchalantly as a perfume, or drags behind her like some exhausted stole, "would vanish," as Sidney put it, "volatilize, with one single, well-written paragraph." Others, according to Sidney, find her mysterious as well. She seems to thrive, he feels, on a kind of vapid mist, on the absence of "fixed points," of what Sidney termed "an explicit presence." He then suggested (serving me, as he did, a fruit salad, with the most perfect, most consummately unassuming air) that only I could write that paragraph. If the spirit ever moved me, he said, even for the sake of "sheer amusement, as a kind of verbal puzzle, let's say," I alone could bring Molly Lamanna into perspective. Even with a single, perfectly observant, penetrating remark I could clear the air. Could shape, press, mold Molly on language alone into something palpable, plausible, true.

And yet, here I am, waiting in a half-heated convertible along the edge of a runway at six in the morning for someone

I don't, in fact, even know; for someone I probably won't even encounter; someone I'd feel grateful enough simply to glimpse, crawling out of a tight cockpit door. Where am I? What exactly have I done to my life? Each day now I recognize less and less of myself. Each day I feel more and more as if I've become hopelessly entangled in an absence. In some deep, existential oversight. Still, Sidney claims that with "one single, well-written paragraph" I could reduce this vision (by which he's implying — gently but insistently — fabulation), and, on language alone, make Molly real.

As if, I write, sitting here in my cooling and now nearly cold convertible, as if there were words for that rush, that flutter, that immensity. As if one could verbalize on light itself, could twist it into so many sharp, incisive syllables.

Reduce her to a phrase? If only I could.

It's six-thirty, and still dark. I've just watched a whole squadron of British Tiger Moths land, one after the other, each of these rather ungainly biplanes bearing the insignia of the Royal Canadian Air Force. The Canadians are down here training on a somewhat clandestine basis for what we've come to call (it's the perfect euphemism): "the inevitable." Despite the heavy secrecy that's supposed to surround their activities, everyone seems well aware of their operations, their sorties in tight formation as well as their simulated dogfights just off the coastline. Everyone, too, seems quite proud to have them. They'll be the first to go, we know that. They'll be leaving long before our own boys do. And they'll be leaving, it's more and more apparent, quite soon, now.

We've been watching Europe, day by day, go under. Within the past few weeks, now, Barcelona has fallen and, along with it, the Spanish Republic. A junta, composed of so many straw men, is being formed in preparation for Franco's triumphant entry into Madrid. It's only a matter of time, now. Since Munich and the annexation of the Sudetenland, everybody here has been counting the days. On last night's news, the Wehrmacht was reported to be massed along the Czechoslovakian frontier. There's nothing, now, to stop them, we know it too well. At any moment, Czechoslovakia, in its turn, will be overrun, occupied, decimated by those methodical, heavily mechanized hordes. And everything we loved, those beautiful cities we traveled through as art students — Vienna, Budapest, and now Prague — that held us astonished in the rich, baroque rolls of their florid mirrors, and gave us our first and perhaps most poignant notions of human glorification, those, those marvelous fugues, those sculpted seminars in pure luminosity, will have all gone under. Under the shadow, the boot. Under the grinding of the barbarian's half-tracks. Gone, perhaps, forever.

Hollywood, of course, has done what it could. Hadn't Joan Crawford been the first to denounce the atrocities in Abyssinia, and Frederic March raised a considerable sum to buy ambulances for the Spanish Republic? The best, as always, came forward. Sidney himself has been active, and immensely generous, with both his time and money, on many of the Anti-Fascist Committees in town, and has enlisted others, many others, in forming what is now called a "Common Front."

But you, Millicent? What about you? In the midst of all this, with all Europe catching fire, what exactly have you done? What causes have you contributed to? Aside from following an exquisite apparition about the city and, through a telescope, along the beach, what can you say you've accomplished in the very same moment the matches were being struck? Were being lit? Wasn't your only vital interest, in fact, going about and purchasing things in absentia for that "apparition," that infant, that sublime child that you, yourself,

could do no more than imagine? Going astutely, from shop
to shop, picking out a skirt here, a bolero blouse there? Hadn't
you, at Saks, chosen in less than an hour, not only a black
silk turban, but so much lingerie, light cashmeres, and chic
imported baubles? Wasn't that your only cause? Your only
interest and activity? Then, returning from Rodeo Drive to
your house overlooking the sea at Santa Monica Canyon, and
rearranging, a bit more each day, your own closets to make
room, shelf after shelf, for that rapidly growing accumulation
of finery? All those soft fabrics in the service of a totally cultivated fiction? The wardrobe swelling — and sumptuously —
for the sake of a pure ephemera? Wasn't that your "contribu-
tion"? Wasn't that what you did, what you're doing, day after
day, with your life?

Now, it's already later. I'd written the foregoing paragraph by
the increasingly faint overhead lamp, when — looking out
through the windshield — I caught sight, entirely by chance,
of a fresh star lying relatively near the horizon. On closer
view, I saw that this wasn't a star, but a planet, its light constant, unblinking. I couldn't, however, recognize the planet,
either by its color or its intensity. I'd just gone back to jotting
a few more words within this journal when, quite inadvertently, I glanced up, once again, and found that the planet
had moved. I found that the planet was moving. That what
I'd mistaken for some celestial body was now located about
two hours west of Venus and closing quite steadily. It was
clearly that of an aircraft, of its running lights. I followed its
slow progress eastward, saw it transit with Venus for fully two,
perhaps three, seconds, then successively vanish and reappear
as if in a set of cinematic frames from behind several distant,
low-roofed structures and the occasional palm that stood like

a dim, sporadic exclamation point against the gradual but now irrepressible blueing of the dawn sky.

Then, it curved. The airplane described a slow arc over the Verdugo Mountains, and, still heading downwind (I could follow the wind by an illuminated wind sock at the edge of the runway), was already, quite clearly, preparing its approach. It vanished twice behind the surrounding hills (the Verdugo's on one side, Griffith Park on another), then suddenly reappeared, terrifically close now. It had entered pattern and, lofting a bit into the oncoming air currents, begun its final descent. Now with its fanned landing lights flooding the runway toward me, what I saw wasn't so much the airplane as its sleek and quite unmistakable front-facing silhouette. It was a Beechcraft "Staggerwing," exactly the model that Molly Lamanna had checked out three hours earlier. The time, at that very instant, was (as estimated) seven-twenty.

I turned off my own engine to hear that of the aircraft, lightly throttled now and held to a single, tenuous cylinder beat just this side of a full stall. The plane's faired, retractable landing gear had been lowered, both downward and out, and even from this distance one could clearly distinguish its neat, streamlined "spats." Now with its flaps, ailerons, perfectly trimmed, the plane touched down faultlessly upon the slick cement runway. As it did, as both its front wheels alighted simultaneously and began spitting rainwater in half-circles off the stale puddles on the airstrip, I heard the aircraft's engine, heavily throttled, roar abruptly, impetuously, even angrily, to a fresh take-off.

Molly, it would seem, wouldn't be reclaimed, restored to earth, that easily. She was off already, and would fully return only after having performed four, five "deadstick landings," her engine cut and coming in, over and over, on skill alone.

On skill, exquisite flair, and, I'd add, nerves as perfectly tuned as harp strings. I'd imagine her then, her entire profile lit marine green from the radium dials on her instrument panel, bringing her craft down, over and over, in utter silence, with that high forehead of hers, the somewhat lifted chin, the whole composure that of one who flies (or simply breathes, exists) with a sublime disregard for her own person. I'd imagine her, brows lightly raised, arched against the oncoming runway, the slightest of smiles — exultations — drawn across her lips, with her entire face lit now not only green from the instrument panel, but the green streaked ruby red in quick, rhythmic slats as the lights of the runway rushed as if upward on either side, and then — in even, pulsating intervals — flashed past.

Molly was back. Molly wasn't ours, wasn't mine, but she was back. She'd returned to earth. That's all that mattered to me: that she was safe, and amongst us once again. Morning after morning, like some entirely invisible mother, I'd wait until my own, equally invisible daughter had returned, touched down, reintegrated what is — after all — our only element. Had merged with that crowded mirror. With that circle of contingencies that we call — somewhat flippantly — a world. Molly, I knew, *could* be said. *Could* be articulated. She wasn't a myth, a mythical escapee of everything we'd come to know and measure ourselves by. Hadn't she just returned? Wasn't she taxiing, that very instant, toward the high, hump-backed Maddux hangars on the far side of the runway? Weren't the very first reflections of a blue dawn already wobbling, like so much irresolute water, from her shining wingtips?

As to Molly, as to Molly's own wishes, there's no doubt: she'd go on and on, forever, if there were a "forever" to fly to. If there were anything else but *back* and *down* as — ultimately — our only destinations. If gravity (like some archaic fate) or simply her own fuel supply didn't, each time, pull her under and hold her as if ballasted to her own relentless repetitions. If there were a word, however, that transgressed, that superseded other words, a word-to-fly-to, I'm certain that Molly would have been the first to discover it. Would have long since set her instruments on to it, and flown, inflexible, until her very being had been absorbed in the all-absorbing folds of its vocable.

"A word-to-fly-to," as if such a thing ever existed. Yet, isn't "Molly" the word that stirs, that continuously incites you? The very vocable, in fact, you yourself fly to how many times each day? That you press like a succulent, or some diaphanous wafer, between your all too anxious lips? Isn't it? Isn't it, Millicent?

March 2*nd.* Now, rereading my last entry, it strikes me this morning that only Molly, among all of us, hasn't a word, a cherished image, a "Molly" of her own whom she, in turn, might evoke. Indeed, she has no one, no one at all. Isn't it this, certainly, that drives her, night after night, to such altitudes, chasing vapors, air currents, flying — as she does — blind into the face of such facelessness?

How one would love to see Molly *encounter* something. Something earthen, even carnal. To see her rub hips, flanks, shoulders against some living surface, pressing her pelvis against some utterly unrelenting response.

See her locked, at last, in the wet, glittering creases of some wet, glittering reflection. Returned; yes, restored at last.

March 3*rd.* The airplane we were so carefully inspecting was indeed a seaplane. Its overall length, including pontoons, was something slightly more than an inch, and its entire body (from propeller to rudder) was constructed out of solid gold.

"Look, look at this one," Vivien Voigt enjoined, because there were two other airplanes, seaplanes as well, both of which dangled from the bracelet's shifting mass of lapping, overlapping charms. The charms jingled dully, I noticed, like distant goat-bells. Spilling with a certain indolence, one over another, they seemed to exist in some quasi-reluctant obedience to the whims of Vivien Voigt's wrist. Whenever her wrist moved, the charms splashed idly, chaotically, after.

We were seated at a small window-side table at the Cine-Grill, talking low over our tall, frosted drinks. Vivien Voigt had called me the night before and announced that she had "something special, really special" to propose. Without giving it a second thought, I suggested that we meet here, in the very heart of Hollywood, at the Roosevelt Hotel. Appearances no longer seemed to matter, now. I've been slipping — letting myself slip — these past few weeks, and finding, in the slow, self-induced fall, a certain, almost voluptuous pleasure. Let it happen, I keep saying to myself. Let it happen.

We went through the charms on Molly Lamanna's charm-glutted bracelet one by one. With a neat, flamenco-like flourish, Vivien Voigt — her arm raised — would shake the bracelet's glittering mass, from time to time, into a fresh disposition. New charms would thus rise to the surface while others, overlapped, would slide under. I noted that each time Vivien Voigt went through this studied little spectacle of hers, the air about us would be charged, suddenly, with the unmistakable redolence of Shalimar.

"I kind of thought . . . ," she said in that rushed, breath-cut elocution of hers, "I kind of thought that this would be a pretty fair exchange, don't you think?"

"And Molly?" I asked.

"She won't even notice. She never notices anything, anyway. What's more, she hasn't worn it in months. It's forgotten already, I can assure you. It was probably forgotten from the very day she got it. Here," she said, "it's yours. It's yours for the taking."

She kept it on, however, rolling it slowly up and down her tanned forearm, or trailing it — its cortège of trinkets — across the starched pink of the tablecloth. She managed to perform each of these rather sham maneuvers with such naturalness that even I, for whom they were intended, couldn't help but be impressed by Vivien Voigt's yet untapped potential as an actress.

Aside from the three seaplanes, we managed to identify, in all that dangling gold, the following:

Two Eiffel Towers

A palette with a half-circle of simulated pigments in applied enamel

A pair of water-skiers

A motorcar, most likely a Lagonda

The initials "M. P." in sleek, swept-back *moderne* characters

A woman in bathing attire, waving

A couple, also in bathing attire, set inside a loop around which *"Souvenir de l'Hôtel Belle Rive, Juan-les-Pins"* was inscribed

A golden toucan inlaid in turquoise

A Scottish terrier

The gold oval of a *jeton* in miniature with *"10,000FF"* incused on one side and *"Casino Municipal de Cannes"* on the other

A second Scottish terrier

Other charms probably escaped us, eclipsed — as they often were — one underneath another. But the hasty inventory listed above represents the better part of what I immediately recognized as utter treasure. For the bracelet was not a simple piece of jewelry, but a collection, a most deliberate accumulation, of personal artifact. It contained, of course, like any charm bracelet, the carefully selected "mementoes" of its bearer's specific history. But unlike most, it offered up an entire set of scattered clues — indices — to an otherwise entirely obliterated past. The charms, I quickly realized, could readily be turned into "keys." Might unlock, someday, some of the sealed doors into Molly Lamanna's memory.

"Well?" she asked. Her fingernail was once again primly stationed between two glistening incisors.

"It's all yours," I told her. "It's nothing very substantial, mind you, but it's what you asked for. It's exactly the role you requested. You begin Monday at a hundred and fifty dollars a week." I had confirmed this with Sidney, only hours earlier.

"Well, it's a start," she said, somewhat laconically.

"It's a start," I agreed.

She began unfastening the clasp of the bracelet with the pointed tip of that very same fingernail she used, occasionally, as a breath-stop. Then, suddenly, she hesitated.

"I'd been hoping, actually, for something a bit more," she said.

"More is coming," I assured her, glancing down at the bracelet. "The more, of course, you bring . . ."

"I know, 'the more I'll get.' But I'd been hoping, in fact, for a contract. A proper, eighteen-month studio contract." Her finger had come free of the clasp now, and with both her hands she was rubbing her hair back from her highly polished temples. Her long hair, like Molly's, was lavish.

"I can give you," I remember telling her, as slowly, solemnly, as I could, "whatever you might wish." I remember, too, in the instant I said this, feeling stunned by my own declaration. It was as if a hidden part of me had once again

released a hidden truth, had disclosed — out loud — what I
wouldn't have dared murmur to myself in my most intimate
moment. But there it was: "whatever you wish," I'd just said.
"Whatever you might wish . . ."

Vivien Voigt was smiling. She had just unfastened the clasp
and was pouring the bracelet — the heavy load of its talismans — into the palm of my hand. My hand dipped, very
slightly, then closed. Clamped shut. The bracelet, at last, was
mine.

"If there's anything," she said, "anything else I can do for
you, I hope you won't hesitate." Never had I heard a word
pronounced with such pure, such perfect ambivalence. "Anything" meant everything and nothing at the same time. No, I
said, quickly correcting myself: it only meant nothing. Nothing and more nothing. It was simply another cheap lure, an
open invitation to that abyss, that netherworld of the spirit,
that I'd already entered, that I'd penetrated, now, a bit deeper
with each day. I didn't need Vivien Voigt's promptings,
either, to do so. To go, with each day, even deeper.

"No," I said, shaking my head. "You've been very kind already."

While Vivien Voigt sipped a frosted daiquiri from a long-
stemmed coupe, I could feel the charms I'd been pressing between my fingers grow gradually warmer. It reminded me, in
a distant, distracted way, of the blue rosaries I'd once had,
years ago, in boarding school. How, in the cold chapel, I'd
smother them in my fist until I had the unmistakable sensation
that it was they, the beads, that were keeping me warm, and
not the opposite; that heat was emanating, even glowing, out
of the very center of so much compacted lapis lazuli. And so
it was now, with the charms. It was their heat, not mine, I
felt radiating outward.

"Certainly," she said, "there must be something, something

else I can do for you, this afternoon." Her gray eyes were as
if floating now over the green rim of her frosted daiquiri,
which, that very moment, she'd brought level with her lips.
Her eyes rose, almost sullenly, to meet mine. "I could tell you,
for instance, about her callers," she said. She pronounced the
word "kah-lahs" in that heavy Boston accent of hers. The accent had, I found, a certain vulgar appeal, a seductiveness of
its own. "You *would* like to hear about her callers, wouldn't
you?"

I didn't say a word.

"Actually, there aren't altogether that many. In fact," she
went on, "they're rather rare, and getting rarer these days. But,
you know, inside an apartment as small as ours, what with the
walls being as thin as they are, you hear everything, if you
understand what I mean. But I've never once — this is the
strangest part — heard Molly. I've heard them. I've heard the
callers, heard them through the paper-thin walls, but I've
never once heard Molly herself say a word, make a single
sound. Never."

How I wanted it to end. How I wanted all this base gossip
that I, only I, had encouraged from the very start — encouraged and collected and, yes, even covertly purchased — how
I wanted this whole traffic of whispers and hearsay and overheard ejaculations to come to an end. How repelled I am at
myself, repelled at dealing with this replica, this *faux-semblant*,
this sham. It's Molly I want. It's Molly I want to protect from
these parasites, these "callers" she so casually, indifferently,
seems to give herself to. But why? Out of what? Boredom?
Curiosity? To revive, perhaps, some deeply buried recollection, some lost memory? Yes, it's Molly herself I'm after. It's
Molly I want to protect and coddle. To be able to run my
hands through her thick, knotted hair, and wash it and be wet
in the same streaming water, and dry it in a huge, heated

towel, and comb it slick and gleaming as a tall waterfall. To hear her breathe, and taste exactly what her breath — quickening — tastes like. To rub her flanks in those natural oils she loves so, and massage her for hours: massage her, as she calls it, "to death."

That it end, this gossip, all this nefarious rumor. This world that's perceived only in the cheap glitter that flies off its metallic surfaces.

That finally, it might finally begin. Might actually start.

March 4th. I left hastily, yesterday. In the hotel lobby, however, Vivien Voigt caught up with me and asked for a lift. Her car, she said, was being serviced, and she had to be at a garden party in Bel Air within that very hour. I knew full well that there were no garden parties at this time of the year but, of course, I took her — it was on my way — and of course asked her no questions en route. If there is one adjective that fully qualifies Vivien Voigt it's that of "available." She's unreservedly available, at least for those who can afford her, and the address she'd given me was clearly that of one who could. I'd long since assumed that even Sidney, at one time or another, had enjoyed Vivien Voigt's very perfect figure, had plunged into that dark cloud of Shalimar, and — who knows — taken a particular pleasure from being in the intimate company of someone so nearly identical to that flower of flowers, his adored wife's adored, inviolable idol.

I thought of all this, driving out. I felt no jealousy whatsoever, begrudged Sidney absolutely nothing. I well knew that, for him, there had never been anyone else, never been a place for anyone else, given that singular fixation, that "focused fire," as he called it, that left him so utterly enthralled in my presence. And, I'd quickly add, so impotent as well. I was his pure untouchable, his projection, the sublimated vision of a deep, deeply self-castigating nature. And so, from that very first night, each of us, in our own way, began drifting apart. Found ourselves more and more astray in a desert of our own making. Yes, each of us, ever since, has scavenged what he could. Sidney, I know, has had his share of starlets, of "Viviens," has been free to pick and choose from that vast Babylonia the Industry maintains. But his affairs have always been short-lived. And, in the end, Sidney has done little more than move from one damp, smoldering, disillusioning romance to another. None of them, it would appear, ever "caught fire."

If Sidney went on to lead one life, I went on — it might be said — to lead a kind of non-life, a life-in-default-of-life, a well-decked, exquisitely appointed vacuity. The "desert," each year, kept on growing and, along with it, that tiny network of thin, ineffaceable tendrils that radiate out of the very extremity of each eyelid. Of course, I had nights here, nights there, my bright, fleeting interludes. Once, I remember, I even had three consecutive weeks in Boca Raton that I qualified, at the time, as "blissful." But I always came back, didn't I? Unscathed, intact, I'd always return to my own unmoved, immovable existence. Now — how many years later — am I, perhaps, at last beginning to learn? To undergo a "Sentimental Education" of my own? At last, at forty-five, am I coming to understand that someone in love, someone at last in love, *doesn't* come back? *Doesn't* return? She, of course, appears, pretends, goes through all the feigned motions of a feigned return, takes her place, seemingly, among the ranks and files of the unruffled, the untouched. Acts outwardly as if she were now cured, and had fully survived her own voluptuous extravagation. That it was "really nothing, in fact." Acts, finally, as if it hadn't even occurred at all, while knowing full well that love is the only thing that actually *does* occur. And that

the very instant it does, one crosses over, and enters the irreparable.

There, she knows, in those immense, immensely desolate
landscapes of the heart, one encounters neither the living nor
the dead, but the blissfully estranged, those that have escaped
category, and wander about weightless, nameless, selfless.
Those drained of all identity, sucked dry of all substance except for that of the curious mirrors that they bear in place of
their hearts: that they carry about like very tiny, itinerant
altars. Within those mirrors, still incandescent (even charred,
occasionally, about their edges), the lovers discern not themselves but the sporadic outlines of their beloved, their elected,
the very agent — that is — of their all-consuming efface-
ment. And that is all that they see, all that they wish to see.
Is all I've seen, seen and dreamt and coveted, these past
weeks: that gorgeous child, her long hair dangling dark
bronze in the gray facets of that mirror that I, as well, bear
instead of a heart. Within it, her eyes are immense, and her
chin floats — ever so slightly — as if buoyed by some secret
effusion. She, for whom certainly I have no existence, has
become, these past weeks, all that I see. That I wish to see.
All, in my own, inner landscape, that *does* exist.

These were my thoughts as I drove Vivien Voigt, Molly Lamanna's glamorous double, through the pompous East Gates
of Bel Air and into that world of so much stage-set property.
Even the very largest estates there appear somewhat miniatur-
ized, plucked as they are from photographs and architectural
renderings. From these, form, style, décor are slavishly replicated, whereas dimension is thoroughly ignored. In front of
one of those shrunken castles or gargantuan doll's houses, we
parted. Vivien Voigt leaned over, kissed me on one cheek,
and in a quick whisper promised to "stay in touch." As she

slid out I noticed for the first time that she was wearing a
rather splendid square-cut emerald on the little finger of her
left hand. I couldn't help wondering where she got it.

March 16th. The days rush past now as if they themselves were
being drawn, drafted, into the general anxiety. They fly by
as if they'd lost all sense of their own duration, and were being
dragged now into some deeper, swifter current: that, that is,
of history itself. Hitler has just yesterday seized Danzig, his
"corridor" into Poland. Every day, now, his pockets bulge fatter and fatter with cities, duchies, entire provinces. Next, certainly, will come Prague, beautiful Prague with its tall turrets
and squat arcades, warm with whisper and gossip and com-
plicity. Our friends returning from Europe tell us of mass mo-
bilizations everywhere, of drawn swords and *partis pris*, of
those who've fled and those — already taken — who've simply vanished, simply "immaterialized." One of our friends gave
us an hallucinating description of the public statuary in Han-
over on one particular night, with all its marble aglow, the
great flanks of its rich, baroque divinities as if coated rose from
the stoked pyre of ten million burning pages, just beneath.

  Here, at home, we're holding our breath. It's only a matter
of months now, we're well aware. But within the Industry itself, the heads of virtually every major studio are bemoaning
the possible loss not of Europe, not of Europe the cradle, the
root, the very underpinnings of our entire civilization, but
Europe the market, the marketplace, the second greatest un-
loading ground on earth for so many streaming miles of punc-
tured celluloid. Some have even expressed outrage that
Europe's preparation for war should attract so much attention;
that the crass spectacle of so many greedy dictators could
enter into open competition with that of the authentic,

inimitable spectacle: that manufactured by Hollywood itself.

As for me, I've plunged under. I'm working with increased ardor now on my rewrite of *Mongol Moon*. The days fly past even faster, and the deadline for the finished script (already twice extended) approaches mercilessly. Here, below, are some of my working notes: they bear particularly on the flashbacks I've introduced into that otherwise stale, monochromatic narrative.

First, Genghis Khan must be *saved* from his own stereotype: from that fixed image (ruthless, saber-wheeling, implacable) in which he has traditionally been cast. Been held, in a sense, captive. Even victim.

He must be *endowed with choice*. Without choice (at least at the dramatically critical moment) there can be no veritable "situation." No scenario worth salvaging.

His heart, spirit, conscience — call it what you will — must be *held in balance*, at least momentarily, between whatever would drive him to destroy Samarkand, before him, and the memory of the girl in the garden, years earlier.

This memory in itself must constitute, in his own torn soul, an alternative. He needn't, that is, destroy Samarkand. He needn't raze the walled cities of Western Asia, one after another. There *is* choice. There *is* an alternative existence which he not only may remember, but — perhaps — anticipate, as well.

How will I render all of this believable? By making it, first, believable to myself. By falling under the charm (if charm there be) of my own reconstitution.

(How, too, can I help but think of Molly as the girl in the garden? As that radiant and — at the same time — obscure, inaccessible creature, belonging to another order — a rarefaction — of reality?)

Khan will appear in the first flashback as a young man, enthralled. He has climbed a tree and is peering down over a garden wall, seeing the girl for the very first time. She is seated on the ground with her back propped against — say — a pomegranate tree. Her skirt lies spread in a pond of embroidered silk about a tiny, corseted waist and a rather ample, adolescent bodice. She should be shown, here, reading a book, entirely absorbed by some *invisible story* when Khan, astonished, first lays eyes upon her. She is exceedingly beautiful.

How will they communicate? Within the five or six flashbacks I'm introducing, it's possible that she might *never* speak. Khan speaks, and at first she flees — but not very far. Behind a tree, say. Or some wrought-iron trellis. Here, we might have a first close-up, preferably in profile, of a girl with long lashes, flowing hair, and a raised, ebullient chin.

Yes, Khan alone will speak. Also, he'll attempt to bring her forth with gifts (an ocelot's skin, for instance, or a game of gold knucklebones). He drops the gifts down onto the ground below (the ground should be dusty, so that each time a gift is dropped one sees, from the slight impact, a slight puff of dust rising). She does nothing to retrieve these gifts, but the next day Khan discovers, each time, that they're gone. He thus knows that the girl in the garden has *received them*. Has *accepted them*.

Khan, throughout, should be seen as both a young warrior, filled with impatience and a scarcely contained lust, *and* a rather self-questioning herdsman: elusive, susceptible, unguarded. Someone, that is, still *capable of falling in love*.

He asks the girl (who is too shy, too intimidated, to reply, and might be — as well — already promised) to place a pomegranate in her straw basket each time she wants to say no; to hold it in her hand each time she wants to say maybe; and to toss it clear up to him in the tree each time she wants to say yes. "Like that," he tells her, "we can talk."

She smiles, and goes on reading. But after a prolonged moment, we see her — in answer to some small question that Khan has put forth — pick a pomegranate off the ground, as if unconsciously, and hold it cupped in the palm of her hand. With the other hand, she goes on reading from her book.

The book, throughout, is paramount. Even when she's not reading from the *invisible story*, she keeps an index finger inserted inside the tiny volume. What is she reading? What does the story recount? Could it possibly already be telling the tale of "the girl in the garden"? Telling, foretelling, the story of what's about to befall them?

Yes, I need to believe totally in this script. I need to believe in it both for the film's sake (how else could I convince a public if I hadn't first thoroughly convinced myself?) and for the sake of my own faith in what we rather obtusely call "humanity." That there *still* might be time. *Still* might be choice. That we might yet, in some obscure, unsuspected, even accidental way uncover the hidden language of human recourse. That a justifiable work of the imagination might still propose, even so tardily, some *alternative* reading: the hope, the glimmer, of some small, overlooked vein in the clogged ore of so much human fatality.

Yes, if I could imagine it, I could — somehow — substantiate it, as well. For it isn't only a scenario that I'm elaborating here, but a tiny — yet crucial — act of faith.

March 30th. Nearly every night now, I await that late-night call from the Glendale Control Tower, telling me that Molly has risen up, as one might say, into her element. That she's left, has quit us, and is giving her "Staggerwing" an airing over the surf-tattered coastline northward, or running now with the full moon fast over the white Sierra Nevada. I rise, dress as quickly, quietly, as possible, and drive out. Even from the cruel distance that I'm forced to keep (seeing Molly minuscule across a wet runway pulling the casque free from her head; observing, even from there, how her hair tumbles free like the soft and flowing abundance from some mythical cornucopia), I simply cannot restrain myself. See her, I must. See her no matter how much damage I might cause what I once blithely called "my self-respect." See her down, and safely amongst us once again. Like a mother, I suppose, putting her child to sleep. Yes, like a mother, I need to put Molly, one might say, *to earth.* Watch her land and listen to her propeller come chopping, stubbornly, to a halt. Yes, back and breathing the same air, the same light, the same shadows. Once again, Molly amongst us.

And even if I never touch her, I want her, at least, within reach. Yes, Molly within reach, moving amongst the same mirrors, brushing against the same roses that squirt like tiny flames in the reflection of the same mirrors.

Yes, within reach. Even if we never touch, never speak, even so. Want her. Want her, even so.

*   *   *

So, once again, I've waited at the end of the runway for Molly's return. And once again, there she is, touching down at exactly the estimated arrival time, making — as ever — a perfect two-point landing, then bringing the heavy, over-powered Beechcraft — still speeding down the slick run-way — back gradually onto its tiny, free-pivoting tailwheel. Yes, once again, there she is. She has taxied up to the huge Maddux hangars, cut her motor, crawled free of the cross-wires between the two heavily strutted wings, set her tie-downs, and, sauntering off now toward the office door, is pulling her gloves free as languidly, lackadaisically, as if all eternity lay before her.

And here I am, once again, turning my key, putting my car into gear, and heading back already along the San Fer-nando Road toward Santa Monica and the ocean. The day has scarcely begun, yet for me it's virtually over. Dawn, though, is bright as jonquils.

April 7th. Vivien Voigt was literally the last person on earth I wanted to see. And most especially there, in public, at what's called a "studio shindig." It was the kind of party that's given to celebrate the completion, successful or not, of some new production. Usually, at these ordeals, everyone drinks too much and hides from their own anxiety at having just lost not only a role but an identity, a momentary place even if it only be in the fictive society of some ephemeral spectacle. No, Vivien Voigt, in this context, was literally the last person I wanted to see. And yet, there she was, moving directly toward me, more radiant, I must admit, than I'd ever seen her, the whole, sheer, loosely hung ensemble of her cocktail dress held together, seemingly, by a single fat sapphire brooch firmly planted high over the rolling muscle of her left hip. The dress itself was in a pale, metallic shade that *Vogue* had

just this season christened, somewhat grandly, "Venus blue."
It was a blue of its own. A wind blue. A shred of something
vaguely celestial that had inadvertently fallen between the
avidity of human scissors.

Why, though, was I there? Why had Sidney called me well
after midnight (something he'd normally never do) begging
me to join him at a party that, he promised, I'd find "absolutely captivating"? Sidney the impeccable, the total embodi-
ment of discretion, of virile delicacy — what reason would he
have to pull me out of bed at that hour (and consequently far
from the late-night phone call I'd be expecting from the
Glendale Control Tower, from that one moment that all the
other moments of the day leapt toward like wild heartbeats:
a thousand moments for the sake of that one that seemed to
escape time, altogether)? Yet Sidney always has his reasons.
Hadn't he, in fact, made his fortune simply by applying his
faultless judgment to an endless succession of problems that
the Studio needed to see immediately resolved? Wasn't that
his art, his craft?

Why, though, this? Why did I have to confront publicly
this duplicate, this glittering imitation of the one person I'd
truly wish to encounter? But there she was, this cheap masquerade, moving toward me at that very moment, her hair
piled high, swept fiercely upward into a limp, overhanging
mass of washed curls. Now, as she came alongside, I could
clearly discern two tortoiseshell combs stuck, at a savage angle, into the midst of that glistening mass, each of them studded with an anarchic burst of blue rhinestones.

Intrigued as I was, I might have gone on examining that
spray of pasted glass if, at that very instant, Vivien Voigt
hadn't smiled. She released a smile that was so beatific, so
angelically round and innocent, and — at the same time —
so utterly impersonal, anonymous, devoid of any emotional

content whatsoever, I scarcely realized (so taken was I by the smile itself) that even if it hadn't been personally intended, it had in fact been aimed not only toward me but, quite expressly, *at* me as well. I was its beneficiary. Then, as simply as that, she swept past. She swept past with scarcely a ruffle of her "Venus blue" cocktail dress, and — unhesitating — continued through the vestibule to the front door, where she took her coat, a wrap of a matching blue, and then, unaccompanied, vanished into the dark, cypress-hedged Hollywood night. And, simultaneously, I realized that the smile couldn't have been Vivien Voigt's, couldn't, in fact, have been anyone's but the one whom Vivien Voigt so slavishly mimicked. And now the smile, the blissful smile, lay, I felt, like the tissue of so much sea mist, already evaporating from the surface of my skin. I touched my cheeks for some lingering trace but, of course, it too had already vanished. "Already vanished," I said to myself, as if it had ever been. As if such things had a duration sufficient to allow for their own vanishing.

And now, writing this so many hours later, I still reach up, from time to time, expecting to feel the stigma of some slight humidity, the still-glowing second skin of that lost benediction.

April 8th. Hadn't Molly told me, the one time I'd actually spoken with her, that she wore white, black and even, occasionally, gray, "but never blue"? Hadn't she? "Never blue" keeps echoing through my thoughts this morning as I recall the flimsy folds of her dress, its silk as if dipped — saturated — not in dye but in clear wind, sudden altitude, unlimited visibility. "Never blue," indeed.

Hadn't I yet learned that nothing she said, or was rumored to have said, had any validity whatsoever? She covered her traces, moved through her own contradictions, a good deal quicker — and with infinitely more dexterity — than any of us could ever anticipate.

April 9th. It was a sudden impulse, a spur-of-the-moment decision. Out shopping, this morning, I dropped into I. J. Fox's and within minutes, bought Molly a cape, a kind of between-season "throw-on" in black Siberian sable.

I knew full well, even as I signed the charge slip, that she'd never wear it, never even know of its existence, for how could she? And even if she did, would Molly want it? Molly, Molly Lamanna, what *does* she want?

Perhaps, though, I hadn't bought it for Molly after all, but for Molly's smile. For the memory — the incandescent memory — of that smile. As if one could envelop an instant, embalm it in the black aureole of so much luxuriant bristle.

April 21st. "There?" he asked.

"Yes, just there," I replied, astonished as always by the "lucidity" inherent in his fingertips.

"There, too, no?" he added. He very gently protracted a somewhat knotted tendon in my left shoulder, and then, pouring a thin film of oil over the entire area, went rhythmically to work. His "vision" of all that dark cordage just beneath the surface of one's skin was perfectly uncanny. Abdul Izmar was never wrong. Now as he pressed and pummeled, my thoughts, once again, came clear; my mind swam free. The immense pleasure of lying naked — naked at last — even in the presence of a blind man (or was it, perhaps, particularly in the presence of a blind man?) seemed to release my spirits. Suddenly, I felt, I had nothing to hide. My thoughts no longer needed to huddle within the dark recesses of my body, but, discharged now, could enter into fresh spaces, patterns, sequences. Once again, could begin creating.

In fact, I was well into imagining the fourth flashback in *Mongol Moon* when I first heard it. It was a voice among the many voices that circulated freely about Abdul Izmar's little house. But unlike the usual voices, familiar to me now despite all their strangeness, this voice was quite the opposite. It was strange, stunningly strange from the very fact of its total familiarity. What, I asked myself, was it doing here?

After a moment, it went silent and remained silent, but I could "sense" it, even "hear" its silence as it stood (I could easily determine) directly behind the heavy hangings in Abdul Izmar's massage parlor. While Abdul worked supplely on my calves, treating them like so much pounded dough, I managed, after a certain time, to ignore (if not simply forget) that very particular stillness, that charged vacuity created by one who scrutinizes; who — perfectly concealed — peers into the world of the totally exposed. Lying there, mesmerized as I was by Abdul's manipulations, I'd even come to visualize, in detail, that fourth flashback in my screenplay. I went on, that is, as ever. In that episode, Khan finally succeeds in wresting a response from the girl in the garden. She picks up a pomegranate and, demurely, cups it in her palm. This gesture, in their private language, signifies "maybe." "Maybe" she'll crawl over the wall and join him that very night. "Maybe," too, under the cover of the new moon, they'll make their escape. "Maybe," wrapped together in a single, flowing cloak, they'll ride off into the dark, "forever and ever." Yes, "maybe" forever, she suggests, implies, her fingertips grasping now the top of the pomegranate as her eyes fill — almost solemnly — with a no longer concealable passion.

(Yes, yes, I keep saying to myself. But first, never forget that you're not only rewriting a scenario, but a tiny moment of human history. And, as you do, you're attempting to break from a vision of fixed destinies, fixed fates: to reinvent, in some small, highly limited context, the rhetoric of the living, the autonomous, of those who'd determine *their own* realities. Yes, even for yourself, Millicent, remember that. Even now, with the world going under a bit more each day, each week, find the means, even the ruse if necessary, for breaking with a language built on the fixed disposition of so many frozen, inflexible stars. On so many lots, irrevocably cast. Let things *decide themselves*, as much as possible. Invent, create, compose in such a way that they do.)

There I was, then, fully "embarked" on my next episode, my thoughts already entirely elsewhere (a typical Wednesday, that is, at my masseur's), when suddenly the spell broke. I suddenly remembered. Abruptly, I became conscious of the room about me, and Abdul Izmar, and the all-too-familiar voice I'd heard, moments earlier, in the next room, murmuring. Now, finally, I was fully present, entirely "there." Abdul was asking me to turn over, and lie upon my back. To do so, I had to stand up, and — for an instant — face not only the curtains — the dark, swirling galaxy of their arabesques — but what stood, perfectly concealed, behind them.

So doing, I heard the silence grow even "louder," "denser." In the brief instant (the second, really) that I stood there, my body slick, glistening with oils, I felt strangely like an actress playing before closed curtains. Or, more accurately, as if I were performing in front of an entirely invisible audience. I felt its hush, the sudden impact of so much focused attention. Of near savage devotedness. I felt it on my hips. Felt its eyes move with the least ripple of my calves, or with the slip of my hair forward as I turned now toward the tall couch, and felt it follow me down, my whole length lacquered, slender, unabashed, a body still in perfect condition, not so much from whatever care it had received as from a single, seamless, uninterrupted history of sheer disuse.

The silence, too, followed me down. I could still "hear" it as I lay there, "hear" it as it, too, grew gradually silent. Assuaged, perhaps. Perhaps even gratified. Yes, "heard" it subside now, and grow still, leaving nothing now but that deep, embedded imprint within me. "Shadow," I called it, that gray ghost of an embryo. The outlines of that tiny, hapless creature whom, once again, I felt stirring against the barren walls of my womb. Felt the minute, powerless kick of its wizened toes. Or the soft, gray, hallucinatory rub of its cheeks. Yes, felt it. Felt it now, as its knees rose to rendezvous, in tiny spasms, with its chin. Felt it, felt it long after the door had closed and another door opened; after the voice, supremely courteous, nearly condolatory, had bid good-bye to Madame Izmar, and that final door, in turn, had — as in a house bereaved — closed quietly behind.

Felt it. Went on feeling its tiny kicks until they, too, finally subsided. Until even the bruises, the tiny, illusory bruises from the tiny, illusory kicks, had left no more trace than that of a vapor, or a breeze creasing the placid surface of some remote body of otherwise forgotten water.

May 12th. I caught sight of the battered green Plymouth, this morning, in my rearview mirror. It was headed downtown along Wilshire, as I was, and moving at a brisk pace. As it came past me, I accelerated. Without forethought, I began following it, maintaining as I went as discreet a distance as possible. The distance would vary a bit according to the traffic and intervening traffic lights along the way, keeping us — our two cars — in a kind of elastic tension that sometimes narrowed to within — say — fifty feet and, at others, stretched to a full block of solid, exhaust-streaming machinery.

Occasionally, in that rush, I'd catch sight of a white, billowing sleeve, its elbow propped against the open window of

the speeding Plymouth. The sleeve throbbed like an organ,
like some living, pulsating tissue in a full state of dilation. It
was this, I realized, this carnal flag, this white, fluttering pennant I was following, rather than any car. It was the sleeve, I
noted, that turned unexpectedly north now on Alvarado and,
within minutes, was winding its way up a short residential
street in the heart of Echo Park. No, it wasn't the car that
mattered as it swung now into an unpaved driveway between
two ragged hedges of unflowering hibiscus (the car dark green
between the pale, powdery green of the dusty foliage), but
the sleeve, the sleeve gone suddenly slack as it vanished now
into the dark interior of the parked vehicle; as the pennant,
at last, retracted.

I kept going, of course. I drove about the rolling, serpen-
tine block as slowly as I could, scarcely touching the accel-
erator, keeping the car — and myself — as if suspended in a
dream-like state of checked anticipation. When I finally returned (probably no more than a minute or two later) I parked
a few yards down from where the sleeve had vanished into
the car, and the car been engulfed within that wedge of dusty,
overhanging greenery. I had no idea, I suddenly realized, *what*
I was doing. What I *intended* to do. I remember that my heart
was beating so rapidly it felt extrinsic to my body: as if, in
fact, it were servicing another's, while the rest of me remained
perfectly calm, self-contained.

Even from where I sat, though, it was detectable. Just
enough air was circulating through the otherwise airless,
pollen-laden atmosphere to carry — through my car windows — no more than a thread, a filament, a drawn whiff of
that unmistakable saccharinity. The scent, one might say, of
some byzantine invert. Or that of some lascivious, still unre-
penting excommunicate. So, I thought, I'd fallen, once again,

for the *faux-semblant*. Had mistaken one for the other, the sham for the veritable. Had let my heart run wild for an artifice, for no one finally but that hollow, heavily perfumed replica of the utterly inimitable.

I turned the key, and started my car up. As I drove slowly past the house, a little girl on the wooden veranda was screaming, "Nicky, Nicky," and kicking at the screen door. "Come on, Nicky. Let me back in," she screamed. She was dressed in a pale, faded calico, the skirt far too long for these times, and scrubbed, probably, down to its very last flower, bleached of whatever garden had once thrived gaily across its printed surface. "Come on, come on, Nicky," I kept hearing as I drove off.

I was, in fact, well over halfway home, on Santa Monica Boulevard, when I decided — but why? — to turn back. I'd been idly, abstractly musing on the inordinate width of thoroughfares here in the Far West when, quite unexpectedly, I slowed to a stop, turned about, and — noting how the shadows exchanged sides — headed once again toward Echo Park. I had no idea of what had prompted me, of what I expected, what exactly I was after.

This time, I parked directly in front of the house — a cottage, really, a cheap, wood-frame structure, nearly a third of which was composed of its veranda. I walked straight up. I was thoroughly dazed, heedless, involuntary. I was, I remember, so intent on entering, not so much the house, as whatever the house withheld, concealed, that I didn't even bother to notice that the battered green sedan was no longer parked in the drive. I walked straight up to the screen door (the same door that the little girl in the faded calico dress had been kicking a bit less than an hour earlier), and knocked. I noticed, as I did, that the insects attached to the screen were clinging, for the most part, from within. I knocked again. A few horseflies lazily exchanged places like tiny, metallic pawns on the crosshatch of some derelict parlor game.

The voice that answered, finally, seemed to come from someone who'd been expecting me. "Please, please come in," it said, not unkindly. I had to open the door, however, myself.

In the sudden dark within, I had no trouble making out the silhouette of a man in his late thirties, standing at the far end of the room. His complexion, even seen in outline, was astonishingly pale, and his limp, baggy clothes, thoroughly exhausted. I could also discern, hidden immediately behind him, the tattered edge of that blanched calico, that faded garden hanging as motionless, as stock-still, as a checked suspiration.

"You're Mrs. Rappaport, aren't you," the silhouette said. "Vivien told me to expect you. Said you'd be here any time, now.

"Please," he added. His voice was gentle. "Have a seat." He gestured toward a wide, upholstered sofa. The sofa itself bore all the stains, scars, rips of so many uninterrupted years of sheer human abuse. Sitting in it, one couldn't help but feel implicated somehow in all that invisible history, all its vanished intent.

"Vivien told me she'd seen you," he continued just as soon as I was seated. "Seen you coming down Wilshire, this morning. Spotted you, just behind her, along Alvarado. Said you'd be calling, that's certain. That Mrs. Rappaport would be paying us a visit because Mrs. Rappaport — how did she put it? — 'needs to know.' "

I sat still, said nothing.

"Told me to tell you, too. Said, 'Tell her everything. Maybe it's better that way. She'll find out anyway, so tell her yourself, go on.' " He stood there, his long arms hanging limp.

"Who are you, exactly?" I asked.

"Me? I'm her husband," he replied, as flatly as that. "I'm Vivien Voigt's husband. Can I get you something?" He moved toward the kitchen door now, and as he did the calico dress scampered free from behind his trouser leg and, rushing down a short, dark corridor, vanished. "I'm drinking White Rock myself," he said. "That's about all they'll allow me, these days. They took the whisky out of my highballs, and left me with that, that and ice cubes." Even his short laugh sounded somewhat dehydrated.

"White Rock would be fine," I answered.

He came back with two tall glasses of soda water. As he handed me mine, the bubbles were still rising in furious little beads, bursting well over the rim of the glass like so many tiny, irrepressible rockets. I noted, as I took the glass, how white his hand was, how thoroughly ascetic. How, too, it trembled.

"Well," he said, settling into his armchair to tell his story, "here goes." He, the silhouette, needed no prompting, either. Occasionally I'd interrupt, ask a particular question merely to clarify some minor point in the full-blown portrait he was depicting of the two of them. Of, eventually, the *three* of them. Of the life they'd led, both together and, later, apart. Yes, Nicolas Sprague, for that was his name, was more than forthcoming. He was profuse.

They'd arrived in Hollywood exactly three weeks after Vivien Voigt had come upon (almost fallen upon) that feature article in *Photoplay* devoted to Molly Lamanna. Devoted to Molly's "rapidly rising star." In fact, when they all came down off the bus, Vivien was still wearing, he distinctly remembered, a small bandage over the birthmark she'd had burnt into her right cheek only days earlier. But aside from the bandage (which very soon vanished), Nicolas Sprague assured me that Vivien was "the living image" of Molly Lamanna herself. "Even I, close as I got to each of them — to both of them — could scarcely tell the difference."

So, there they were, Vivien Voigt, her husband, and their child (probably already in the self-same calico dress, but considerably less faded), standing in front of the Union Bus Terminal on North Cahuenga and Hollywood. Between them, they had twenty-seven dollars, and not a "soul, a living soul" to contact. Not a single number to dial. "It's damned hard, you know, trying to be a serious young screen actress, these days. Dragging a little family about when you have high hopes and ambitions. When you know that overnight, with a bit of luck, you too could become a star. A starlet, at least.

"But Vivien's good. She's solid. It's her that found this house here in no time. In no time, too, she was returning with the rent. Sure, she'd come back at odd hours. Sometimes not until morning. Sometimes she wouldn't even come back at all, not for days. For days we wouldn't see her. But then, just like that," he said, snapping his fingers rather damply, "there she'd be. Smiling and all. Vivien standing over there in that doorway," he said, pointing toward the screen door, "smiling as if she'd never left.

"Then," he said, "one morning, they *both* came. They both stood there in that very same doorway, identical. Her and her. And for the life of me I couldn't tell one from the other. Couldn't tell my own wife from an absolutely total stranger. They both looked so beautiful, I tell you, standing there.

" 'You'd better get the kid out,' Vivien said to me.

" 'Why's that?' I asked.

" 'Get the kid out, understand?' she said. 'Ask the neighbors to look after her. It's only for an hour or two.' And then: 'And don't forget to come right back yourself.'

"So that's exactly what I did, left Priscilla off a few houses down the block, and then returned, and there they were, her and her, like two mirrors, like one body caught between two mirrors so that you couldn't tell one from the other. And each of them, standing there, was undressing the other. Just like that, as slow as they could. Undressing one another just as if I wasn't even there. As if I wasn't watching their every move.

"No, it's not what you might be thinking, either. Even naked, with Vivien taking Molly Lamanna's earrings off last of all, lightly, delicately, like plucking tiny buds off some overly precocious fruit tree, so that the two of them were standing there just like God made them, it still isn't what you might be thinking. Even when I tell you that Vivien then asked me to join them, be as naked as they were. Because that's what Molly likes. Likes couples. Likes a man on one side and a woman on the other, but not like a man and a woman, if you understand what I mean, but like a kind of father and mother. Loves coddling. Yes, coddling, that's what she likes.

"So finally there we were, all three of us in that one bed, with Molly in the middle like some gorgeous, overgrown baby, her hair spread all over in every which way, and already sound asleep from the moment her head hit the pillow, with me on one side staring over her naked shoulder at Vivien, and Vivien staring at nothing, really, but maybe the blank ceiling overhead. And that's just exactly what happened. Or — should I say — that's just exactly what didn't happen. Because nothing, actually, ever did. I'd lie there, and after a while I'd start smoking, watching the smoke curls rise in order to keep from thinking about that warm creature lying beside me, her body identical to the one I'd married, and legally, at least, had a right to. So I'd blow smoke rings, and smell her, and notice how her smell — it was something natural like flowers — got even stronger as the dark came on. As the dark got darker and the two of us lay there, waiting for Molly to awaken or to roll over and lie with her arms wrapped around whichever one she happened to awaken against. What's more, it didn't make any difference to her, whatsoever, which of us it was. She'd just lie there, her whole body warm, moist from so much sleep, breathing a bit less heavy with each minute. Until she'd finally awaken. Then, just as she did, she'd pull herself loose. Come free. Act as if she hadn't even seen you. As if you didn't even exist. She'd get up and walk around, look out the window, check the weather. Even, sometimes, do some exercises. Then, in her own good time, she'd start getting dressed, and brush out her hair as if there were no one in the room but herself. As if, for that matter, there were no one else in the whole world. Not that she was vain, mind you. She wasn't vain in the least. Only solitary, like. Only the loneliest person you could ever hope to encounter.

" 'Vivien,' I whispered the very first time it happened. Molly was lying there, sleeping stark naked between the two of us.

" 'Vivien,' I said.

" 'Hush,' she answered. 'Don't bother her. Let her sleep, let her be. She's like that. She's kind of odd, if you know what I mean. Let her be.'

"And odd she was. Once, I remember, a little while back, the three of us went to the beach. We left Priscilla with the neighbors, and went to a little beach north of Malibu. We were swimming and splashing about in the surf, kind of roughhousing with the waves. Then, all of a sudden, Molly began talking to a couple of strangers, a man and a woman, who were hiking together down the coastline. We'd seen them coming from a long way because the beach there was completely deserted. They were tall, tanned, athletic-looking people. Not young, either. But perfect strangers. And just like that, after only a few minutes chatting together, the three of them simply left. Molly left with these perfect strangers without even saying good-bye. Not even a wave. Not even some small sign of parting.

"So off they went, the three of them. Molly left us with her car, her clothing and her handbag, and took nothing more than the swimsuit she was wearing and a beach towel wrapped around her shoulders. We watched them, the three of them, without saying a word. Saw them as if disappear into the sunset. Followed them with our eyes until they seemed to dissolve like three grains of sand into that tiny gold wedge the beach makes between the rocks on one side and the ocean on the other.

"Molly didn't reappear, either, for several days. Her studio, I hear, was kind of upset. But then, from what I understand, there's little, precious little, they'd do against Molly Lamanna. She's pretty well protected there from what I hear. Pretty well untouchable." At that very instant, Nicolas Sprague looked quite expressly at me, as if, at this point in his narrative, I might know more than he himself; might — at least here — be able to prolong the thread, the whisper, the tenuous rumor that, like so many others, held Molly Lamanna — even fortuitously — to some vaguely appreciable context, some semblance of a living reality. But, of course, I couldn't. I might have furnished a few details here and there, but in fact I know so much less about Molly than Nicolas Sprague does. I know so much less about her, even, than I thought I knew, earlier. Because with Molly every freshly acquired scrap of information seems to cancel, annul, undo all those that preceded it. One's sense of Molly Lamanna, over time, only dissipates.

Nicolas Sprague poured me a fresh glass of White Rock. As he did, his little girl, who'd come out of hiding to hear us and to observe, surreptitiously, every move I made, came up alongside him and, as he poured the soda water, stared at me with a bland, doll-like intractability. "Come here, Priscilla," I said. "Come and I'll braid your hair. Would you like braids, dear? Would you like me to braid your hair?"

She stood perfectly still now, and stared at me with that same, near lunar inflexibility, her two eyes wide, bewildered, big as teaspoons (the eyes, I thought somewhat offhandedly, of an infant insomniac). "Come," I said. But she wouldn't move. She kept her distance, stood in the tiny, invisible circle her tight shoes made with the worn boards of the floor, while her father sat back in the armchair facing me, and continued, told me how Molly's visits had dwindled with time, had now virtually ceased.

"It's Vivien, of course, that brought her. Kept bringing her. Kept saying to me, 'You make good use of this time, understand? Question her, get quotes, confessions. Find out what she's thinking. What she's really feeling. You're a writer, now *write*.' Because that's the reason Vivien brought her in the first place. Not simply to fall asleep. Not simply to lie there in our bed like a big, beautiful baby, with each of us on either side keeping her company, coddling her like, but to make copy out of. Write articles about. Write — and why not? — a whole book about. There's a market now for books about young stars. From the moment they sign their first major contract, there's a market, Vivien kept telling me, for that kind of thing."

So, I said to myself, somewhat bemused, Nicolas Sprague, it turns out, is a writer, a journalist. A would-be biographer. So *this* was the reason that Vivien, who'd so meticulously hidden both her husband and child, not only from public scrutiny, but from any acknowledgment whatsoever as to their very existence, had smuggled Molly into the house at Echo Park. Had introduced her clandestinely to her mean little secret. Molly, she knew, would be too oblivious even to notice. Or, noticing, wouldn't care one way or another. She had her own preoccupations. She filled her days with work at the Studio, and her nights (at least three or four times a week) chasing vapors at some ungodly altitude in that elegant, overpowered Beechcraft that she piloted. No wonder she needed sleep, I thought. No wonder, too, she needed to feel "coddled," protected. For Molly's thoroughly exposed, and has no real knowledge of the world, it would seem, except to the extent that it always leaves her, in a sense, a bit weary. A bit worldless.

Nicolas Sprague continued. He went on to tell me how he'd probed Molly for answers to even the simplest, most basic questions. How he'd done so sometimes before the three of them (as if by some silent, unspoken, unspeakable agreement) crawled naked into bed together, or — at others — long after they'd arisen. There were whole evenings, too, spent on the very sofa I was seated on at that moment, with Molly sipping sarsaparilla, or leaning against a pillow, or cushion, or someone's — anyone's — shoulder, or sometimes against nothing at all, but sitting upright, mute, a bit vacant. "But it got me nowhere," Nicolas Sprague confessed. "Nowhere at all. It was like interviewing a ghost. How can anyone ghostwrite for a ghost, I ask you. I mean, for every question I'd ask, I'd get a kind of hollow response. I'd draw a blank. Listen," he said. "Just listen to this." He got up to fetch, presumably, some copybook, some vacuous little catalogue of "Mollyisms."

While he knocked about in the next room, his daughter, whose caution had turned gradually to curiosity, moved toward me now in small, sporadic, carefully chosen steps that took her more sideways than forward, so that when she finally reached me she was standing not in front but alongside and even slightly behind me. Her calico dress, with the faded print of its once flourishing garden, rustled, almost crackled now, from all the heavy starch it had been washed in.

"Listen," Nicolas Sprague said upon returning, a notebook under one arm. I could feel the little girl's eyes fixed intently upon my hair, my neck, the wide hoops of my earrings. Her curiosity, I sensed, was turning now into fascination. Perhaps, too, in her mind, she was staring into one of those myriad images of her own future, one of those premonitory mirrors. I reached out and took her very gently by the shoulder. She sat down closely, almost complicitously, alongside me.

"Listen. Listen to this," her father repeated, having run now through several scribbled pages of a disorderly, loose-leaf notebook. "These are the kinds of things Molly would say. These, actually, are her very words:

" *'Being a star is exactly like being a non-star,'* she told me. *'Trouble is, non-stars don't realize that.'*

"That's what I mean," he said rather irately. "That's the kind of double-talk she reasons in. I'd ask her a question, say, about Hollywood, how she liked it, where she shopped, what nightspots she frequented. *'Hollywood?'* she'd answer, as if I were referring to some lost continent, or something. *'I suppose one place is just as good as another. Or just as bad . . .'*

"I mean, you can't write an article, let alone ghostwrite a book for some would-be celebrity on material like that. It gets you nowhere." I watched him turn the tall, loose-leaf pages, his long fingers white, nearly leprous from so much sunless reclusion, no doubt. The fingers would suddenly go still, seemingly freeze each time his eyes alighted upon a particular phrase, upon some lapidary quote, some dark spark drawn, extracted, from the radiant absentee herself. "Here," Nicolas Sprague would say, utterly perplexed. "Listen, listen to this.

" *'I only know what I haven't seen. I only care to know what I haven't seen. It's only that that thrills me.'*

"Or once, when I asked her about her beliefs, what she really believed in, she answered just as glibly as that: *'I'm waiting, actually, to have each and every one of my assumptions unconfirmed. Then, maybe, I might begin.'* Those were her very words. That's exactly the way she said it. I have a whole notebook here, Mrs. Rappaport, full of riddles like that. I've got page after page of totally unquotable material. Of worthless ramblings. Of junk, really." He kept flipping through his notes, selecting — here and there — a particular statement, an especially obtuse, bewildering remark. What Nicolas Sprague read, however, was not at all what I heard. What I heard was the running comments of someone profoundly estranged, the involuted terminology of some totally detached, alienated spirit. Of a creature uprooted, unearthed, speaking in the idiom of the placeless. I found it utterly fascinating. I could have easily, even happily, gone on listening to Molly Lamanna's remarks all afternoon long. For all their estrangement, they contained — it seemed to me — the shattered segments of some lost, elemental vision. Like the fragments, for instance, of an abolished metaphysic. Or the broken sections of a scarcely legible inscription running along the pedestal of some long since vandalized temple. Yes, I could have gone on listening for hours. Every quote contained — in some small, shattered, yet irreducible way — a wisdom of its own.

I remember, most of all, the very last words that Nicolas Sprague quoted. Apparently the three of them, Molly, Vivien and Sprague himself, had watched the sun go down, one evening, several months earlier. They'd been sitting in the very same sofa, watching the sun catch in the scrolled fronds of the tall, stately palms, then sink — a dense flame dissolving into the luscious polychrome of a late Southern Californian twilight — when Molly suddenly declared, whispered really (more to herself than to any other), muttered in a soft, plaintive suspiration: *"There's nothing there. There's nothing out there, not a single, blessed thing."* She kept saying this, according to Nicolas Sprague, shaking her head very slightly and staring, squinting really, beyond the tall, lanky palms and the slovenly mass of the city, rolling westward, to where the line between earth and air dissolved into a single, gaseous, apocalyptic rose. *"Nothing,"* she went on, *"no matter what they say, keep saying, nothing, there's nothing out there, you hear?"*

Now, this evening, inscribing the above passage into my journal, the word *"nothing,"* Molly's *"nothing,"* echoes down the corridor of my thoughts like the hissings of the Sibyl herself. I think of Molly disconsolate, inconsolable, the recipient of her own dark, irrecusable speculations. I think, too, of Sprague, his fingers — white as ivory — flicking through the scribbled pages of his abandoned notes. Of his daughter, his pale daughter, Priscilla, toying with each of my earrings, running her thin fingers over my blouse as if attempting, by touch alone, to memorize (even in the dark recesses of that desolate cottage) some of the elemental attributes of womanhood. Some of those tiny, inviolate details that she would have to learn, even scavenge, one at a time, entirely by herself. Yes, I think of both of them, both Sprague and his daughter, captive, doomed to those shadows, that darkness, banished for the sake of preserving Vivien Voigt's publicized status as an unmarried, unfettered, unreservedly available female in a floating market abounding with available females. And yes, Vivien, too, I think of Vivien. Vivien, rubbing Molly's charm bracelet — that cluttered collection of gold talismans — up and down over her richly tanned forearm, or shaking them like a gypsy — like gypsy loot — from her wrist. *Nothing*, I reiterate. *Nothing, there's nothing there.*

No matter what they say, keep saying, nothing, nothing, you hear?

July 7th. Summer began with a rainstorm. And, ever since, the rains — heavy, sporadic, semitropical downpours — haven't ceased. They're not unwelcome, either. Day after day, now, the rains have been falling into the most static, most motionless, most ominous period of time that any of us has ever experienced. Everything, since May, has simply stopped. Come to a total standstill. We're all living, we know, at the very edge of a historic interval, at its tenuous extremity. We wait — the world waits — for its sudden, savage, unequivocal expiration. Every morning, now, Sidney and I, over breakfast, listen in utter silence to the latest news reports. It's only a matter of weeks, we know. Maybe even days. And, in the meanwhile, here we are, fussing with flowers, playing mahjongg, inspecting the dailies, doing — that is — what people out here do, but, at the same time, feeling caught in a kind of insidious web. Over each of us, a paralysis of sorts has fallen. It's as if even our least thoughts were being held in abeyance. As if our breath itself had decided to hesitate. To hold itself in check. As if nothing could really happen now until — inexorably — everything does. Until, that is, Europe explodes.

So, in the meanwhile, we have the rains. I record them here with gratitude as the one event worth entering. As, at least, our one solace.

July 17th. Molly's been on location, now, since May. She's with a film crew somewhere in the desert: in New Mexico, I believe. The silences in this journal will speak for themselves,

I trust. Or should I say the "silences compounded" since Molly herself says nothing. Molly's a mute. One can only speak about what she *doesn't* say.

How I miss her. Even if I never so much as see her, how, still, nonetheless, despite everything, I miss her.

July 22nd. Sidney told me this morning that the presidents of virtually every major film studio in Hollywood have installed Teletype machines in their private offices, and follow the hour-by-hour news reports emanating out of Europe with all the monomaniacal curiosity of jilted lovers. With all the dismay of cuckolds. Hollywood is furious. Already, work on quite a number of soundstages has been interrupted, and much of the production scheduled for shooting in the next months has simply been abandoned. Everywhere one hears the words "reassessment," "fresh priorities" being touted. Producers suddenly speak of nothing now but the search for "new markets," "the wooing of an entirely new clientele," and the like.

The production of *Mongol Moon*, along with those of so many other projects, has been delayed, postponed until the first days of September. For me, this is a great relief. I have yet to finish my own revisions, which — as I've noted — not only constitute a simple rewrite, but a thoroughgoing reappraisal of its contents. I'm still intent on saving Samarkand; still determined, too, to give Genghis Khan the opportunity, at least, of redeeming his own soul. And, in so doing, liberating himself from the role in which history, traditionally, has cast him.

Why, I ask, can't a creative act of the imagination save a historical character — even retroactively — from his own barbarism? Why can't many disparate acts of the creative imagination, acknowledging some hidden, overlooked goodness in the human spirit, save each of us from the otherwise implacable workings of an irreversible destiny?

I still need time to complete my revisions, bring them, with both ease and conviction, to something that touches upon the inevitable. Happily, I've just been given two more months to do so.

August 3rd. Molly, my Molly. Her name came up unexpectedly at a cocktail party last night in Brentwood. We'd gone there with C. G. to celebrate some pontiff's eightieth birthday. Attendance, more or less, was mandatory. While chattering with someone whose very face I've forgotten about some subject too mindless to retain long enough even to allow for its forgetting, I heard her name. I heard it mentioned and, as I did, in the very same instant, it literally rang, resounded, bell-clear. Its resonance stood like a sudden marsh flower, abrupt, petal-sharp, erect amongst so much surrounding morass.

Someone (I think his name is Brent Batterton) was telling a story a bit loudly, a bit drunkenly, about how Molly Lamanna, once, had stolen an airplane. How some young man, a flight instructor in Tulsa, Oklahoma, had apparently been giving her a hard time, and Molly, who was flying then for her livelihood, picking up whatever work she could as an aviator, had stomped out of the young man's office and stolen — in full daylight — his very own airplane. The plane, it turned out, was a Waco Tapperwing which had been fully rigged to perform as a skywriter.

No sooner was Molly up five hundred feet than she opened the vapor valve and wrote, in a set of broad, wonderfully looping, intersecting white characters, not only the instructor's name, but the following phrase for anyone within half a mile of the airport to read:

YOU GO TO HELL SLOAN MITCHELL

That's exactly what she wrote, according to Brent Batterton, in that studious, highly applied script she was trailing out of the aircraft's exhaust system.

Then, she headed off. Apparently she was well over a hundred miles out of Tulsa and bound, full speed, westward, when she did the wildest thing. She turned back. She returned, not to the airport but over the very center of the budding skyline of Tulsa itself. There, once again, she opened the vapor valve and, in that same, studious, concentrated script (probably much like her own handwriting on paper), diligently inscribed against a cloudless sky:

TO HELL WITH YOU TOO TULSA OKLAHOMA

The beginning of that vaporous inscription had already begun dissolving, tattering in a light breeze, well before she'd reached the end, but virtually everyone in Tulsa, Oklahoma, had received its message. In fact, according to Batterton, people in Tulsa still talk about it today, and not obligingly, either. Molly then retraced her air route westward and landed, without a single drop of gas, on some small airstrip near Red River, Texas. She simply abandoned the aircraft and went on by bus, train, car rides, still headed westward. No one, least of all Sloan Mitchell himself, ever pressed charges.

Quite aside from the hilarity of the situation, I immediately recognized, throughout the entire anecdote, Molly's imprint. Stubborn, solitary, thoroughly her own person, she'd never allow herself to be "manhandled." Quite the contrary. What's even more unmistakably Molly, however, in this tiny portrait, is her habit — call it ritual — of declaring her own colors, revealing her true feelings, *only on the point of departure.* Yes, it's always leaving that she throws us a glance, gives us some precious sign, offers up some tiny trickle of language that we turn, quickly enough, into the living relic of the already volatilized. Of the adored one, the single, retainable substance.

August 7th. So I go on accumulating what I can: anecdotes, gossip, clippings, whatever. They're all parts of Molly's image, certainly, but so far everything I've gathered remains much too disparate. Too scattered. It lacks (like so many spilled beads) a thread, a sense of the continuum, a sustained narrative of its own. In short, a story. How I'd love to capture Molly in the very quick of things, in some set of inexorable events. See her caught, finally, like the rest of us, within the living shuttle of circumstance, sequence, of history itself. For Molly alone seems subject to none of them. She has neither a past (the memory, that is, of a past) nor anything more than the most superficial attachment to any present. She's *hors catégorie,* really. She's nowhere at all. She reminds me of some word that has fallen, almost arbitrarily, out of usage, and ultimately out of recall. Been removed, effaced, obliterated from the lexicons. From culture itself. Has no grammatical applications, now, whatsoever.

Molly, my treasure. My unnameable. How I'd love to gather you, having no other means of gathering you except, like so many bunched stalks, within the arrangements of my own deployed paragraphs. Yes, hold you. Hold you there, at least, like so many wet stems, like so many wet, loose, overhanging petals, hold you. There, there, at least there.

August 13th. She's back. Sidney mentioned seeing her on a soundstage yesterday, "sporting," as he put it, "a fabulous tan."

That little vicarious scrap has made me — all day long — inordinately happy.

August 14th. And yes, sure enough, Glendale Control telephoned me a bit after midnight, last night. Molly's not only back, she's *up*. And, yes, there's Millicent, Millicent again, speeding down the dawn-slick boulevards (the wonderful smells at that hour of fuel, wet cement, bougainvillaea), and headed — as resolute as she is unreflecting — toward Glendale's Grand Central Air Terminal. Yes, once again, there she is, parked already at the far extremity of that long, ruby-lit runway, waiting, a fictive mother for her fictive daughter's return. For the winged one herself, the recalcitrant. For that part (that part of herself, too, she recognized) that forever escapes. That belongs finally only to the buoyant, the weightless, the blissfully irreducible. That — that very moment — idled no doubt at an altitude that only reluctantly, now, had begun turning blue.

August 17th. While waiting, once again, at the edge of the airfield, I passed the time listening to swing (Artie Shaw, mostly) on an all-night disc-jockey program. Then, at five sharp, came the news. It couldn't have been worse. Everywhere in Europe there's been a breakdown in last-minute, last-chance negotiations. One after another, now, the doors of the chancelleries are closing. Everywhere, now: total mobilization.

Molly, no wonder you fly. No wonder.

August 19th. Last night, I had my telephone calls transferred to the Trocadero. Once again we'd committed ourselves (been committed, really) to an evening of pure inanity. I spent whatever spare time I had (between dances, chatter) scribbling the

broken syllables of our two names, Molly's and mine, on anything at hand: the back of envelopes, notepaper, whatever.
This morning I was rather fascinated — troubled, too — to
see what I'd been scribbling, the night before. By separating
and then recomposing the discrete sections of our names, I'd
come up with an absurd set of riddles. Of nonsense rhymes.
Here, for instance, is one of them:

> *Mol sent Mil*
> *Sends Mil a scent all*
> *All all*
> *Ends*
> *All*

And another:

> *O Mol*
> *Milly's all lee*
> *All lil*
> *All lilies*
> *Mil*
> *Ascend Mol*
> *Mol*
> *All lee*

Clearly, I'd resort to any means whatsoever, including the
most ludicrous. Anything, that is, that might bind (no matter
how superficially) our hopelessly separated lives. Yes, even
this. Even to wrapping the broken syllables of our two names
about an arbitrary column of sound. Yes, even this.

I'll take whatever I can, even if it's only from myself.

August 24th. So it's happened, the irreparable. Sidney and I
over breakfast this morning listened — dumbfounded — to
the news. Hitler and Stalin have come to an "arrangement,"

it seems. Have signed what they apparently call a "nonaggres-
sion pact" with one another. Who would have thought such
a thing possible? Who could have guessed at such a monstrosity? Hitler's free now. There's nothing, no one, to stop him.
Europe's his. Our political friends (and virtually all our friends
are political, these days) have expressed — in a flurry of
phone calls — panic, embarrassment, outrage, as the case
may be. A few, and among them some of the most politically
committed, have taken refuge in their own already outdated
rhetoric, or in so much hollow apology. But the world's already rushed past them. Past all of us, in fact.

The cage is open; the monster's out.

August 25th. Yes, yes, my Molly, no wonder you fly. No wonder, too, that I've spent the whole afternoon, this afternoon,
in my greenhouse, whispering to roses.

August 26th. Walked all morning along the beach. What with
the surf heavy, walked as if in a gauze of spume, wonderfully
enveloped. Wonderfully removed. What has happened? What
is happening? What is the world about to do to itself?

Even at Glendale, these past days, the air traffic has grown
almost exclusively military. The Canadians have just left for
England, the poor dears. "Chaps," we came to call them. Now
it's our turn, it's our own boys, by whole squadrons, running
night patrols or practicing stellar navigation, who hoard the
one, heavily trafficked runway; who flood the air lanes, night
after night.

Soon, there'll be little room left for Molly. The runways,
the airfields everywhere, will have been entirely taken over by
the military. Soon, in fact, there'll be little room left anywhere
in the world for those rare spirits who have managed — by

their own acuity, or flair, or cunning — to avoid the world, altogether.

August 27th. Each day, now, I walk farther and farther down the beach, southward. Happily, the rains have subsided and I can let myself go, a bit more with each day. Today, I got as far as Venice, had a fruit drink, and then returned as slowly, reluctantly, ponderously, as I could. I let the wind work on my skin, flapping my tennis skirt taut against my thighs, filling my blouse. Yes, there's at least that, I thought. At least that.

That, and the gulls, and the hooter buoys at the tip of each pier. And this, this little trickle of sound that somehow manages to thread its way through nothing, nothing at all.

August 28th. The rains have returned. It rained torrentially all morning, then cleared up in the early afternoon. Walked as far as Ocean Park. Saw a family of dead porpoises, washed ashore.

August 29th. Rained all day without a let-up. Wrote. Wrote poorly.

August 30th. Today was a day you'd never return from. You enter this — this phrase — as deliberately, almost as pedantically, as you can in the one space that's left you, and then repeat it: "Today was a day you'd never return from," as if by sheer repetition you might secure some hold on so much shattered experience. Yes, today was a day to end days. An end day. A death day, one might call it. You'll measure time, from now on, by whatever happened before, whatever happened after, but today, today itself, today was a hole pierced through time's very heart. As vacant. And as unsoundable.

Here, as carefully as I can remember, can call forth particulars, was what occurred. Sidney had come up to my studio (something he normally never does) and, after knocking gently at the door and excusing himself a bit too profusely, had begun pacing up and down the highly polished floor tiles, his polished shoes clicking sharply with each step. He looked tense, distraught; his normally even demeanor clearly shaken. He was turning the thick, platinum band of his ring about his little finger as he paced back and forth, looking — whenever he could — out through the studio windows. As he did, his hair shone.

"Millicent, don't you ever wish you'd been a painter?" he asked me.

"No," I answered, a bit puzzled. "No, not in the least."

"No, of course not. What an absurd question. Please forgive me."

"What is it, Sidney? What's troubling you?" He was wearing a very smart, chocolate-brown sharkskin suit, and — perfectly matched — a saffron tie fastidiously knotted between a pair of starched, sea-blue collars.

"Words," he answered. "Words trouble me. I can never quite grasp them. They're always shifting, always saying something different than what one means. They never quite fall where one wants them to. Never quite settle. They kind of blow about, don't you find?" He reached down and thumbed through a recent issue of *Vogue*, stopping here and there for a particular photograph, an especially striking advertisement. "Images, prints, pictures, these — these — I understand. They're my livelihood, my terrain. But words . . ." He hesitated, turning toward the window and the view beyond. "They're like so much shadow. They get tossed about like so much shadow, don't you think? There's simply nothing to keep them. They're so weightless . . . unsubstantial."

I draped an arm limply about his shoulders, and together, side by side, the two of us gazed out through the window on to the roof of the greenhouse and the moving foliage of the garden, below. It was all sunny outside and smelled wonderfully fresh, vivified by the morning's rain. I could hear the gardener's shears, somewhere in the midst of all that greenery, clipping away, sometimes as if squeezing through a thick section of wood, then snipping, snipping at the lighter branches with a kind of deft, bird-like syncopation. There was a heavy sea breeze running through the foliage and — yes — the breeze was pushing the shadows one way, then another. "Look, look at them," Sidney said, staring down. I especially noticed the shadows cast by the low, outlying branches of our ragged cedar. In the heavy breeze, they seemed to be fanning, in a wide, prescribed arc, their own allotted section of lawn. They swept rapaciously across, then, at the far end of their trajectory, came sweeping, with the same rapacity, all the way back. Either way, there was no end to their dark, incessant shuttle. Eternally, they had nothing to chase but themselves.

"Last night," Sidney began, the tone of his voice just perceptibly changing, becoming ever so slightly constricted, "last night, I wanted to tell you, I was at Miss Palomar's. I paid a visit to Miss Palomar's. It's something I rarely do, you must understand, but last night I simply couldn't restrain myself. It's something I desperately needed." I held Sidney a bit tighter about the shoulders, and let him feel the pressure of my fingertips. Miss Palomar's is, according to all, the most elegant, the most respectable, and easily the most exquisitely provisioned "house" in all Hollywood. I know that Sidney, like many of the studio executives and top stars in town, would occasionally leave his car parked and his chauffeur waiting in Miss Palomar's long, looping driveway, while his each and every whim received — one might say — lavish attention.

Between the two of us, it was part of an unspoken understanding. There was nothing, no small pleasure, that I'd ever deny Sidney. He was as perfectly free to lead his life as I was mine. If, by default or simple misfortune, mine had turned into a kind of non-life, that was my affair, not his. Together, in any case, we had our implicit understandings. This, certainly, was one of them.

"Of course, Sidney. But don't let it disturb you. It shouldn't, you know. It shouldn't disturb you in any way whatsoever."

"It wouldn't," he responded, "but last night . . ." and here, he hesitated, "last night, you see, something went wrong. Went very wrong." And there, just then, with those very words, I entered immediately into his preoccupations, felt as if accomplice to his own anxieties, partner to his hidden pain.

"Vivien, Vivien Voigt," he continued, and the very instant he mentioned her name, I heard myself say: of course, of course. I would have expected Vivien Voigt to belong to Miss Palomar's rigorously selected personnel. Maybe, even by Hollywood's standards (which are the highest), she's Miss Palomar's most attractive and — I wouldn't doubt — most accomplished "hostess," or whatever they're called. I remember Vivien Voigt suggesting: "Why don't you ask your husband?" only so many months earlier. Of course, I thought. I remember, too, how I'd immediately suspected (or perhaps foreseen) some kind of liaison between the two of them, even if it were for no more than a few purchased moments of some cold, yet lascivious, even mutual act of self-gratification. No, none of this surprised me. It neither surprised nor disturbed me. Not in the least.

I ran my hand under Sidney's lapel, and reassured him.

"Don't fret about nothing," I told him. "Come, let's go down-stairs and mix ourselves some whisky sours."

"No," he replied, "you don't understand, Millicent. You simply don't understand, my beloved."

"But of course I do," I insisted.

"No," he said, shaking his head. "It's like with words. They say one thing, and mean another. Like with words, Millicent. Like with words . . ."

"Come," I said, "I'll mix the drinks this time."

"I'd made the appointment a day earlier, by telephone," Sidney went on in that haggard voice I was so unused to. " 'Vivien Voigt,' I'd specified, and was immediately given an appointment, a time, even a room number. It couldn't have been more explicit. But when I got there, the room was mostly dark except for the light streaming in from the open door of the bathroom. I could just make out Vivien's profile, her shoulders tucked under the covers and her hair spread out all over the pillow. But she didn't move, didn't say a word. She just lay there, wordless, like a large, limp doll; just lay there, I tell you. 'Vivien,' I called out, and she smiled. Smiled, and said nothing. Lay there like a gorgeous stranger, and kept smiling at nothing in particular except maybe the ceiling, or the lamps, or the dark ashtray on the night table, alongside. Pleasuring in nothing, absolutely nothing, I can assure you, but limp, doll-like. Lying there for the exact length of the ordeal itself: until, that is, I'd finished. Thoroughly finished. Lying there almost amused in a curious, removed, speculative kind of way, and all for the sake of that somewhat twisted little masquerade of hers, that comedy of exchanged identi-ties, of being, or pretending to be — even for the ten or twelve or fifteen vile, debasing, self-punishing minutes it took — someone else, anyone else but the amnesiac that she really is, lying there, lying there, I tell you, just like a gorgeous doll, smiling at nothing in particular, smiling maybe at the dark ashtray, alongside."

While I listened (listened with a kind of sustained, paralytic fascination), my thoughts, strangely enough, flew forward. Turned instantaneously cold, methodical, efficacious. It wasn't a matter of what I'd say, or how I'd react, but of what exactly I'd do. What exactly I'd need. What clothes, shoes, accessories. How much ready cash, which checkbooks, how many bags I'd have to pack for at least — say — the first weeks. First months. Because now, suddenly, irreparably, the present had been demolished. The present wasn't. The present was this violent cessation I'd just felt, sweeping — cardiacal — throughout my entire system. The present, if anything, was what, with fortune, one might possibly survive.

"Just lay there," Sidney continued, contrite, broken. "By the time I realized what I was doing, it was too late. Too late, Millicent. I couldn't stop myself."

I remember how he followed me from room to room as I fetched pens, notebooks, a flask of Tabu, some recently published novels, throwing one thing after another into whatever sacks, satchels, hatboxes came to hand. I couldn't, I remember, move quickly enough. As I crammed clothing, helter-skelter, into my suitcases, my maid — silently, diligently — removed them just as rapidly and, piece by piece, paired my gloves, my shoes, folded and stacked my blouses, then lay them all, immaculately, into the very same suitcases in which I'd stuffed them only moments earlier. As for my dresses and gowns, she hung them, straight as weighted curtains, into a single, heavily hinged, brass-padlocked steamer trunk. This, we quickly decided, would be sent on separately.

"Nothing, there was nothing I could do, Millicent.

Nothing," Sidney said, following me from room to room. The very last things I packed, I remember, were of course the most essential: this, this journal, and several of my most precious jades. Yes, the journal and the jades. We'd travel together, keep one another company, I remember thinking. I remember, too, the impassivity in the eyes of my favorite Kuan Yin, or was it — I wondered — simply acquiescence, even a deep-seated exhaustion from having been exposed to too much human traffic? Its expression vanished altogether into a felt sack, originally designed, I wouldn't doubt, for some gaudy ornament. Some self-aggrandizing centerpiece.

"Forgive me," Sidney was saying.

"Forgive me," he kept repeating, as I climbed into my car, the gardeners, that very instant, having just finished loading its trunk and backseat with bags, hatboxes, the whole paraphernalia of flight. I remember, too, as I slid behind the steering wheel, noticing with total attentiveness, just alongside, a particular blossom, a tiny, self-enveloped jasmine, hanging as they hang at that hour in a white waterfall of long, suspended, ever-unfalling droplets. I remember its petals, pronged shut, were as if lacquered in dampness, in wet. Was that wetness, I wondered, the dew, or simply that of the light sprinkling the shrubbery received each morning?

I remember, as I drove off, thinking about that one particular blossom. That damp jasmine. I remember how it hung, pudendal, like a droplet itself in the very midst of my thoughts, monopolizing all others. How it hung, hung there — magnified — as I drove off.

August 31st. Yesterday, I checked into the Miramar Hotel in Santa Monica.

". . . *checked,"* I repeat, "*into the Miramar Hotel in Santa*

Monica," as if — once again — I needed to write each thing twice, have it reiterated, have the reiteration in sorts weigh upon and ballast the slightness, the immateriality contained within the phrase itself. Keep it, in a sense, from blowing away.

September 2nd. I was having breakfast out on the terrace this morning when the waiter, as he poured my tea, asked if I'd heard last night's news. I remember that in the very same instant I let a sugar cube slip into the steaming tea and saw its wake ripple blonde, concentric, across the taut, wobbling surface, I learned that Poland had just been attacked. That war had begun.

I remember, too, ridiculously enough, looking for my lost sugar cube. Stirring my cup to find it, retrieve it. Stirring my cup long past the time the sugar had thoroughly dissolved into the now cooled, untouched tea itself.

September 4th. Calls — essential calls — are being forwarded here from my home. While I talk, I can gaze through the open windows and watch small, ragged sections of the ocean shuttle back and forth through the fronds of the heavy palm grove before me. The ocean, here, is no more than that: a blue, near-purple succession of blindingly bright, unpredictable intervals. It's whatever the wind, rattling through the royal palms, chooses — at any particular instant — to disclose.

P. A. called at ten, and told me that she'd just heard, moments earlier, that England had declared war. She called back almost immediately after to tell me that France had just done exactly the same thing. War, she said, might now be considered "official."

I can't keep my eyes off the fronds. Off the sudden

segments of near-purple, between the fronds, that rise, plummet, flash past.

September 5th. There'll be no problems, now, finishing the rewrite of *Mongol Moon.* The Studio called this morning and asked for the revised screenplay by next Saturday. Production, apparently, is about to begin within three weeks, exactly as rescheduled. I told J.F. that he'd have the finished work on his desk by the day after tomorrow. "There are no obstacles, now," I told him. "Nothing to keep me from bringing it to a rapid conclusion."

And there aren't, either. Despite the series of flashbacks I'd introduced — the episodes dealing, that is, with Genghis Khan as a young shepherd-warrior and his relationship with the girl in the garden — despite every device I'd employed, every imaginable means to establish some form of "civilizing agent" that would keep Genghis Khan from razing Samarkand and slaughtering its entire population, it's clear, now, that I've failed. I've found utterly nothing to stop him. Nothing to keep Genghis Khan, in his own unbridled ferocity, from — finally — himself. The "hidden, overlooked goodness in the human spirit" that I'd so much sought after I clearly hadn't found. To the contrary. History's not to be rewritten. Not to be reinvented afresh. History's exactly what's locked and doomed, doomed like the metronome, to its own inflexible recurrences. To the punctual reenactment of its own, innately barbarous nature. Art certainly was what we meant, but history, history — each time — was what we got.

Yes, from here, it would be easy. In the very last flashback, the girl in the garden will fail to appear at the appointed time. Will break her promise. They won't elope, after all. Won't ride off together, as they'd dreamt, into the rocky moonscapes of the Mongolian steppes. For this, for this broken rendezvous, Khan will never forgive her. Will never — by extension — forgive humanity itself. His life, from then on, will be devoted to an unbroken succession of wars and conquests in which city after plundered city will serve as the hapless substitute for a single, unrealizable act of personal vindication.

Here, within the corrected script, I've written explicit instructions. Khan's armies shall storm Samarkand through all four of its portals simultaneously. Nothing, nothing, I insist, shall be spared. As much violence as the Hays Office will allow (which is virtually limitless) should be employed. Simulated rape, murder and dismembering, the impaling of children, the whole saturnalia of horror, nothing, nothing should be considered too barbarous. Too atrocious.

"Some hidden, overlooked goodness in the human spirit"? "Goodness," indeed. At virtually the very same instant that Genghis Khan, in this morning's rewrite, sets Samarkand ablaze, the Wehrmacht is breaking into Kraków. Laying it low.

September 8th. What are you going to do with yourself now, Millicent? The completed rewrite was delivered to the Studio yesterday. What words will you find, now, to bury yourself under? What lid will you use for sliding over so much unsanctified shadow?

September 9th. Walk, keep walking, Millicent. Keep your whispers somewhere within reach of your own hearing. Don't lose the thread, the trickle. And since it's the shore you're walking along each morning, listen to the shorebirds. Watch how the gulls wheel. How, as they vanish into the spume that rises from the waves' explosions below, they leave nothing but their squeals. But their thin whistles, trailing.

Listen, listen to them.

September 11th. One doesn't age in fixed increments, but in sudden, sporadic, unpredictable leaps. I've felt this acutely, these last days. Since leaving my home. Since separating from Sidney. How carefully now I scrutinize each wrinkle in that tiny delta of wrinkles at the eyes' very edges, expecting — each time — to find some fresh, irrefutable sign. Some recent affluent in the intimate geography of one's own attrition.

As to Sidney, I would have permitted him anything except that. Anything. Any and every conceivable act of adultery, no matter how dissolute, except that. "Adultery," in any case, isn't the word. "Incest" comes closer, much closer.

September 13th. I ran into G. G. in the lobby. Neither of us knew that the other was staying here, and were delighted by the surprise. A kindred spirit, I thought to myself, looking at the extreme gravity of her expression, situated as it is at the very heart of her inimitable beauty. She goes swimming each night in the ocean, and — like myself — takes long, solitary walks along the beach, each day. She wears, as she was wearing this morning, white slacks, a white blouse, and never more than the lightest mascara on her already lovely eyelashes. I adore her. And, I find, she's not above adoring me, either.

"Don't suffer too much," she advised me in that heavy voice of hers that possesses as much personal cachet as her wide, cupped shoulders. "Don't," she said, guessing, perhaps, by my appearance, at my own inner state of affairs. "People aren't worth all the suffering we afford them. All our silly suffering. Don't," she repeated, leaning her hand lightly against my shoulder. "Not worth it," she said, shaking her head. "People aren't worth it . . ."

We decided to meet that afternoon for tea. "For fruit juice," G. G. specified. "For fruit juice," I agreed, and then watched her move past the glass doors that the bellboys, either side, had swung open with a perfectly synchronized, matched set of near military flourishes.

September 14th. Am I, I wonder, suffering, as G. G. suggested, for people (for, that is, a particular person), or simply for myself? For that projection I've fabricated, created quite on my own, that exquisite mirror into which — each time I've gazed — I've virtually drowned. That empty effigy. That shell of a thousand imaginary miscarriages.

September 15th. A large part of the Polish army, caught on the far side of the Vistula, and hopelessly outnumbered, capitulated yesterday. The vise tightens.

September 16th. Warsaw, we hear, is now totally encircled. FDR's silence, ominous. What now? Where now?

September 17th. Inordinately hot, all night. All night, heard the heavy blades of the black ceiling fan slap the air sullenly to what seemed an even higher temperature. As a tiny palliative, I took Molly's charm bracelet off my night table and ran it — its full jingling length — over my wet skin. It felt cool at first. Felt astringent. I ran it over my belly and between my breasts; let it linger — fresh as a sudden rain puddle — in the crook of my neck. I then repeated the movement. Over and over I dragged the sluggish, overlapping charms across the slick of my sweating torso. Each time I did, they grew warmer. Grew wetter. Then, I remember, I extended the itinerary. I let the tiny *troupeau* of blind, obedient amulets linger a bit between my thighs, then slip, two or three at a time, over my sex, then scamper in a thin line back over the flat of my belly and — in half-turns — between my breasts, upward.

I must have fallen asleep finally repeating this movement, this gesture, this exercise in self-assuagement. No wonder, then, that the charms reappeared — perfectly replicated — in a dream I had sometime before dawn. In that dream, however, the charms were no longer gold but gray. But ash gray. Otherwise, down to the last detail, they were identical. Didn't I recognize the three seaplanes and the water-skiers? The Eiffel Towers and Scottish terriers? But most of all, most vividly, as if deliberately soliciting my attention, was the little loop inscribed *"Souvenir de l'Hôtel Belle Rive, Juan-les-Pins."* Within the loop, the couple of stereotyped bathers, stamped out in metal, appeared — or, rather, reappeared — as two very distinct and even identifiable individuals. I had no idea who the man might be, but the woman, unmistakably, was Molly Lamanna herself. She was waving and laughing joyously as she did.

La nuit porte conseil. When I awoke, this morning, everything, it would seem, had fallen into place. Had come totally clear like a landscape, emerging suddenly out of so much turbidness. Here is what the dream said: what the dream, without the least deliberation on my part, "gave me." I'd no longer have to go searching, now, for Molly. I had something better, it told me: "something" in my very own possession. I'd no longer need to drive out to Glendale, night after night, to await surreptitiously her arrivals; to watch her through the cache of my windshield, as dawn after dawn she'd touch down, returning at last to the same ground, the same earth as the rest of us. I'd no longer need to feed on whatever "morsels" Vivien Voigt chose to serve up, or the various screen magazines publish. No longer need to follow her through a penny telescope from the Santa Monica Pier, doting on the twinges in her thigh muscles from a distance of two, three hundred feet. No, I'd no longer need Molly now in order to become, even vicariously, part of her. To go even deeper, perhaps, than she could herself.

No, I'd no longer have to behave like a salamander feeding on mythical fire. Here, briefly, is what I decided, this morning. I shall use these charms as "keys," as exactly what I've always suspected they were. And, like all good "keys," I shall let them open the very doors they belong to. I shall leave as soon as I possibly can for Europe. For France, and the Côte d'Azur. Yes, door after door, room after room, secret after secret, I shall let them open what they will. *Whatever* they will.

Shamelessly, if need be, I'll let them lead me into the very antechambers of Molly Lamanna's lost memory itself.

September 27th. But quickly, Millicent, quickly. Yesterday, the Polish government capitulated. Go while you still can. While there's still something left.

Don't linger, go.

September 28th. Warsaw itself, outlasting its own government, has fallen. Now, Millicent. Go now.

September 29th. The tickets for a passage over on Pan American's new "Flying Clipper" service were easy enough to obtain. "No one's flying in *that direction*," the agent declared with more than a trace of arrogance.

September 30th. While I was packing, Vivien Voigt dropped by. I simply had no time now for Vivien Voigt. Not even for the recent stories — the specious glitter — concerning Molly that she was trying to dangle before me. I had my own Molly, now. I didn't need hers, or anyone else's.

Yes, I had a Molly of my own, now.

October 1st. I'm packed, and ready. I leave for New York tomorrow night; for Marseilles, by flying boat, Thursday.

October 2nd. I left Santa Monica without saying good-bye to anyone. No, that's not quite true. I said good-bye to G. G. over the house telephone. *"Bon voyage,"* she wished me, and added, "and eat lots of *fraises des bois,* it's the season. And remember, don't trouble yourself too much. Don't fret. The world's not worth it."

Dearest G.

October 3rd. Lovely cloud formations — "anvil tops" — flying over the Mississippi basin. Cirrus in tiny, upturned curls crossing Tennessee.

Read in the evening newspapers we picked up at the Nashville Airport that Polish filmmakers were publicly executed in Warsaw, yesterday. They're apparently the first to go. Stories of this sort are now becoming, it seems, part of our daily lot.

Landed at La Guardia well past midnight. It was raining hard.

October 4th. Called no one. Was no one I wanted to speak with. Stayed in the same suite at the Sherry Netherland as last January. There in the hallway stood the exact same lamp Molly Lamanna had used to inspect the little beaded bag I'd just offered her. The reflections of the bag, I remember, played like so many blue, rotating sequins, bathing her lovely face in a wash of cool, cerulean fires.

*　　　*　　　*

October 5th. Last January! Ten months already! Well, Millicent, we pick our mirrors, don't we? We pick our mirrors and then we fly into their very heart. We might vanish in the process, but we fly, don't we? We throw ourselves into the very thick of so much shadow, so much dark, then beg whatever reflections we may. Amongst so much debris, whatever glints, splinters, crystals we might happen upon.

"Now," I heard myself say as the "Clipper" lifted up off Long Island Sound and headed, with a near empty load, into a heavy bank of black clouds. The clouds would last — we'd soon discover — the entire length of the dark, turbulent Atlantic.

"Now, now," I kept saying. Kept hearing myself say.

PART THREE
(Stefan Hollander, 1989)

So HERE I AM, once again. It's exactly half a century later, and — I'd quickly add — none the better for it, either.

At this very moment I'm flying into Los Angeles just as Millicent in her journal (in as far as I've read in her journal) prepares to land near Marseilles. But, for the moment, we're both in air. Despite the fact we're flying in opposite directions, separated by a fifty-year interval in time, we're both as if held — suspended together — in this frail bubble of space. What with the disparateness in both time and destination, perhaps it's language alone — sheer sound — that holds us within this "frail bubble." Maybe, who knows, language is the "frail bubble" itself.

Now, venturing a few pages forward, I could easily picture Millicent's "Flying Clipper" alighting upon the slick surface of the Étang de Berre; could picture, at sundown, the necklace of lights surrounding that pearl gray basin as the hull of the huge flying boat thudded — four, five, six consecutive times — before streaming evenly over the water, trailing now a triple wake as it settled slowly, gradually now with deceleration, and came to rest — perhaps half a mile later — on both its hollow gray belly and its fat outlying floaters.

"Europe, Europe at last," I could easily imagine Millicent exclaiming.

That, in fact, was as far as I read last night. As far as I got in that thin, unique copy of *M.L.*: the sole surviving account of Millicent's pilgrimage through what she so aptly called "the shadows." My reading, however, wasn't without its interruptions. Some time earlier, I'd invited my brother over for dinner, and while the two of us, last night, let *fajitas* spit over the mesquite branches of an open fire, I told him, in résumé, the strange story of Millicent and Molly. Of a love story, essentially, without lovers. Of one that struck me as so entirely abstract, illusory, forlorn, without even the least hope of encounter, let alone requital.

"But maybe," my brother suggested, "we're like that. Maybe we're stranger, and certainly lonelier, than we think we are. Maybe, too, 'the shadows,' as Millicent calls them, are more attractive than we suspect. Than we'd wish to admit. Yes, 'the shadows.' Maybe," my brother continued as if musing himself on the subject, " 'the shadows,' if we only knew, would be full of all kinds of meaning. Full of . . . ," and here, he hesitated a long moment while carefully selecting the exact word, the precise quality he sought, ". . . Light," he finally uttered. "Yes, full of light."

Then suddenly, he changed subjects, drifted off, started talking about some hydraulic project he was responsible for out on the Pima Reservation. But long after he'd left, last night, I kept wondering whether my brother hadn't had an affair himself with "the shadows." When he'd disappeared, for instance, several years earlier for several months running, and returned as if altered, strange, never again "quite the same," hadn't he perhaps been smitten himself by "the shadows"? By the light — as he'd suggested — that hid at the very heart of those "shadows"?

So, long after the dear man had left, his pick-up trailing a thin veil of dust into the dry, dewless, moonlit night, I went

on wondering what he knew. What he knew, that is, that I
didn't, that I hadn't experienced, hadn't even suspected.
What, in the absence of which, had turned me into a semi-
professional collector of bric-à-brac, a man with a marked
penchant for filling, interring, those very same shadows —
those vacua and lacunae — that others, such as himself, such
as Millicent Rappaport, had gone on to explore.

I went back to reading the journal. Ensconced as I was in
my white, deeply cushioned chaise longue with a swing lamp
over my shoulder, its narrow beam flooding the journal's
heavy, hand-pulled pages, I returned to what I could only
consider now as a ledger, an account book of shadows, of
mysteries, of figures flitting across a basically imponderable
décor. And, of all those figures, the most mysterious of all —
more than Millicent, more even than Molly — was the unmentioned, the unnamed, perhaps the unnameable Luis
deSaumerez himself. Who was he? And why had Millicent
designated him not only heir to her considerable fortune but,
more poignantly, the sole recipient of her memoirs: the ex-
clusive beneficiary, in a sense, of the one memory she must
have felt worth preserving?

No, hard as I looked, Luis deSaumerez (aside from the
handwritten inscription in the flyleaf, added so many years
later) was never mentioned nor alluded to. I'd already read
well over half the journal from Millicent's first encounter with
Molly at the Sherry Netherland to her departure, ten months
later, for Europe, but no: no deSaumerez, nor cryptic set of
initials that might possibly designate deSaumerez, ever
emerged. Furthermore, I'd glanced forward, thumbed quickly
through those pages I still hadn't read, but with no more suc-
cess than before. DeSaumerez was clearly not part of the published account. For me, he remained a "shadow" unto himself.
Perhaps the "shadow" of shadows.

Why, furthermore, was Plinsky, the Los Angeles attorney, so anxious to retrieve a journal that had no real intrinsic value except, of course, to a collector; both to retrieve and reclaim the journal as property that now belonged — he insisted — to the law firm of Bliss, Plinsky and Lee. The law firm that had become, he continued, the rightful heirs to Millicent Rappaport's estate, now that Luis deSaumerez was dead. Or — I'd quickly qualify — now that Luis deSaumerez had been proclaimed "legally deceased."

Well into the night, an index finger marking the unread pages of the journal, I went on puzzling over the trouble Millicent had taken in having her memoirs published, copyrighted, and then — except for this one copy — destroyed. Why was it so meaningful, even imperative, that deSaumerez, apparently a total outsider to anything contained within its pages, be its sole recipient? Its one designated reader?

I felt, in a curious way, involved. Even more, I felt responsible to Millicent, to Millicent's very last wishes. This wasn't, after all, my journal, but Luis deSaumerez's. It would be up to me, if there was some small chance he were still alive, to restitute the slender volume, place it into his very own hands. And, if he were truly dead (not only certified as such but verified as well), it would be up to me to find some next of kin, someone at least close enough to deSaumerez to treat Millicent's journal as something more than mere merchandise. More than mere legal pawn.

I also felt a sentimental, even (call it what you will) an emotional attachment to Millicent herself. All afternoon, in reading the journal, I felt myself — I must admit — "falling" for Millicent Rappaport. For her natural elegance, for that stateliness of spirit she so infallibly exuded. I imagined her physically as rather tall, rapid and gracious in her movement, her blonde hair bobbed in later years and several shades lighter than the tanned skin in which it rooted. From the temples back, it seemed to rush as if streamlined by some continuous yet otherwise imperceptible current. I imagined her, too, in linen. In loose, satin blouses with wide collars that hung limply over an ivory or moss-green linen sports jacket. And yes, at her wrist, more limply yet, I imagined Molly's charms. I imagined their soft jingle.

So it's Millicent I'm involved with. And, if it was Millicent's wish that this journal belong to deSaumerez (or, by extension, to someone sufficiently close to deSaumerez), then I more than willingly accept the charge. At the risk of sounding pretentious, I might even say that the journal ends not with Millicent's last words, but with the volume itself, and the way — the exact way — in which I dispose of it.

I fell asleep thinking these thoughts. When I awoke well into the night (the desert, at that hour, so much more "desert" than merely "suburban Southwestern," the coyotes now incredibly close, perhaps even scavenging about in the back yard: nature itself — once again — encroaching, reclaiming its own lost, hopelessly mismanaged acreage) my thoughts had come perfectly clear. *La nuit porte conseil*, as Millicent had written. I decided that, in the morning, I'd leave for Los Angeles. That I'd see, if he were available, Jasper May, the Studio archivist, and whoever else might help me trace, track down deSaumerez or any of his kin. I felt, in fact, as if I'd been engaged by Millicent herself. As if she'd charged me with this very particular mission. That by my action, the efficacity of my gesture, the journal — at long last — might reach its destination.

"Come ahead, come ahead," Jasper May implored when I telephoned in the morning. He responded with all the gaiety, the flamboyance, of a retired tango champion. "Yes, yes, it's Saturday, but even Saturdays, I can assure you, our 'catacombs' here remain open. In fact, if you wish to know, they never close. Yes, by all means, come ahead. Yes, yes, three this afternoon would be just perfect, Dr. Hollander. What's more, I've been intending to telephone you, these last days. I have a little surprise for you. Not much, but something. A little 'whiff' you might call it, a little rumor that might help you on your way. Not much, but maybe more than enough. We'll see, won't we?"

So here I am at fifteen thousand feet, and already the pilot has begun his descent into what cannot too broadly be designated "the Los Angeles area." I must admit, however, that for all its spread, its pollution, and its reputed mindlessness, I adore Los Angeles almost without reserve. I might not have a single friend who'd share this enthusiasm (most especially among my Angeleno acquaintances who all feel "doomed" to live and work within its unending confines), but I still remain stubbornly — even passionately — attached. Already, flying over the golden roll of the surrounding San Gabriels, and seeing — even from this altitude — the gradual and finally the massive convergence of power lines toward the city itself, I feel an excitement I simply never do for any other place on earth. I'd like to think of it, in fact, as "my city." How much of this attachment, however, is due to the place itself and how much to its myth, I cannot begin to say. One's vision of a place is so unalterably determined by one's very first glance, one's first, superficial encounter, and mine — as a child — with Los Angeles (with Hollywood, to be more exact; with Beverly Hills, to be even more exact) was nothing short of dazzling.

It was during the summer of 1944. It was only five years, that is, after Millicent had walked the beaches, daydreaming about Molly, the wind wrapping her skirts taut about her tanned thighs. Five years since she'd awaited, dawn after dawn, Molly's returns out at Glendale's Grand Central Air Terminal; had waited for her "child," her "spirit," her "heavy-haired angel" to abandon those inviolate altitudes and descend, alight, taxi up to her hangar, enveloped — dawn after dawn — in the sleek, metallic trappings of the still young century.

But most especially, it was five years since Europe had caught fire. Since the war would render a large part of the civilized world unrecognizable. But, for a child of eight, wonderfully sheltered and spoiled beyond measure, staying with both mother and brother at the "Pink Palace" itself, life was a dream. I remember the "Wham Girl," Esther Williams, teaching me each morning at seven how to backstroke, and starlets (they were *then*, in any case) such as Marsha Hunt and Gloria De Haven treating me to strawberry sundaes as a kind of lure or recompense for listening to their endless (and, for me, incomprehensible) tales of emotional woe. Those tales doubtlessly touched upon one torrid situation after another, but I understood — was meant to understand — perfectly nothing. So I diligently sipped at my sundaes while gazing at those strange sisters. While marveling at their smells, the freshness of their clothes, at what — even at age eight — I apprehended already as "their difference."

Yes, I was surrounded, enveloped, even coddled in myth. Didn't the mythlings themselves keep me in sweets? Didn't I shag tennis balls for Katharine Hepburn all summer and — two bungalows down — see Spencer Tracy's feet, still in their sandals, rammed through the screening in the screen door with Tracy himself — on the far side, the dark side of the door — in a universe of his own?

With time, of course, the myth faded. For everyone, I suppose, Hollywood gradually lost its magic, its impalpable

luster, its power to create, out of so many purchased particulars, a genuinely public mythology. But for years (*those* years,
certainly, and late into the 1940s) it remained our reference,
not only the source of our styles and fashions, but the mirror
from which we drew our gestures, learned how to smoke and
kiss, to hold a cocktail and tip a hat, how to squint into endless sunsets and dance — as they say — until dawn. But best,
best of all, how to hold a door open, and let — fabulously
preened — the "goddess" through.

For then, in those years, it was different. I couldn't help
thinking (as our Whisperjet dropped low over the San Diego
Freeway, flaps down, and entered its final approach into Los
Angeles International) that then, America didn't end in an
ocean, but a projection room. That perhaps, in a sense, it
always had. That that, perhaps, was an essential part of its
destiny. One might easily imagine that even the whole inexorable migration westward could have had, as its most secret
ambition, not the acquisition of property but, inevitably, the
seizure of some precarious identity, some image of itself, its
first explorers and trappers and frontiersmen thirsting already
for that most ephemeral of all metals, that flickering substance
in which, one day, they'd see their faces slashed diagonally
by the deep shadow of their own lowered brims. Yes, it was
easy enough now to imagine. To imagine that steady "push"
westward, that "manifest destiny" of sorts, as they came, one
after (and often over) another in that gradual, often groping,
but continuously irrepressible movement, following the sun as
they came until the earth under them simply gave way and
ended finally, no, not with an ocean, but — pressed to the
land's very limits — with the promise of some form of response. Of self-recognition. Of some set of images that,
nearly a full century later, would not simply terminate, accumulate there in so many luminous flickers, as if in a bank

of flickers, but be refracted backward as well. Would be sent now flashing across the whole breadth of the nation in which they'd first originated, restituted in a sense, but unrecognizably so: deformed, distorted, trumped up now by the marketing of image, the plundering of history for the sake of spectacle, the celluloid running autonomously, now, spinning — out of so much decimated fact — a mythology of its own.

We touched down at that very instant. Amid the heavy, midday air traffic, it took quite some time to taxi to the terminal itself. I had no more baggage to claim than the briefcase I already held in my fist. In it, along with toiletries and a single change of clothes, was Millicent Rappaport's journal, both in its original, hand-printed edition and in two sets of photocopies I'd had made just before leaving. I picked up a rental, and within twenty minutes I was checking into the Hotel Shangri-La, easily one of my favorite haunts on earth. A lovely Deco structure with a stringent, marine motif, its white flanks seem as if embossed by the tall, voluted heraldry of so much shaggy, overhanging palm. The building itself was completed in 1939, in what I'd come to call "Molly's year." My taste, at least in such matters, is thoroughly consistent.

The ocean-side suite I'd reserved from Tucson was already filled with afternoon sunlight. A breeze was blowing in stiffly off the water and through the tall palms. As it did, the long, vertical slats of the ivory-white venetians rattled flatly. With each successive gust, they'd dilate, light then dark.

I'd no sooner opened my briefcase and removed a single starched blue shirt than the telephone rang. "I'm very glad to know that you've arrived safely," the voice said heavily. "I'm glad, too, to see that you're behaving in such a responsible manner, Dr. Hollander." It was Plinsky, of course. His every word seemed as if chased, as if scarcely outrunning the emphysema that tugged, as it were, at the shirttails of his every syllable. "Glad, very glad," he continued, "that you've decided, and well within the time allotted, to return what is, after all, stolen property. Not that we ever, ever were led to believe, Doctor, that you were acting with larcenous intent. No, we never did, please rest assured." He paused an instant, just long enough, I surmised, to catch his breath. Then he added as flatly, unequivocally, as one could: "Four. Between four, say, and four-fifteen. Just drop the property off at our office — you have the address, don't you? It will be a pleasure, a great pleasure to meet you, Dr. Hollander. Four, four-fifteen, remember. No later."

I would have gone on to tell Plinsky that I had no intention whatsoever of surrendering Millicent's journal, but he'd already hung up. "Four, four-fifteen, remember. No later," had been his last words. I never even had time enough to ask how he knew I was in Santa Monica, how he'd been informed — virtually to the very instant — of my arrival.

I sat on the edge of my bed, looking out. I watched how the breeze clicked through the blinds, set them tapping one against the other like the blades of so many desiccated palm fronds. I could have gone on watching this slow, serial movement, letting myself be drawn a bit further with each moment into its light hypnosis. But the afternoon was passing, and passing quickly. I got up, washed, changed shirts, and — after fetching my briefcase — took the stairway down into the Shangri-La's gracious lobby. There, I deposited the original copy of Millicent's journal in the hotel's house vault, and came out into the afternoon air feeling — I must admit — immensely relieved.

In my rented Mustang, I joined the heavy, streaming traffic, taking Santa Monica Boulevard past the endless succession of foreign car dealers, toward the Studio where Sidney

Rappaport had once been Associate Producer and where, today, Jasper May served as Director of Archives, presiding over its infamous bone heap as a heart might be said to preside over so much memory. Courteous, even convivial, Jasper May greeted me with all the honors due to one who dealt in veritable relics, in "genuine articles." Millicent's journal alone, as a pure artifact of Hollywood's "Golden Age," exuded — quite by itself — a considerable luster. But when I offered Jasper May a photocopy of M.L. for his archival files, he laughed it off quite lightly. "No, good heavens, no. What would we want with *that?*" he said, jovially enough. "Here, you must understand, we're only interested in original materials, you see. Why, in our catacombs, our crypts, what would we do with duplicates, replicas? What good, for instance, would a perfect plaster cast of one of Mary Magdalene's knuckles be, for Lord's sake? No, really, can you imagine?" And here, the good Mr. May broke into a high-pitched, thoroughly self-delighted laugh. As he did, I saw the bow tie at his collar, the "tiny, cajoling dwarf" that I remembered from our first encounter, rise as if quivering into a kind of mute hilarity. "No, no, it would be like offering me a carbon copy of Theda Bara's autograph. Now really, Doctor!" Then, changing tone altogether, Jasper May went on to explain the true nature of archival properties.

"You see, it's not the echoes we're interested in here, but the voices themselves. What remains of those voices, those lives. I'm referring to such things, for instance, as their baubles and stickpins, their gloves and brooches and hand-painted fans, *that* sort of thing. What they'd actually touched and fondled. The combs, for instance, that they'd run through their hair. Or the sashes they'd wrapped about their silk robes and, at the precise moment, let fall to the floor. That's what we mean by authentic materials. Not to speak of their words. Of their postcards and *billets doux,* their memos and memoirs and written confessions. For these, you see, are the very stuff of genuine relic. The very flesh and bone of memorabilia. And it's these, you see, and not the endless copies, replicas, duplications, that we not only identify and classify and tag, but embalm as well. Yes, embalm. For there's no other word that quite so accurately describes our day-to-day practice of preserving the past against . . . well, against itself, really.

"Now," he said with only the slightest trace of facetiousness, "as to that unique copy of yours of Mrs. Rappaport's journal, it will wend its way here, sooner or later. All things do, you know. All things, you know, eventually do."

Jasper May was smiling his mischievous smile, pivoting back and forth very slightly in his swiveling, lavender-back armchair. Then, checking his own movement to make his next remark all the more pertinent, he asked, surprisingly enough, about Plinsky.

"Tell me, now, about Mr. Plinsky. Has he been giving you a hard time these days? Since yesterday, he's been calling here, calling at least five times in as many working hours, asking after you. Oh yes, you're much in demand, Dr. Hollander. I only spoke with him the first time, told him nothing, of course. What was there, after all, to tell? But he's been the bane of our dear secretaries, ever since."

I knew, of course, nothing about Plinsky aside from the two telephone conversations I'd had (or, rather, been subjected to) in the last day. To the contrary, it was Jasper May himself, serving once again as an endless source of boundless information, who informed me. According to the good Mr. May, it had been only a month now since Luis deSaumerez had been declared, by the State of California, legally deceased. The required statutory period of five years had, in fact, just expired. And now, with that expiration, and in default of the appointed heir, the law firm of Bliss, Plinsky and Lee was charged, as privy to Luis deSaumerez's estate (to what was once, that is, Millicent's), with the distribution of something over fifteen million dollars to the charity that they considered, still according to Millicent's stipulations, "both the most worthy and the most needful."

Jasper May was smiling. "Now tell me, Doctor, who could be more worthy and needful on this earth than Bliss, Plinsky and Lee themselves? Who more deserving? Oh, one needn't worry, either, they'll find the means, the 'loophole,' some clever legality too subtle for even the law courts to challenge. They'll create, I'm certain, some fictive, nonprofit, charitable organization unto themselves, and reap Mrs. Rappaport's millions in the process. Poor little dears. Can't you imagine them discussing their dire needs around some vast swimming pool tiled like a sultan's in a fairy tale? Can't you? Oh, but that's the law, these days. That's what jurisprudence has come to, it seems."

I could at last begin to understand why the journal — the reemergence of the journal — had created such a stir. Clearly, Bliss, Plinsky and Lee, at the very moment of coming into control and, inevitably, possession of such a vast fortune, didn't want "intruders." Didn't want some well-informed collector in the very neighborhood asking well-informed questions. The journal, they must have felt, both in regard to its contents and its true proprietorship, could only cause trouble.

This was a good deal more than the little "whiff" that Jasper May had promised me. I was very grateful indeed, and told him so.

"Oh, but *that's* not the little surprise I had in store for you. That's not it at all. Oh dear," he said, and I noticed, as he did, how his bow tie seemed to collapse slightly, its four petals as if wilt. "No, I'm afraid that what I have to tell you is quite slight. Quite inconsequential. You see, around a week ago a woman in about her midforties, a Hispanic, and not very *bonita*, I can assure you, dropped by. She had something she wanted authenticated. Yes, she sat just where you're sitting now — no, not in the least *bonita* — and brought out of her handbag, but slowly, slowly as the day is long, a stuffed little black purse, fat and ugly and smooth as a sow's ear. Oh, but so slowly I could have answered three phone calls in the time it took her to pull out of that sow's ear then a knotted, tightly knotted, black handkerchief. She looked down at the handkerchief, then up, then down once again, trying to decide, I suppose, whether she was doing the right thing. Then, in a single, nearly uninterrupted movement, she unknotted the handkerchief and poured its contents out over the very same table that you're facing, this very instant. The contents kind of clattered against its glass surface. And lo and behold, what was it but a piece of Millicent Rappaport's estate jewelry, and one I could immediately identify, thanks to an estate inventory, with no trouble at all. To wit, it was a rather bizarre amalgam of charms, most of which seemed to have originated in France sometime in the late nineteen-thirties. They just lay there," Jasper May said, pointing to the edge of the glass table before me. "Just lay there like so many little marine specimens that had just been washed ashore. Just lay there like that.

" 'This OK?' she asked me.

" 'How do you mean, OK?'

" 'This hers? This really belong once to her? To Missiz Rappaport?' she asked.

"For me, there was absolutely no doubt. I immediately gave the bracelet a signed tag of authenticity. Aside from the estate inventory description, I'd actually seen the bracelet in a photograph of Mrs. Rappaport, taken in the last years of her life.

With her elbow propped against a garden table and her long, elegant fingers forked across her cheek, the charms seemed to drip down her wrist like some viscous liquid. Yes, I wrote out the tag without the least hesitation, and then this woman, this Hispanic, took it, and — sad, stupid, foolish of me as it was — I let her go without bothering to ask her her name, her address. You see, Doctor, this is what I meant when I called my little surprise 'a whiff,' a thread really, rather than a proper clue. It's so slight, so inconsequential. But wait, Doctor. Because there's a bit more.

"About two hours later, maybe three, a somewhat infamous dealer in cinema artifact telephoned me from across town. And what do you think the dear man wanted? Nothing less than a verification on the very tag I'd just that morning signed and attached to Millicent Rappaport's charm bracelet. He told me that he himself was on the point of purchasing that very item, and simply wanted to be sure — doubly sure — as to its authenticity. Well, I might never have got the woman's name, but I certainly got *his*." Jasper May leaned across his desk and scribbled something on a block of paper in the manner of a house physician prescribing a rather mild barbiturate. "Here," he said, handing me the dealer's name and address. "If you're interested in Molly Lamanna, you must, by necessity, be interested in Millicent Rappaport. Try it, try it anyway. You really have nothing to lose, do you?"

Then, as I got up to leave, Jasper May added, "Oh, and don't forget to give me a ring and let me know how it went. I'm always more than curious to hear *who* exactly gets *what*. In Hollywood, you know, it's never the person who should."

Mat Martz was exactly the kind of character one would expect. A kitsch figure himself, dealing in kitsch (but only of the most glamorous, most mythical sort, and at the most hopelessly exorbitant prices), he operated out of his own home, a typical middle-class, blue stucco duplex off Romaine Street. Yes, he was exactly the kind of character one would expect: both overweight and overbearing, he peered through a pair of unwashed, tortoiseshell-frame glasses with eyes that had probably never taken the trouble to see, perceive, observe anything for the sake of itself, but simply (as if serving as some kind of mercantile instrument) to appraise, evaluate, determine. "We're here for people like yourself, Doctor. For nice people, serious collectors. For myself, I wouldn't do it. Do it for what, for money? Who needs it, anyway?" He showed me about his cluttered "office," a living room long since abandoned to the steady and now seemingly replete stockage of illustrious *bibelots*, bric-à-brac, desiderata.

Apparently, he'd sold Millicent's charm bracelet (Molly's, that is) a good fifteen minutes before he'd actually purchased it. "A standing order, I've got standing orders from all over the world. Merchandise like that I can sell ten, twenty times in a single day, there's no limit, I tell you." The bracelet itself, Mat Martz continued, had been acquired "at the asking price" by some scrap-metal potentate from Yokohama. "Nice, nice man, a real gentleman." Then, mistaking me perhaps for yet another curio hunter, Martz tried to interest me in a gray cashmere beret that Greta Garbo had once, reputedly, worn, or the black chiffon scarf that Ginger Rogers trailed from one hand as she danced "The Continental" with Fred Astaire in *The Gay Divorcee*. "Original materials, tags and all. I can assure you, you can't go wrong. It's a veritable investment, you'll double your money in six months. It's me that loses, each time, not my client. What do I do it for, I keep asking myself, what?"

He then pulled out of an open safe-deposit vault a manila

envelope in which, carefully bound in elastic bands, lay wad
upon wad of cellophane sachets. "Rita Hayworth," Mat Martz
exclaimed with great proprietorship. "Her hair. It's her hair.
When Orson Welles had it cut for *The Lady from Shanghai*,
someone, someone real smart, picked the clippings up off the
floor. I bought the whole consignment years later, the whole
lot in one go, and I've been peddling it out ever since, a few
grams at a time." There must have been over fifty cellophane
sachets altogether, and in each — gone now a rather luster-
less burnt orange — a tiny wick, a quick flare of what had
once been the most glorious, most flamboyant head of hair in
cinema history. "Priests," Mat Martz continued, "priests,
funnily enough, go wild over the stuff. There's a padre in
Costa Rica who sends me a money order for a few grams every
four or five months. He just can't get enough of it," he
said, shrugging his shoulders as if to say that the quirks and
fancies of his clientele had nothing to do, finally, with
what ultimately mattered: his own, scrupulously kept balance
sheets.

Surprisingly enough, when Mat Martz at last realized that
I wasn't in his "office" to purchase memorabilia but to obtain
a specific address, the name of a particular client of his, his
tone scarcely changed. "That's what we're here for, my friend.
To help others, that's our business, after all. You get what
you want, and — as for us — you help us cover our costs,
our overhead. That way, everyone's satisfied, right?" So I had
to pay, and pay dearly, a hundred dollars ("cash only," once
again), for the scribbled name and address of someone who
probably had no bearing whatsoever on this gathering intrigue, this mystery that only thickened as I attempted to
chase down its last surviving participant. As I paid, I felt as if
I were leading myself further and further astray. Acting on
such slender evidence (on "a whiff," as Jasper May had put it),

I wondered if I weren't, quite simply, knocking on the wrong doors a full half-century too late.

Consuelo Innes, for that was her name (the name I had just been given, or rather had just purchased like a single, irresistible share in some improbable gold mine), lived in something more than a shack and a good deal less than a cottage a few blocks from the San Pedro shipyards. To get there, I'd taken the Harbor Freeway directly southward. Off to my right, a late, molten sun had gradually flattened, gone oval against the horizon, and lay burning — through the gauze of so much industrial discharge — a deep vermilion.

In places such as San Pedro, I'd often noticed, nature — as if in compensation for all else — seems to thrive. Without the aid of gardeners, sprinkler systems, and the general fussing it receives in the happier suburbs, never had bougainvillaea, hibiscus, jacaranda seemed to flourish so profusely. Not even driving through Bel Air and Beverly Hills had I seen fruit trees so clogged, even burdened, by their own produce. Yes, almost in default, even defiance, of all else, nature in San Pedro abounds.

I found the house easily enough. Two perfectly matched dwarf palms on either side of a short, sandy footpath not only marked the address but virtually obliterated it as well. The more-than-shack, less-than-cottage lay secreted just beyond and beneath the double palms as if attempting to hide from public scrutiny its own misfortunes. Huddled now in the gathering dusk, it lay, an improvised assemblage of so much blistered clapboard and asbestos roofing. Whatever remained of its once white coat of paint seemed to glow, now, nearly fluorescent in the last, lingering, shadowless light. It reminded me of the hull of some barge, long since run ashore.

When I knocked, the screen door skipped a bit backward

from my knuckles. The door was latched, but loosely. I waited a moment, felt fairly certain I'd heard the sound of something — someone — emanating from an adjoining room within, then knocked again. The sound went on, unabated. I waited. I waited long enough to hear the sound finally turn to a voice — to two, clearly distinguishable voices, a woman's and a man's — before I knocked yet once again. But by then both voices were already dissolving into so many mute whispers, hisses. So many quick, guttural exclamations.

I walked about the block, downhill and back, two, maybe three times, then returned to this "something more than a shack." This time, however, when I knocked, the door sprang forward and jammed against a far stop. I found myself staring into the dark shell of a room in which only a few glints — skeletal outlines — were visible. "*Momento, momento,*" a woman shouted from what was clearly the only adjoining room. "*Momento,*" she called out, as if impatient not only with the inopportuneness of her caller but with some zipper in her skirt or catch on her brassiere.

Now, with the screen door inadvertently fixed open, I could peer into the dark room inside and discern a kitchen with its kitchen table, its minimal utensils dripping from their hooks like the pure, indispensable artifacts of poverty itself. Against the blue, chalk-washed walls, a number of straw-backed chairs stood rather stiffly as if at attention, while overhead, hanging from each of the four blades of a manifestly broken ceiling fan, glistened — in a slow, corkscrew spiral — an uncoiled streamer of flypaper. It hung there with its heavy load of captured and now perfectly extinct victims. The streamer would tremble slightly, quiver metallic from the life struggle of some fresh arrival, then, after an instant, go perfectly, irreparably, still.

Just then, an adjoining door opened and, almost

immediately, sprang shut behind. I could see, but scarcely, a woman outlined against the blue, chalk-washed wall. Her arms hung rigidly, and when she spoke her voice was hard, almost raucous.

"Who you? What you want?" she asked, seeing me standing there in her open doorway. "Huh, what you want?" Strangely enough, she didn't so much face me as the wall alongside, so that what I saw (but even that, obscurely) was more of a profile than a face. Rather, it was more the silhouette of a profile of a face than a face itself. Her black hair, coiling over her cheek, poured into a loose, disheveled chignon that lay limply against the nape of her neck.

"Who you?" she repeated.

"A friend," I replied.

"Friend? Friend of who?"

I waited a long moment, then answered with as much deliberation as I could possibly summon: "I'm a friend of Millicent Rappaport's."

Her silence — a long silence — spoke for itself. I knew from that very instant that I'd knocked at the right door, had just given exactly the right answer. The mere mention of Millicent's name had created what might be called an eloquent silence. Even, a loquacious one. Yes, the name had created a silence, and the silence — in circle after circle — seemed to surround and envelop us. Somewhere within those circles, those complicities, doubtlessly lay — of this, I was certain — the deposits of that second name, unmentioned and still unmentionable: that of Luis deSaumerez himself.

"How you know Missiz Rappaport?" she asked angrily. She was still standing there in profile, in silhouette, a dark, encrusted cameo against a ground of chalk blue. "How you know her, huh?"

"She was my aunt," I lied. I lied just as Millicent had, over and over, to Vivien Voigt. I lied — at least I'd like to think — for the sake of that buried truth, whatever it be.

"Aunt? She no aunt. She have no family, nobody. Who you, huh?" I felt I was getting closer and closer, now. She hadn't come upon Millicent's charm bracelet by chance. Hadn't sold it to Mat Martz without some sense of the consequences. She stood there like a blind woman, facing the wall before her. "What you want? What you want, huh?"

"Luis," I replied flatly. "I want to talk to Luis."

"Get out," she answered. "Get out, get out," she kept repeating, still as if addressing not me but the wall before her. No one, I thought to myself, would ever trouble to conceal a dead man with such vehemence. Such vitriol.

"I must speak to Luis," I told her. "There's something that I must give him. It's a book. A book from Millicent Rappaport. Millicent Rappaport wanted him to have it, but the lawyers . . ."

"Which lawyer?" she interjected, still standing there in rigid profile.

"A man called Plinsky. Plinsky's trying . . ."

"Plinsky's *una puta mierda*. What Plinsky want? What you want with Plinsky?"

"The book. Plinsky wants the book. It's mine now, it's in my possession, but it belongs to Luis, do you understand? It's a gift from Millicent to Luis. It's urgent that he gets it, that he gets the book."

"Leave it," she replied. "Leave it there, on that table," she said, standing rigid as an Assyrian bas-relief with one eye as if quivering so much black in the midst of so little silver. With an index finger, she was pointing to a small table alongside me.

"No, it's Luis's. It's Luis's book, not yours. Not mine. It's him I have to give it to. It's what Millicent Rappaport would have wanted. Would have wished."

"On the table, leave it on the table," she repeated sharply.

At that very instant, I heard footsteps on the sandy path behind me, and turned to see an elderly Chicano with a squash-shaped face and a heavy, overhanging moustache coming toward me. He was dressed in khaki work clothes and had the low, deeply wrinkled forehead one would associate with an Olmec. He and Consuelo Innes entered immediately into a rapid, angry exchange in Spanish. She was telling him to leave; he was saying no, that he wouldn't leave, that he had the money tonight and had no intention now of leaving until he'd received what he called his "satisfaction." He drew a few creased bills out of his pants pocket and held them between the thumb and crooked forefinger of an incredibly broad, squat hand, cracked like so much sunbaked alluvium.

They went into the dark adjoining room inside, while I waited a good hour, perhaps more, sitting out on the crabgrass in front of the more-than-shack, less-than-cottage, and listened to the particularly aggressive sounds of Saturday night traffic, all the sudden accelerations and the equally sudden slamming of brakes. Now and then, a few stray bars of "house music" would drift down the street from a passing car like the thin, insipid vapor of some remaindered perfume or hair lotion. Added to all these were the more and more frequent sounds of police sirens, circulating like so many wind instruments in and out of a whole, somewhat sinister orchestration.

After the elderly Chicano had finally left, hobbling down the sandy path between the paired dwarf palms, Consuelo Innes called me from her doorway. "*Venga*," she said passively, with sudden resignation. "Come," she beckoned, "come on in." It must have been something after ten o'clock at night when I finally stepped into her kitchen-cum-living-cum-waiting-room, and sat down on one of her stiff, straw-backed chairs.

"Here," she said. "You want a drink?" She handed me a shot glass of what smelled to me like mescal. I noticed that even as she poured she continued to keep half of her face concealed, stepping sideways occasionally to assure that that half remain (like the moon, I thought) in perpetual obscurity. "Not *bonita*," Jasper May had forewarned me, but what I saw (the half, that is, that I saw) was sensuous, carnal, and even if Consuelo Innes had, as they say, "let herself go," there still remained all the innate, underlying features of an inextinguishable femininity.

"Luis *no aquí*," she began. "Luis come sometime, come for an hour, maybe two, come to sleep. Sleep quick, leave fast. 'Too dangerous,' he say, 'too dangerous here.' Sure, Luis come, but never know. Never know *que hora, que día, que mes, no sé, no sé*," she said. I watched her pour herself another shot of mescal and drink it down — her chin out, her hair back — with a single, deep, remorseless swallow.

"If maybe you could give me an address," I suggested.

"*Una dirección? Una dirección?*" she wailed. She was part laughing, part jeering. "Sure, I give you an address. *La mitad de las basuras en la ciudad de Los Angeles*, that's his address. Half of the garbage cans in the city of Los Angeles."

"I don't understand," I replied.

"It's wherever there's a bit of fish still clinging to the fish bone," she explained in Spanish. "You understand, now? That's where you'll find Luis deSaumerez. Wherever a spoon hasn't scooped all the melon clean of its rind, that's his street number, his telephone number, his *dirección*. Understand?" she went on, still in Spanish. "Wherever there's just enough shadow left inside the broken rim of some cast-away straw

hat, that's where you'll find him. Where you'll find Luis
deSaumerez's poor, worthless, burned-out head, that's where.

"Five years, now," she continued. "For five years, Luis *loco*.
Bad," she said, turning now to English. "He got it bad, real
bad." With three pronged fingers she made a twisting gesture
over one temple as if suggesting that some large, if invisible,
bolt had come undone in the region of Luis deSaumerez's
mind.

"Crazy, they make him crazy . . ."

"Who?" I asked her.

"*La ley*," she said, "the law. The law make him crazy. Law,
the lawyers, people like Plinsky make him crazy, that's who."

"Why Plinsky?" I asked. I was getting now to the very heart
of the matter, and knew it.

"Why Plinsky?" she parroted. "Why Plinsky? *Porque Plinsky
es un agente de la ley y porque la ley es el mal*," she said. "Because
Plinsky is an agent of the law and because law is evil, that's
why." She stared at me sideways as a fish might, the white of
her eye quivering silver once again against the black of its iris.
"Because law destroys, that's why," she went on in Spanish.
She was speaking quietly now, but under the quietness one
could sense a scarcely concealed ferocity. "Because law sets
fire to people's homes. Sets fire to anywhere you might live,
and anywhere you might work, and anything — yes, anything — you might touch. *Como en un cuento de hadas*. Like in a
fairy tale. Everything you touch turns — no, not to gold —
but to fire. You touch a book, and it burns. You buy a black
negligee and, a few weeks later, it goes up with the rest of
your belongings, your clothes, your furniture, everything.
Quemado, quemado, quemado, that's what the law does. That's
what the law's about. About flames, about ashes."

Luis, it seemed, had bought a little grocery shop at a cross-
roads near Tallahassee, and soon after he'd signed the papers

and paid the first instalment ("*Too* soon after," according to Consuelo Innes), it burnt. It burnt in a matter of minutes, clear to the ground. And nothing, "absolutely *nothing*," was left. "The law makes sure that *nothing's* ever left," she added. So a few months later, perhaps half a year, Luis went ahead and bought a gas station somewhere down the same road with a single room overhead for the two of them to live in. And, sure enough, a month or two after that, driving back one day from downtown, they both could already see the smoke rising higher and higher over the skyline, "like a huge black cauliflower," as Consuelo Innes put it. "It hung just over where we lived and worked. Just over the one place on earth we could call our own.

"And, as we got still closer, my heart going kind of crazy inside, beating faster and faster as we drove, out of sheer terror, slower and slower, we began to see, rising up through the smoke, the glow, the glow going yellow, then orange, then red, rising higher and higher as we got closer and closer still. *That* — *that's* what the law does. It sets your life on fire, I tell you. Over and over, I tell you, it sets your very life on fire."

So that finally, several years later, when they saw the smoke rising high over another skyline in some other city that they'd escaped to, saw it rising for the third, fourth time, they would know that the law had caught up with them once again. That the law was paying another visit, doing its work, accomplishing its mission. That they would never get far enough from it, that the law would always catch up, no matter where they went. "That the law," as Consuelo Innes put it, "is *inexorable.*"

She poured herself another shot of mescal. As she lifted it to her mouth, I noticed on the dark, linoleum-covered table top all the small interlocking circles that past glassfuls had left.

Altogether, the circles read like an illustration of the perfectly inextricable. "Yes," she said, still in Spanish. "That's the law. That's what the law does, but at the time we didn't know this. Didn't yet know that the law was all about fire and ashes. But then, how could we?" The scarcely concealed ferocity in her voice had given way, now, to a tone of lassitude, exhaustion.

I stayed on at Consuelo Innes's house for at least two hours more. During that time, she had three clients. While she attended to them (two of them had arrived together) I waited as I'd waited before, sitting out on the crabgrass in front of the house until I heard the inner door spring shut and the outer door, onto the porch and the sandy path, come unlatched. Then, after the footsteps had vanished, as if drawn and finally absorbed, diluted into the rest of the Saturday night sounds on the bluffs over San Pedro harbor, I picked up the conversation (it was really a monologue, punctuated, here and there, by a question on my part) from wherever we'd last left off. Consuelo's narrative, her life story, to say the least, was captivating.

Her story began, in fact, not at the beginning but with her first encounter with Luis deSaumerez. From that moment on their two stories would turn, inseparably, into one. They'd met, apparently, at Tampa Bay Downs Racetrack during the winter season of 1959. Even though both of them were "Hispanics" and belonged, more or less, to the same class, the same social milieu, she found him entirely different from anyone she'd ever encountered. DeSaumerez's culture, his bearing, even his idiom — she immediately recognized — were something entirely "other." *Un ceceor*, she laughed: someone who lisps. He was terribly handsome in those years, with a high forehead, broad black eyebrows, and clear, "water-clear," gray eyes. She said that she fell in love with him at first sight because of his eyes, and then because of his language, and

lastly — but most profoundly — because of his manners. She
had never met anyone with such exquisite manners. He'd
come out of nowhere, apparently; he had, seemingly, no
origins. But his manners bespoke heritage, tradition, a deep,
even if lost history of their own. He'd been in an orphanage,
in several orphanages as a child, but had managed to escape
one after another in fairly quick succession. He then took
whatever work he could find — mostly odd jobs — before
becoming, as he was at that time, the skipper of a small,
broken-down trawler. The trawler belonged to a fleet of
shrimp-fishing boats that worked the offshore waters of the
Gulf of Mexico from Key West all the way across to the
Yucatán.

A few months, however, after Luis deSaumerez and Consuelo Innes met, his fortunes — at first figuratively and, soon
after, literally — changed, and in a most unexpected manner.
Returning from a two-week run in the Gulf, he was met one
morning in September by a rather tall, utterly striking woman
with bobbed blonde hair and an ivory-white linen suit. She
was standing on the dock, in Tampa, waiting for him. Altogether, the two of them spoke for no more than five minutes.
They stood in the shade of an awning that hung taut over an
ice shed, and talked quietly. The woman, whom deSaumerez
would always refer to in later years as "the Lady on the Dock,"
asked him, in those five brief minutes, a brief series of questions. The questions would leave deSaumerez totally perplexed. He couldn't even begin to comprehend, let alone
answer them. In his own courteous way, he had to shake his
head to one after another. The questions all touched upon
people, places, a historical context he knew nothing of. But
the encounter with "the Lady on the Dock," for all its brevity,
would not only change deSaumerez's life: it would determine
it, forever.

The lady, of course, was Millicent Rappaport. They met, that one time on the dock, then never saw one another again. She vanished as she had emerged: seemingly out of — and into — nothing. But a full year later, the first bulky envelope in a series of envelopes arrived at the one address deSaumerez ever maintained: that of General Delivery. The first of these came addressed to General Delivery, Tallahassee, Florida (where deSaumerez had recently been hired as a foreman in a cannery), notifying him that Millicent Rappaport had died a month earlier and had designated him in her testament as her sole beneficiary. He was to receive, and perpetually, in monthly distributions, such-and-such a sum from a trust fund that she'd established exclusively in his name. This, for Luis, it turns out, wasn't so much the beginning of his good fortune (literally as well as figuratively) as its very end.

Four years later came the first fire. It came just after Millicent's highly respectable law firm had closed its practice and left its clientele in the hands of a new partnership, namely that of Bliss, Plinsky and Lee. It was soon, very soon, too soon after — Consuelo Innes insisted — that their little grocery shop, purchased with the proceeds from several monthly distributions, burnt to a crisp, one Sunday night, in something less than seven minutes.

Began, thus, what might well be called a desolate litany. For their lives together, over the years, would be marked by a succession of criminally set fires (so many, in fact, that Consuelo Innes was incapable of recalling their exact number). The fires themselves served as a kind of black calendar, a timekeep of the irreparable. They'd look back on one charred ruin after another, and measure the time that they'd spent in a particular place, recall even the place itself, according to the particular blaze it had terminated in. Each blaze would signal the end of one residence, and the beginning of another. Because the two of them never stopped, couldn't stay. They kept moving in a vague, permanently improvised manner westward, following in a slow, erratic but inexorable movement the original drift of the nation in its historic conquest of what it would come to call its "Territories." Except that here, in Consuelo Innes's account, it wasn't a matter of conquest but of a steady, implacable dispossession not only of a person's property and chattels, but — bit by bit — of his very sanity as well.

I noted down a few, but only a few, of the dates that marked that hapless migration westward. The flames not only chased them from place to place, residence to residence, livelihood to livelihood, but in a patient, even impassive, but always implacable manner, seemed to *await* them as well. Dormant, the flames would as if bide their time among the oily rags and jerry cans stashed away in the dark toolsheds of whatever town the couple had just come to settle in. Wherever they settled, however, it would never take more than a year or two for the kerosene to be spread and the match to be struck. Never more than a year or two to find them, once again, driving an empty car away from a still fuming foundation, or, if the car too had been set afire, destroyed, awaiting the next train at a local train depot, and whiling their time away with a chessboard (if they still had one) or a borrowed deck of playing cards. For after a certain period, after so many deliberately set conflagrations, they came to acquiesce. They came to realize that they'd never escape what they'd eventually (but only eventually, only after so many years) come to designate as "the law." That they'd been chosen to suffer "the law," to be its permanently accursed subjects.

Here, then, are a few of the dates and places and, wherever

indicated, some of the circumstances surrounding "the law's" very particular visitations. Here, at least, is what I noted down or recalled from Consuelo Innes's account:

1964: Tallahassee, Florida; as mentioned, deSaumerez's grocery shop is destroyed by a verified act of arson.

1965: Tallahassee, Florida; as mentioned, a service station with a one-room, overhead living quarters, purchased in the latter part of that year by Luis deSaumerez, is also destroyed by a verified act of arson.

1966: All applications, on deSaumerez's part, for either personal or property insurance, will henceforth be systematically refused. This will remain the case each time and in whatever state and under whatever circumstances he applies for such insurance.

1967: DeSaumerez sublets an all-night diner on the outskirts of Panama City, Florida. No incidents.

1968: He and Consuelo make a tidy profit, working every night, all night, from this small affair. Again, no incidents.

1969: DeSaumerez purchases the all-night diner in the last month of the year.

1970: On January 7th the diner goes up in flames. Once again, the local fire department attests to a verified act of arson.

1971: Mobile, Alabama. A first indication of mental disorder: deSaumerez has grown increasingly insomniac. He can't close his eyes now without immediately seeing flames. The longer he keeps his eyes closed, the higher the flames rise.

1972: Starkville, Mississippi. Again, deSaumerez purchases a combination service station/one-room living quarters. But now, for the first time, he fully expects its imminent destruction. He awaits the disaster, from week to week, month to month, with a curiosity bordering on the morbid.

1973: Without any apparent reason (unless the law firm of Bliss, Plinsky and Lee could be endowed with the power not only to create but to prolong deSaumerez's every anxiety) the Starkville fuel station doesn't go up in flames until the very last day of December. Once again, the local fire department attests to a verified act of arson.

1974: Plaquemine, Louisiana. DeSaumerez is employed as a day laborer in a cotton gin. He no longer sleeps nights and has begun suffering, for the first time, from chronic hallucinations. As ever, his mail (and consequently his monthly distributions) reaches him through General Delivery at the post office of whatever town they happen to find themselves in. To assure the safe receipt of those distributions, deSaumerez must notify the attorneys in Los Angeles each time that they move. He still, of course, hasn't made the connection between the lawyers' machinations and the successive acts of arson of which both of them are victims.

1975: DeSaumerez's hallucinations worsen. From Consuelo Innes's account, all the symptoms of a fairly advanced state of paranoia have become increasingly apparent.

1976: With the better part of two years' income deSaumerez offers Consuelo's aging parents the funds necessary for purchasing a house of their own in South Miami.

1977: Three weeks after the elderly Inneses move in, the whole house catches fire, and is destroyed within minutes. Seriously burnt, Consuelo's mother must remain swaddled in bandages for the rest of her life. That life doesn't last long. She dies in late November.

1978: Consuelo remains disconsolate. The two of them move on to Port Arthur, Texas, and then, after several months, to Shreveport, Louisiana. They practice all kinds of desultory jobs from fruit- and cotton-picking to construction work.

1979: Laredo, Texas. With an intent bordering on the maniacal, deSaumerez buys a small lumberyard. Even more maniacal, perhaps, the arsonists, or hired hands, or whoever has been employed to burn them out of every dwelling and pursue them across the southern half of the nation, bide their time.

1980: The night the lumberyard finally goes up in flames, deSaumerez is admitted, under duress, to the psychiatric ward of the San Antonio City Hospital. He's immediately bound into a straitjacket. His mouth remains wide open for two weeks as if he were screaming, but no sound comes out. After three weeks, he's released from the hospital due to lack of both bed space and adequate personnel.

1981: Gallup, New Mexico. DeSaumerez picks up and loses one odd job after another. He is now no longer capable of behaving in any consistent way whatsoever. Added to his own chronic insomnia, deSaumerez has now begun "wandering." He often roams into the high plateau country near Gallup, and several times has to be "recuperated" by the local sheriff's office of whatever county he's happened to stray into.

1982: Florence, Arizona. His tendency to "wander off" has become increasingly acute. A number of times he is discovered in a delirious state in the midst of the surrounding desert by Pima Indians who are out gathering brushwood, or hunting. They take deSaumerez in, shelter and nourish him, restore him to his senses. Later, deSaumerez will tell Consuelo that these Pimans are the only friends, aside from herself, that he has ever had.

At this point, I asked Consuelo Innes if the two of them had ever married, had ever even contemplated marriage. "Never," she snapped back. What with one fire after another, Luis considered it *"demasiado peligroso,"* too dangerous, she said, to marry. In fact, he felt that the only way to protect Consuelo from what they hadn't yet designated as "the law" was to keep her as publicly disassociated from himself as possible. As removed in terms of deeds, contracts, legal affiliations as he possibly could. This, in a sense, *was* their marriage: this flight, this continuous escape (for nearly half the length of their lifetimes) from what, in fact, they'd never escape: that fire that licked like water about their ankles each and every time they attempted to settle anywhere.

1983: Castroville, California. Consuelo works permanently now in the artichoke fields. Luis's condition has worsened. One day the two of them take the bus together as far as the ocean. They go swimming in the Pacific for the very first time. Luis, Consuelo remembers, was happier that day than she'd seen him in years.

Perhaps, she suggests, it's because he'd reached the land's very edge. There was nowhere further, now, to escape to. The chase, in a sense, had ended. Or, she adds, maybe he was happy simply to be in water, in the ocean, in somewhere where the flames wouldn't reach them. When, however, the sun began to set over the water in a wild, scarlet conflagration, in a gaseous outburst, Luis broke into tears and wouldn't stop crying. He wept all night, Consuelo remembers. Then, in the morning, he stopped weeping and opened his mouth wide, wordless, as he had with each crisis, and remained that way all day. The next day he began moaning, and the day after that, still moaning, allowed himself to be committed.

Once again, however, due to an insufficiency of both staff and bed space, deSaumerez was quickly released. He's shuttled from one state asylum to another. None, however, can keep him for more than a few days: time, that is, to receive only the most superficial treatment. He roams, now, continuously. From town to town, he begins living off garbage and dressing in castoffs. "Too dangerous, too dangerous," he keeps telling Consuelo in regard to their ever more sporadic encounters. Clearly, he is trying to protect her at all costs. The curse, the "*maldición*," he realizes, is upon him, not her, but like some contagious agent it must be kept from infecting Consuelo, as well. So, even as he enters — bit by bit — into his own private madness, he continues protecting Consuelo. Goes on protecting her in the only way that he can: by excluding himself increasingly from her life.

1984: It is hard to determine, from Consuelo's account, when exactly the two of them came to realize that the cause of all their suffering wasn't that of some fate, some predestined force, but the inexorable workings of what they could at last designate, now, as "the law." It's in this year — 1984 — that they decide to enter into a kind of clandestine existence. To avoid detection, deSaumerez no longer collects his mail, still being delivered in care of General Delivery. Thus, his monthly distributions, after remaining unclaimed at the local post office, are returned after two weeks to "the sender": namely, the law firm of Bliss, Plinsky and Lee. In May of this very same year, the same law firm declares that their client has not only vanished, but that there is cause to believe that he has died, as well. They file papers with the State Attorney's office to this effect. Thus begins the mandatory five-year period of time at the end of which Luis deSaumerez may, by state law, be proclaimed "legally deceased."

1985: Consuelo Innes settles into a three-room bungalow in San Pedro. To make ends meet, she takes on boarders. The boarders, quickly enough, become paramours, and soon after that, "clients." Thus she enters, insidiously, into the trade. Luis's visits, over the same period, become rarer; his mental condition ever more precarious. When he does visit he never fails to bring Consuelo some scavenged shellfish, or a canned pineapple, or a little fistful of stolen flowers. If Consuelo is "occupied," he'll wait, but won't linger. He's always gone well before dawn.

1986: Consuelo moves to the present address, to this "more-than-shack, less-than-cottage." Luis's visits now have become even rarer, even briefer.

1987: Repeatedly questioned by both the San Pedro Police Department and a series of state investigators, Consuelo is obliged to corroborate the fiction of Luis's disappearance, if not death, since the very first months of 1984.

1988: After a half-year's absence, Luis appears one night. Instead of making love, he weeps in her arms. His tears, Consuelo tells me in Spanish, were the tears of love. "The same towel that dries one dries the other," she explains. "The same, the exact same."

1989: Consuelo has been selling the very small amount of estate jewelry that Luis inherited from "the Lady on the Dock." The last piece to go, she tells me, is a charm bracelet. This was sold, she specifies, only a week ago. As to Luis, he scarcely ever visits anymore. When he does, apparently, he only weeps. He takes Consuelo into his arms, and weeps. Weeps, then leaves. Slips cautiously back into the long night he now so rarely abandons.

This, then, was her story. Was their story. I'd listened to Consuelo Innes's account until well past midnight; had watched her — her dark, hieratic profile — as she went through the terrifying chronology of their lives together, year after year, disaster after disaster. It struck me, in fact, only some time later — driving back on the late-night freeway toward Santa Monica — that I'd never once seen the far side of her face. That she'd kept it, all that time, perfectly concealed. Kept it (as she couldn't have kept it from all the full fluorescent exposure it must have received in Jasper May's overlit offices) in that eclipse of her own making. In that vanity of shadows. I could only guess, as I drove toward the ocean, which one of the fires (Tallahassee, Panama City, Starkville?) had taken half of what must have once been a beautiful countenance. Had simply washed it away like a wave, leaving (after a certain time) not even a scar, but an absence, a dearth of feature, a hallucinating omission. Leaving (in place of an eye, an eyebrow, the curve of a nostril) what must have appeared now as some horrendous oversight on the part of a perverse, or simply oblivious, nature.

Returning now toward the ocean, I decided to send Luis, the next morning, Millicent's journal. To send him, that is, that one, surviving copy of the journal in its unique edition. It was his, after all, not mine. I'd send it, I decided, to Consuelo Innes's address by registered mail, return-receipt-requested. That way, at least, the journal would receive the protection of the postal service. It would be in safe hands, that is, until the day Luis himself received it. Under the circumstances, I couldn't do better. Millicent's wish would at last be satisfied, and my "mission" — as they say — accomplished. What's more, I'd eventually receive, as a kind of memento, the scratched signature of the fugitive himself, the juridically deceased. Yes, this was the best, the very best I could hope for.

On the way back, I stopped at Venice Beach. Entering Rebecca's, I suddenly realized I was once again entering the world of the wanted, the socially integrated, the financially blessed. Even their high, animated chatter, their brief, effervescent outbursts of laughter rang of the infallibly prosperous. They were, it seemed, almost all people attached to the Industry in one capacity or another. I sat up on a bar stool, ordered a lobster Newburg salad and a glass of Chablis, and watched them, those of an entirely new generation, nurtured and raised upon a vision of sheer mythlessness. They weren't unattractive, either. They simply never intrigued, never drew one *under* into what Millicent once called "the shadows." They shone, sparkled, but never radiated with that darker luster of those jealously self-contained. The fiercely private. Yes, those whose aureole glowed not so much from what they emitted as from what they so defiantly withheld. I thought, of course, of Molly. I thought, too, of Millicent, in the high privacy of her adoration, tracking Molly, tracing Molly's lost memory across the south of France.

I was anxious to return to my hotel. It was getting very late (at least by my own Southwest desert standards), and I wanted to rise early and finish reading the remainder of Millicent's journal. There wasn't much left, either. Back at the Shangri-La I had a call put through for six in the morning. Then, once upstairs, I opened my windows and let the ocean air, as if ushered forth by the palm fronds, enter every part of my bedroom, ruffling the linen and curling the limp collars of my pajama tops.

Somewhere, I knew, on the far side of this vast, unending, urban agglomeration, Luis deSaumerez was most probably picking through garbage at that very instant. Deprived of not only an immense fortune, but of his very sanity, he was someone I could only imagine out of so much composite image. As I stretched out, however, under my fresh linens, and closed my eyes, I suddenly *saw* Luis deSaumerez. He was, as if conjured, holding a fish bone up to a bare streetlight. I could see him inspecting the full length of — say — a red snapper, examining the delicate artifact of its now almost entirely depredated skeleton. Yes, I could imagine him admiring this skeleton as if aesthetically, and forgetting — for the moment — to nourish his now discounted, officially nonexistent body because he was still too busy admiring the delicacy of the fish's bared structure. Still too preoccupied — fascinated — by its infinite intricacy.

PART FOUR
(Millicent Rappaport, 1939)

OCTOBER 8TH. The wind was everywhere. All the way to Antibes, as we drove through the small towns, the awnings were drawn stiff with mistral, and — on the straightaways past — the leaves of the rhythmically planted planes throbbed taut, flattened against their mottled, olive-green boughs. There were occasional military convoys all moving in the opposite direction northward, and a general air of pre-paredness wherever we passed through. The wind only added to this somewhat skittish atmosphere one immediately senses upon arriving. Like the leaves, things here — the endless little phenomena of the quotidian — seem as if pulled, stretched, tested against their own slender points of attachment. Every-thing strikes one suddenly as tentative, provisional, under question, subject to a constant, albeit obscure, scrutiny. I closed my eyes occasionally and let myself be taken by the scents of Provence, while the driver (who happens to be the Studio agent in the Midi) filled me in on the finer subtleties of France's steady self-betrayal. I only half listened to what he was saying. I kept my eyes closed and pleasured in the sound of the trees ticking past, in the smells of this rich, pungent soil, so redolent, at this very moment, of the grapes that are being picked, trimmed, and then laid — like so much brook trout — into their flat, rose-papered cases.

"Disastrous," he kept saying, referring to present-day French policy. "Utterly disastrous." His name is Jean-Jacques Doréac, and, despite his perfect manners, he let me know, within minutes of leaving the Marine Terminal at Marignane, that the one thing on earth he most desires is an entry visa into America. He's quite desperate, too, poor man, to obtain one.

"To get out, you must understand, is the only answer. Get out as quickly, as quietly as possible. Doréac, you see, is a borrowed name. I'm not even a French national, and the French — many of them, at least — are becoming quite tribal, these days. Quite territorial. They're after people, you understand, with borrowed names. They're after people like Jean-Jacques Doréac."

Half listening, I marveled at the kilometer stones whisking past, at their perfect frequency. They're so much part of the intensity one feels upon arriving in France: not that of miles, but of kilometers. Of a space in-gathered, contracted and, in the process, as if magnified. How I thrill to it, that sudden absence of all things slack and superfluous. Here, there's never a thistle too few, or a vine row too many. The *route nationale sept*, and everything either side of it (rocks, orchards, belfries, clouds), is a single, uninterrupted lesson in *rapprochement*.

"I'll do whatever I can," I promised Doréac. "I'll use whatever influence I have at the Studio, I can assure you."

For all his anxiety, Doréac is a rather gentle, mild-mannered young man for whom I feel an instinctive liking. We stopped at Le Luc and had lunch together in a restaurant under a trellis that was still thick with blue grapes. The grapes swung like blue lanterns in the mistral, causing the whole trellis to heave on its wires like so much extended rigging. It was lovely there, sitting beneath it, and watching the wind ripple across the surface of our wineglasses, wrinkling the *rosé* to a

thin, quivering tissue. Yes, everything, it seems, is being
pulled, tugged at, and not simply the napkins and tablecloths,
but a whole inner world of once unquestioned, unquestionable
certitudes. Everything, suddenly, is slipping. Even my own
memories of Europe, my cherished images of its cathedrals
and squares, its crammed antique shops and pampered rose
gardens, all of it now seems like exactly that: like so many
images. Like the back of so many playing cards that have
slipped free of the hand and got lost in some sudden, frenetic
reshuffle. Clearly, nothing's the same.

"Disastrous," Doréac said, pouring me another glass of
Tavel. I noted his long, aquiline nose and the rich curl of his
thick hair, and suddenly, unpredictably, I felt afraid for the
man. Certainly he must be expressing some premonition,
some instinctive reading of what might possibly befall him.
Don't we all, in a sense, carry hidden within us those glimpses
forward? Carry, amongst our oldest memories perhaps, that
ultimate vision, that final memory upon which, someday, our
eyes will close, and forever?

We lunched on *feuilleté de lotte cardinal*, followed by assorted
goat cheeses and glass bowls of those tiny *fraises des bois* that
G. had so heartily recommended. Over coffee, with the table
cleared, and at what I considered a propitious moment, I at
last brought up the reason for my visit; for, at least, requesting
the assistance of the Studio's agent in these parts.

"But I must ask you first for your total discretion," I told
Doréac.

"Count on it," he answered with such immediacy that I
knew I could confide in the good man without the least hesitation. I brought out from an attaché case a set of glossy,
eight-by-ten photographs of Molly Lamanna, each of them
taken at a different angle, showing her in various moods,
poses, hairstyles, fashions. I spread them across the tablecloth

separating us. "I'd like you to go to the Hôtel Belle Rive in Juan-les-Pins tomorrow morning. I'd like you to speak with the manager or at least the concierge, and tell him who you are; show him — if need be — your Studio credentials, and then ask if he's ever seen the young woman in these photos. Tell him that it's urgent. That it's Studio business. That we're searching for her — her name is Molly Lamanna, yes, L-A-M-A-N-N-A — because we're hoping to have her star — say — in some upcoming production. Say anything, anything you wish, but find out every possible thing that he, or anyone else, might know — or, rather, *remember* — about her. It's crucial," I told Doréac.

"Please," he responded in a quiet but unequivocal way, "count on me." His tone suggested an immediate comprehension of a situation he could in no way be aware of. Decidedly, Doréac was a man of experience.

We arrived at Antibes toward twilight. After checking into the Hôtel du Cap, the two of us stood out on the terrace together and admired the view. The bay was astonishingly active. Everywhere yachts and little *bateaux de plaisance* were carving the waters with their wake, and, beyond them, a surprising number of seaplanes were landing and taking off, skimming across the already bejeweled reflections, causing the reflections — for a brief but glittering instant — to shimmy. Viewing all this, one would be hard pressed to remember that only a few weeks earlier the Second World War had broken out.

"Lamanna, you say."

"Yes," I replied, "Molly Lamanna."

"Shall we have lunch, say, tomorrow?" Doréac suggested. "By then, I'll have made my inquiries. Perhaps — who knows — I'll already be able to give you answers to some of your questions."

"Question," I gently specified. "There's only one."

We decided to meet here, on the terrace, at twelve-thirty tomorrow. As Doréac turned to leave, he asked: "And you won't forget, will you?" He was referring, of course, to the visa. Poor Doréac. I looked at his long, sad, quietly desperate eyes and, for an instant, I swear that I could see him — his entire body — as if shrouded in darkness, or smoke, or the pale, insidious film of some perfectly obscure, perfectly unavoidable fate.

"*Je ferai de mon mieux,*" I said.

"*Merci,*" he replied. "*Merci de tout coeur.*" And then, as quickly as he'd said this, he was gone, absorbed not so much by the hotel lobby as by his own precarious existence. He seemed to vanish back into himself.

October 9th. Doréac was good to his word. At twelve-thirty sharp, we met out on the terrace and walked down underneath a canopy of parasol pines to lunch at Eden Roc. He was smiling quietly to himself as we walked. Clearly, he'd had a successful morning. While the two of us sipped dry champagne under a rattling white and yellow umbrella, the bay just beyond us chopped by the wind into an endless flotilla of high, spuming whitecaps, he told me what he'd learned. "Successful," indeed, he'd been.

"First of all," he said, "her name isn't — or at least wasn't — Molly Lamanna, but a certain Mildred Pearl. The hotel manager at the Belle Rive took one glance at the first photograph I showed him, and — as he did — threw both his arms up in the air, and exclaimed: '*Quelle histoire, quelle histoire!*' There'd been a drama, you see. A terrible crisis." Doréac began detailing the circumstances of this crisis: how, one morning (it was a Saturday in late September, exactly two years ago, the manager remembered), "Madame Pearl," returning from an early-morning swim, was handed a telegram that had just arrived from Madrid. She read it once, then twice, then opened her mouth wide and began screaming. She began screaming right there in the midst of the hotel lobby. She wouldn't — couldn't — stop, either. She held the telegram crumpled in one hand like a tiny blue handkerchief, and went on screaming and screaming until finally the house physician arrived and somehow managed to administer a sedative. Then, after a moment, after a long moment, she dropped the telegram to the floor, and sat down in a sofa and started pulling quietly but persistently at her long, extraordinarily long hair. Everyone remembered her for her hair because, apparently, it was so beautiful. She kept pulling and tearing at it until she was taken — led, really — by three bellboys and the house physician himself up to her bedroom. There, she was given a second sedative. Within a few minutes, she was asleep. A nurse would watch over her all day and all night as she slept, and well into the afternoon of the day after, when she'd awaken. When she awoke, surprisingly enough, she was fine, perfectly fine. She didn't quite understand what the nurse was doing in her room, but made light of it, and altogether behaved in a calm, relaxed, even cheerful manner. The nurse reported that the two of them even joked together about some small trifle or another.

When she came down into the lobby, however, she walked straight up to the concierge's desk and — leaning over it — whispered as quietly but imploringly as she could into the concierge's ear whether or not he happened to remember her name. "She couldn't recall a thing," Doréac explained, "not a single thing."

"Mildred Pearl," she was told. "Mildred Pearl," she kept repeating to herself with all the application of someone attempting to retain the numbers of some complicated combination lock. Then, just as simply as that, she let the numbers — the three syllables — spill once and for all from her mind. Her memory, now, no longer existed. With the receipt of that single telegram, her past had been — with one blow — obliterated. It no longer was.

She was smiling, apparently, as she left the hotel. She moved through the revolving glass doors and came out onto the street. From there, she never returned. She was seen wandering along the Croisette at Cannes that same afternoon, and then roaming about the beach near St. Raphaël the next morning. On both days, she was wearing the same clothes: a blue bolero and a white, pleated, ankle-length skirt. Then, from there, she disappeared altogether. In fact, she wasn't seen or heard of again along the Côte d'Azur until this very morning, two years later: until, that is, Doréac entered the lobby of the Hôtel Belle Rive and pulled Molly Lamanna's photographs out of that tall, thin, manila envelope, and presented them to the hotel manager. "*Quelle histoire,*" as the manager had said, throwing his arms up over his head. "*Quelle histoire.*"

"But there's a bit more that I must tell you," Doréac added. "Because a day or two after Mildred Pearl, or Molly Lamanna, or whatever name she goes by, had vanished into sheer air, leaving all her belongings in her hotel bedroom, a telegram came from her brother-in-law in Avignon."

"Her brother-in-law? But how?" I exclaimed. "By whose marriage?" With a small, seemingly inconsequential phrase, I felt that Doréac had just opened an immense door. I had no idea, either, onto what that door might lead, if not, perhaps, an abyss. Had I gone too far? Was I about to learn a good deal more than I'd wished? Than I'd bargained for?

"I can't say," Doréac replied. "I can only tell you exactly what I was told."

"But Molly," I insisted, "was Molly Lamanna actually married?"

Doréac shrugged his shoulders. "All I know is this: the brother-in-law came down from Avignon on the very same day he was contacted, and recuperated all of Mildred Pearl's belongings. Apparently, he was in tears. He was beside himself, and couldn't stop weeping. Here," Doréac offered me. "This is the very best I can do. Here is the brother-in-law's address." He handed me a calling card. *"Professeur Giacòbbe Lampronti, 7 place des Carmes, Avignon, Vse.,"* it read, plus a telephone number: *"427."* I slipped it into my wallet, under a photograph I always keep of Molly sitting high in the cockpit of some seaplane. Her hair is blowing wildly about, half masking her lovely face.

Molly, my Molly, had she really married? Could this actually be? And, if it were, how could I possibly begin to justify the jealousy I felt invading every part of my being? Molly, who owed me nothing, who scarcely acknowledged my existence, who might not even recall my name — how could I expect, in return, that high, quasi-religious fervor that I offer up unto her name, day after day? How could I ask her to light, as I do, a half-circle of candles about an image of rolling curls and heavy, heavily lidded, inconsolable gray eyes, fixed — if anything — on some distant cloud bank? Have her devote an entire cult, as I do, to an utter untouchable? A pure vacuity?

I turned to Doréac, who was busy flaking thin, opalescent slabs of sea bass loose with his fish knife, and asked, almost offhandedly, if he had any idea what the telegram had said. What the message contained that had sent Molly Lamanna, nearly instantaneously, into total amnesia.

"Of course," Doréac responded with perfect aplomb. "*Que son bébé était mort.* That her baby was dead. That Mildred Pearl, or Molly Lamanna, or whatever you wish to call her, had just lost her little child."

October 10th. Giacòbbe Lampronti wore gloves — gray gloves — and spoke in nearly a whisper. I had to lean over somewhat to catch his quick, inhibited syllables, because everything he said — or, rather, murmured, mumbled, elided — was well — *very* well — worth hearing, indeed. Giacòbbe, after all, was Molly's "brother-in-law." He had not only known and loved her as such, but cherished every memory of her as an ornithologist might the very few numberable occasions on which he'd spotted (perhaps through the pulled curtain of a sea mist) the glide of some reputedly extinct shorebird, its stalk-like legs tucked neatly behind, and its long, faintly turquoise neck section craned, imperturbably, forward. "Milly," he called her. "Milly" was for Mildred, of course. But, I'd quickly add, for Millicent as well. Yes, yes, for Millicent as well.

Doréac and I had reached Avignon late last night. Upon arriving, I'd gone straight to bed, but what with the mistral knocking the tall shutters against their loose latches, and slamming doors a bit everywhere throughout the half-empty hotel, I'd slept poorly. I awoke for perhaps the fifth and last time somewhere around dawn, and got up. Wrapped in my black negligee and smoking one cigarette after another, I jotted down yesterday's entry. "*Que son bébé était mort, que son bébé était mort.*" How could one have guessed at such a thing? How could one have known? I was anxious (too anxious, perhaps) to meet Lampronti. To hear, at last, the entire story. About Molly. Molly's lover, Molly's baby: yes, *all* of it. Wasn't it

like some sudden unearthing, a random strike in an otherwise
abandoned mine? The unexpected glitter of so much mne-
monic ore?

I waited until nine, then called. Lampronti's number wasn't
private: a caretaker went to fetch him in an adjoining apartment. While he did, I watched how the wind pulled the
smoke free of the chimney pots on the far side of the square,
drawing the smoke flat across the backs of the corrugated, red
roof tiles. Over the roofs themselves, I could just make out
the gold domes of the elms, already well gone with autumn.
In the wind, the elms heaved slightly, as if in a single, inseparable mass.

"But I don't even know who you are," Lampronti protested
over the telephone. I had just asked whether I might speak
with him in regard to Mildred Pearl.

"Meet me," I said, somewhat insistently. "Meet me, and I'll
show you. I have some pictures, some recent photographs that
I'd like to show you."

"Photographs? Recent photographs of Milly?" he responded
in that urgent whisper of his. "But Milly's gone. In all likeli-
hood, Milly's dead. Who are you, anyway?"

"Molly's not dead," I replied, then quickly added: "I saw
Milly last month. Last week, even. Milly's alive, she's well, I
can assure you. Meet me, and I'll show you proof. Abundant
proof."

"But this is all impossible."

"Meet me," I repeated. "Meet me now, this morning."

"But I teach mornings . . ."

"Meet me here, at the Hôtel d'Europe, at one this afternoon. I'll be expecting you," I said.

Doréac departed only a few minutes before Lampronti arrived.
He gave me several telephone numbers where he might be

reached in the event he could still be of service, but felt —
and no doubt rightly — that he'd completed his "little task";
that he'd brought me, after all, to the very last appreciable
source of information. He couldn't, in fact, have done better.
I thanked him profusely, and once again promised that I'd do
everything within my power to obtain for him an entry visa
into the United States. I wouldn't fail, I assured him.* He
then asked, almost incidentally, if I knew who the Lampronti
were. I must confess that I didn't. Doréac, briefly but deftly,
sketched the portrait of a very ancient Jewish family, "a dy-
nasty of sorts, all doctors and scholars," who've lived in northern Italy and contributed profoundly, if quietly, to Italian
culture ever since the beginning of the Renaissance. Several
generations of Lampronti, in fact, had written a Hebrew-
Italian lexicon that theologians still considered definitive.
"You'll see for yourself," Doréac promised me. "Giacòbbe
Lampronti is likely to be a most astonishing young man."

Doréac took my hand. Dear Doréac. As he left, he seemed
to vanish, once again, into that very same premonitory darkness he'd first emerged from only three days earlier. With his
eyebrows arched, he seemed to be saying: You won't forget,
will you? I won't, I won't, I assured him, waving back. Then
he turned the corner and was gone.

The "most astonishing young man" whom he'd promised
appeared only a few moments later. He seemed, in fact, as if

---

* But fail him I did. His papers being forged, and his identity unverifiable,
the State Department, despite heavy pressure from the Studio, refused to
grant Doréac entry. In 1945 I checked for his whereabouts and learned that
he'd been rounded up in the Rafle du Vel' d'Hiver by French police, and
perished a year later at Auschwitz. Lampronti, I'd quickly add, didn't fare
much better. He joined the Resistance in 1942, and after two years of
valorous conduct was captured by the Gestapo near Cereste in the Basses-
Alpes. He was placed against a wall and shot three times through the heart.
(M.R., *1959*)

conjured, invoked by Doréac; as if he were Doréac's "last act."
And "astonishing," indeed, he was. I had just lit a cigarette
and made a note in my agenda regarding Doréac's visa, when
Giacòbbe Lampronti arrived in the heavily mirrored, heavily
chandeliered lounge. Holding a gray fedora in one hand, and
wearing gray gloves, an exquisite gray pinstripe suit and black
shoes so glossy that they appeared wet, Lampronti, replicated
at least five times over within the *jeu de miroirs*, was the image
itself of arrested elegance. He looked, in all his genteel finery,
at least ten years out of date. I expected him to bow slightly,
and kiss my hand, but happily he didn't do either. He introduced himself rather stiffly, and acted altogether as if under
severe constraint.

"Please," I said, patting the cushion alongside me, "won't
you sit down?"

"I have no idea who you are," he answered rather petulantly. "I have no idea what you want."

"Please," I said, and opened out my hand.

He sat down, but at the opposite end of a somewhat roomy
sofa. Crossing his legs and cupping his propped knee with
both hands, he looked back with a disarming mélange of
timidity and disapprobation. He had lovely eyes, I quickly
noted. I'd put Lampronti, I knew, into an impossible situation.
He was too polite to have refused my invitation, but far too
private, too discreet, not to feel — at the same time — somewhat violated.

"Look," I said, tapping the ash of my cigarette into a deep
crystal ashtray. "Look, look at these." I opened the tall manila
envelope I'd been carrying, and spread — across the marble-
top coffee table — the exact same photographs of Molly Lamanna that Doréac had shown the hotel manager the day
before. "Look, look carefully," I said.

Lampronti not only looked, he scrutinized. He compared

one to another, brought a tiny pair of spectacles out of his vest pocket and peered — squinted, really — into photograph after photograph. He seemed more like a botanist, suddenly, or a marine biologist, examining specimens, than the scholar that he actually was, poring over — say — a particular manuscript.

After a long moment, I heard him whisper to himself. *"Dio,"* he whispered. It came out more as a sigh, a prolonged suspiration, than as a deliberately articulated sound.

"Dio, Dio," he kept repeating, kept breathing really to no one but himself as he inspected one photograph after another, questioning each and — in the same instant — recognizing, acknowledging, indentifying in each the unmistakable portrait of the young woman whom he had once known as Mildred Pearl.

"Questo è impossibile," he said to no one, once again, but himself, as if still incredulous before these now irrefutable proofs. *"E ella, dov'è?"* he asked.

"In Hollywood," I told him. "She's in films. She's making pictures."

"E come sta?" I was quite certain that Lampronti, dazed as he was, had no idea he'd been addressing me the last few moments in Italian.

"Well, very well," I said, "but as you know, something happened . . ."

"Yes," he replied in that rushed whisper of his, "something happened . . ."

"And ever since," I continued, "she's remained totally amnesic. She can't remember a thing, the poor girl, not a single thing. Her entire past, from her childhood to her very last days in France, was as if eradicated. As if washed away . . ."

". . . washed away," Lampronti repeated, following my every word as if the next might alight at last on some fixed instant, some image of Molly — of Milly — substantial enough to hold on to, such as a bit of flotsam in the midst of so much rushing water.

"It's as if," I continued, "she hadn't had a past . . ."

". . . had a past," Lampronti echoed, still dazed.

"Hadn't had a child . . ."

". . . a child."

"It's as if she awoke one morning in America without even a name she could call her own, and began life all over again at the age of twenty-five or twenty-six. Yes, even her age, you see, one would have to guess at."

". . . even her age," Lampronti repeated, still utterly astonished by the reappearance — even in image — of someone he clearly felt had been eternally lost. He kept mulling over the photographs, one after another, with a care and attentiveness that one could only call reverent.

"Milly," he'd murmur from time to time, as if his breath alone might stir the effigy from the glossy celluloid it found itself caught in. There was one particular photograph that showed Molly Lamanna laughing with her eyes closed and her long, disheveled hair thrown backward. What with her arms crossed behind her head and her elbows spread wing-like, she appeared the image itself of release, boundlessness, joy. Lampronti, I remarked, couldn't keep his eyes off this particular picture. He went on murmuring, breathing — across the slick, impassive surface of that glorious likeness — the two syllables of her lost name.

"Listen," I said, feeling for this total stranger a sudden intimacy. For weren't we, after all, fellow votaries? Didn't we share a common, if estranged, idol? "Listen," I said, leaning over and placing my hand on top of his. "Between us, between the two of us, each of us knows what the other doesn't. You know everything that happened before. And I, everything after. Yes," I said, pressing Lampronti's hand, "between the two of us, we could bring Molly, could bring Milly together. Could tell Milly's story to one another in a way that even she couldn't. Milly's *ours*, don't you understand? She's ours for the telling. Ours for so many words, if we both truly want her . . ."

Lampronti was silent for a long moment. When he finally looked up, pulling his attention free of the now carefully stacked photographs, he asked me quietly, gently, I might even say lovingly, "What exactly do you wish to hear?"

"Everything," I replied, with such a sudden vehemence I surprised even myself.

"But where, where would we begin?"

I smiled. "With lunch, perhaps. It's warm enough to eat out on the terrace under the trees. Wouldn't it be pleasant to begin there, under the trees, having lunch?"

Curiously enough, it was I who began. It was I, after all, who'd instigated this entire situation, and anxious as I might be to hear Lampronti's half of the story, Lampronti was just as anxious to hear mine. Molly, in his eyes, now appeared as a kind of miracle, *une miraculée*. He was pressed to hear every detail, every event in Mildred Pearl's sudden transformation — call it metamorphosis — into someone he'd only begun to call, but with great hesitation, Molly Lamanna.

Of all the specific questions he might have asked, the first, in a way, was the most indicative, the most revealing. "Tell me," he asked in that urgent whisper of his, "does Molly, does Molly Lamanna fly?" It was like attempting to match fingerprints, or two images, with a view to creating a perfect composite.

When I assured Lampronti that — yes — she still did, still flew, his eyes, I noticed, went suddenly damp. He nodded, almost solemnly, and said nothing. He was now thoroughly assured. He sat there, I remarked, with a certain radiance about his being in the leaf-splashed light that blew with the mistral, high over both of us.

So I began. Leaving most of my lunch, a *raie au beurre noir*, untouched, and taking only occasional sips of a chilled *blanc de blancs* from Cassis, I began the story of Molly Lamanna. I started with her repatriation in New York, her "recovery" (if one could call it such) and her steady, job-by-job migration westward as a barnstormer, a skywriter, as anything, in fact, that would lift her off the surface of the earth and keep her, as long as possible, in air. I told Lampronti how she'd flown film back and forth between location sites and the Studio laboratories in Los Angeles, and had happened upon an acting career quite by chance. Wasn't it Sidney himself, my own husband, who had noticed her in her grease-stained overalls at the edge of an improvised runway in the very heart of the Mojave, and invited — urged — her to take a screen test as soon as possible? I enumerated the titles of Molly's films, and Lampronti duly noted them down. Clearly, the more I revealed about Molly's life — her "second life," that is — the more enthralled he became. I went on to mention her curious indifference to Hollywood, and even to her own growing reputation as "a rising star." None of it appeared to matter. She had no sense whatsoever of a career, if career was the appropriate word, except to earn enough money to purchase an airplane of her own — a seaplane, I believe — because there was nothing else that Molly Lamanna seemed to care for. She had no family, neither friends nor lovers, nor any material attachment to anything on earth except flight. Except the sudden release from any and every constraint on her own jealously coveted autonomy as — night after night — the runway as if vanished from under and, elevators up, she soon

attained those phosphorous, moon-lit altitudes that she lived
for, thrived in, and from which she'd never return, I'm quite
convinced, if she ever discovered the means not to. I'd even
come to believe that those altitudes, in some mysterious way,
might resemble her as a mirror, perhaps, might come to
resemble, after a certain time, some endlessly diaphanous
face.

Lampronti, who'd scarcely begun eating, had now entirely
stopped. He sat there, perfectly still, for however long it took
me to summarize this "second life" of Molly Lamanna's. Probably, seen through Lampronti's eyes, it was more of an "after-
life," some elysium of the spirit that had allowed Molly to
wander about in its charmed gardens long after she'd been
given up for irreparably lost. There was simply nothing Lampronti didn't want to know. Did Molly still read as abun-
dantly? (I couldn't say.) Was she still painting, every day? (I
was utterly perplexed by this question, but had to answer, of
course, in the negative.) Did she still love massages, and smell
of talc and olive oil? (Oh yes, yes indeed, I answered.) But
most of all, Lampronti's questions, strangely — and signifi-
cantly — enough, touched upon aviation. What kind of aircraft was she flying, these days? Was she flying solo? Flying
nights, as she used to? Returning, whenever possible, at dawn?

"Because, you see, that's how it all began," Lampronti suggested.

"Began?" I asked.

"How they all met in the first place. How they all came
together, the three of them. How they all fell in love."

Now it was my turn to sit as if paralyzed, my fork and fish
knife on either side of the scarcely touched *raie*, as Giacòbbe
Lampronti, in that hushed voice of his, leaned toward me,
and whispered: "But, of course, you know nothing about this,
do you."

I sat still, silent, as if caught at the very edge of a perilous dream.

"About Lea and Amedeo, my sister and brother, I mean. You know nothing, do you."

"Nothing," I assured him.

"Not that there's anything to conceal. But it's easy, too easy, to misconstrue, you understand. To think things about them that . . . ."

"No," I said, "please continue."

"There was a moment then, it's gone now, when some of us," Lampronti explained, taking a quick sip of his Cassis, "people like Lea and Amedeo and myself, were filled with a very strange elation."

"Please," I said, "go on."

"It's as if something momentous were about to happen, like the birth of something. Of a new age, for instance."

"Yes, yes, go on. I understand."

"It's as if things had got so bad by nineteen thirty-five, nineteen thirty-six — fascism had reduced our lives, at least outwardly, to such a parody of existence — that some of us felt that the wickedness we were living through was simply the herald, the annunciating angel in horrendous disguise, of some entirely unforeseeable dawn."

"Yes, of course."

"And so it was with us, with my brother and sister and myself. We'd all be witnesses, we thought, to that 'birth.' That 'new age.' Then, too, it's only fair to mention that each of us was steeped in — drunk on, you might say — messianic literature. We'd been reading, for instance, for months at a time, Gershom Scholem and Walter Benjamin, as well as the classic texts, the esoteric ones, that is. We spent a small fortune, I remember, having copies smuggled across the Italian frontier.

Paying the fascist authorities considerable sums for those thin, seminal works on the imminence of human redemption.

"That's what we read. But with them, with Lea and Amedeo, it was different. They had, you see, a special relationship. They'd read out loud to one another, sitting on the same settee, and often, being by far the youngest (sometimes they'd call me their 'little boy'), I'd sit across and listen, while one of them read and the other, from time to time, with what seemed to be an inexhaustible fascination, would toy with a lock of the reader's hair. Would wrap it, over and over, about an idle forefinger.

"For them, you see, for Lea and Amedeo, the words were aglow. Were ablaze with the very same exalted light as they themselves. They seemed to recognize one another in those utopian visions, in those images of some form of ultimate deliverance. They existed, you see, in a world of their own. In a love of their own. And they did absolutely nothing to hide it. Even at the Lido, that last summer, I remember them at the hour of the *passeggiata* walking arm in arm, or dancing, just like lovers, on the esplanade at the Excelsior. This isn't to say that they actually were lovers. I'm fairly certain, in fact, that they weren't. But that, at least, is how they appeared, and how they must have first seemed to Milly — to Molly, that is — that first day. That first afternoon when they saw one another on the beach at Cap d'Antibes."

"But why Antibes?"

"Antibes, really, was circumstantial," Lampronti explained. "Lea and Amedeo had just managed to escape from Italy, and were on their way to Spain. They'd decided to volunteer as nurses, as nurses' assistants, for the Spanish Republic. They'd left Italy one night in a terrible rush, alerted by a friend of our parents that the authorities would arrest them within the next few hours. We were all under continuous surveillance, of course, both as Jews and as intellectuals, but Lea and Amedeo were under particular suspicion for what was called 'seditious behavior.' They barely made it. Papa had always kept a small, two-passenger seaplane, a Caproncino, tied to a covered dock alongside the lagoon. We'd all grown up taking rides, each summer, in this rattling, red and green 'Flamingo,' as we called it. We loved it, and it left us with some of our happiest child-hood memories. Once, I remember, Papa and I flew it as far as Chios. We spent a week there with friends, eating shellfish and sea urchins. Papa was giving himself a vacation from a long, laborious work on Aramaic derivatives, and told me that there was no cure for intellectual fatigue quite like eating a basketful of raw, writhing sea urchins. And that's exactly what we did.

"But even our Caproncino, now, was in trouble. It, too, was about to be seized, confiscated by the fascist authorities within the very next days. So Papa urged Lea and Amedeo to take it, to make their escape in the 'Flamingo,' saving the air-plane at the same time as themselves. They took off well after midnight in a heavy mist. 'Three ethereal spirits,' Papa would joke, long after they'd left. But there was too much sorrow in his voice for those of us who still remained at the dining table to take him lightly.

"And so there they were, at Antibes," Lampronti contin-ued. "They'd been there for something over three weeks, and were still waiting for clearance papers (both for themselves and the seaplane) to arrive from Spain. But, of course, nothing was forthcoming: the civil war would bring Spanish bureau-cracy to a near total standstill. So Lea and Amedeo waited, and while they waited they whiled away their time reading along empty beaches, going for strolls — promenades — along the Croisette, and, two or three times a week, taking their

Caproncino up in the late afternoon for a run westward down the French littoral.

"It was after one of those runs in late April that they returned, one day, and landed near a small, deserted beach. They fastened the lead of their seaplane to a bobbing offshore marker, and swam ashore. It was then, that afternoon, that moment, that it happened. That they all laid eyes upon one another. That they 'encountered,' if you like, Mildred Pearl. For Milly was lying there alongside a low, candy-striped cabana and, like themselves, like Lea and Amedeo, was wearing perfectly nothing. She simply lay there, stark naked, and watched them wade ashore. She didn't reach for a towel, nor turn over onto her belly. She simply lay there, propped up on both elbows, half smiling, but not necessarily at them, not in the least troubled by their sudden arrival but fascinated, intrigued. She had two black Scottie dogs that scurried about her not tall, not altogether lean body, her somewhat fulsome breasts tanned to the same darkness as her shoulders. But the dogs, for all their playfulness, never strayed. They remained close to the young woman as if they'd been charged with her protection or, at the very least, her entertainment.

"And so, there they were, all three of them for the very first time. Nothing happened, of course. Nothing was said, or exchanged. But already, like three players on the first page of a closet drama, all the elements had been, if not introduced to one another, at least presented. Lea and Amedeo, after sunbathing for a certain time, went back into the water and splashed about. I can easily imagine them, too, singing arias to one another in the shallows, or riding each other's shoulders across the cool, sun-lacquered surface of the water.

"When they returned to the beach, they noticed that the young woman, whose cabana was no more than a hundred feet away, was rubbing herself down in suntan lotion. Her

skin shone across that short distance like wet copper, while
her heavy, honey-brown hair covered both her shoulders in a
delta of thick, tentacular loops. They tried not to notice, not
to stare. But both Lea and Amedeo felt profoundly distracted.
Even disturbed. Something between them, as Amedeo would
write me, had been broken, severed, and suddenly as if pro-
jected — concentrated — upon a perfect stranger. They both
felt this. They both felt this at the very same instant and, I'm
convinced, with the very same intensity.

"When they got up to leave, it was Lea who waved. She
gave a tiny double twist to her wrist, and waved at the young
woman lying there across that short, sunlit expanse. The
young woman didn't wave back, but she smiled. She smiled
with the perfect reserve of the utterly self-assured. Both Lea
and Amedeo interpreted that smile as something radiant. Yes,
'radiant' was the word Amedeo used in his letter. 'Radiant.
Radiant and glowing.'

"Two days later, they came back to the same beach and at
the same late hour of the afternoon. And, exactly as they'd
anticipated (or, at least, hoped), there she was, lying alongside the candy-striped cabana once again, sunning herself in
the nude. Just as before, she did nothing to conceal that nudity. Nor, one might add, anything to exhibit it, either. Like
Lea and Amedeo, she didn't seem to feel the slightest necessity to dissimulate any part of herself. Didn't seem to feel that
her nudity was nakedness. That afternoon, however, two
things happened. The matched pair of Scottie dogs, who'd
been so protective of their mistress the first day, came rushing
down now to greet Lea and Amedeo as they waded ashore.
The dogs then scurried back and forth between the three of
them like mute little messengers. They continued doing so for
the brief time they all found themselves within each other's
reach. Once again, however, nothing was said, nothing was

exchanged. The identical little black dogs (like each other's shadow) rushed back and forth between the three of them, bearing — as they did — an ever more embarassed burden of unmitigated silence.

"When they left, perhaps half an hour later, it was Lea, once again, who waved at the young woman. And it was just then, at that very instant, that the *second* thing happened. For the young woman waved back. She waved with a single, leisurely, unexpected curl of her hand. But she waved, nonetheless, and her wave was received like a treasure, a windfall. A 'blessing,' my sister and brother would call it as they swam out to the 'Flamingo' and prepared the seaplane for its brief flight back to its anchorage at Antibes. 'A blessing, a blessing,' they kept repeating.

"Now, they began seeing the 'Flamingo' itself as an agent of that 'blessing'; in a metaphysical sense, as its very vehicle. They no longer flew down the coastline as far as Cap d'Agde or Narbonne, but lifted the craft just high enough to clear the parasol pines at Cap d'Antibes. Then, circling the gulf on the far side of that narrow peninsula, they'd bring the 'Flamingo' down to land, skim really, across the surface of the water. They'd then taxi over to the bobbing red marker that lay anchored off that white crescent, and fasten their leads.

"Their next two visits to that beach, however, would leave them deeply distressed. For on neither occasion was the young woman there. They both felt forsaken, as if some silent arrangement between the three of them had been broken. As if some trust had just been betrayed. On the following visit, however, about a week later, they would see (even through the smudged windscreens of their twin cockpits) the two little black dogs, far off, frolicking against the bright sand.

"This time, everything was different. Or nearly. Amedeo,

in his letter, described how Lea, acting on impulse alone (on something Lea would later term 'a kind of premonition'), walked directly up to her. She crossed the hundred feet or so of secluded beach that separated them, and — upon reaching the young woman — kneeled down alongside her, and began oiling her prone body with her very own lotions. The young woman didn't stir. To the contrary, her body remained perfectly still, perfectly supple as well, under the pressure of Lea's fingertips and, several moments later, Lea's palms. She didn't stir except, according to Amedeo's letter, when she rolled over and let Lea cover her shoulders and breasts, her belly and thighs, and the full length of her legs with the amber-red oil. Her face, all that time — turned to one side and wrapped in that wild mass of brass-brown hair — did nothing to hide a perfectly child-like, utterly guileless smile. She'd closed her eyes, but the smile, nonetheless, burnt through the closed lids as if the lids were diaphanous. Clearly, she was in no way displeased.

"This would be the third and last time the three of them met on the beach. Lea leaned over the young woman a moment or two after she'd closed her eyes, and ran her lips across the young woman's brows, as if to seal them with a mute whisper. Then, Lea got up and silently left. The young woman must have fallen asleep, the smile still fixed to her face, while Lea and Amedeo, after a moment, rejoined their seaplane. Taxiing out as quietly as they could, they took off at a distance that in no way would have disturbed the sleeper. From there, once again, they returned to Antibes harbor.

"Once more, but only once, according to Amedeo's letter, my sister and brother would make their way back to that charmed beach. But this time, to no avail: 'she' wouldn't be there. I could easily imagine them, that last time, walking over to that low, abandoned, candy-striped cabana and, spreading a beach towel exactly where she'd spread hers, lying down exactly where she'd lain.

"They'd have to wait a full month, in fact, before they'd see her again. It was a month of rain, of folded umbrellas and deserted beaches. It was a month, too, full of restlessness, anxiety, dismay. It was during that spell, if I remember correctly, that Lea, but most especially Amedeo, began writing to me — and in great detail — about what had just befallen them: how a total stranger, without a single word being exchanged, had virtually transformed their very lives. As they wrote of these things (Lea as much as Amedeo, finally) they'd slip more and more into that increasingly mystic, increasingly arcane usage of theirs, so very dear to each of them. The young woman's wave, for instance, was now interpreted not only as a 'blessing' but as a 'sign,' 'a divine indication.' A portent, in itself, of 'the forthcoming.'

"*Carissimi*, how little they saw. How little they allowed themselves to see. As long as they felt enveloped in what they called 'a visionary perspective' they thought themselves secure, protected, immune. I'd followed their beliefs, though, as far as I could; had shared many of their views and let myself be influenced to the very limits of the plausible. But beyond that I couldn't go. I've often wondered, though, whether it wasn't despair itself that drove them into the very heart of those euphoric visions. Drove them deeper and deeper as Europe, the idea of Europe, steadily collapsed, as the most basic tenets of the civilized world were swept aside like so many playing cards. As they themselves felt more and more the depth of their own alienation. Yes, often I've wondered whether what they came to call the 'paradisiacal' wasn't simply the last refuge for a certain, historic exhaustion." Giacòbbe Lampronti, at that very instant, looked out of the window, then back; took a long sip from his drink.

"In any case, during that month — during those rains —
they wrote me a letter virtually every day. It was vital, as they
put it, that I become the 'witness' to what they considered 'a
potentially redemptive experience'; a 'witness' to the realiza-
tion of some 'secret agreement,' some 'unspoken promise' that
existed between themselves and that lovely creature, that
'Eve,' as they now called her. Once again, they wrote about
how, with a single glance, their entire lives had been turned
outward, away, and fixed upon that 'single, glistening figure'
who lay no more than a hundred feet across the sands. Both
of them, clearly enough, had not only fallen in love with that
'glistening figure,' but had invested her with every mystical
attribute imaginable. Such, now, was their adoration.

"So, locked in by the long rains, they kept writing to me,
day after day. The gray sea, they wrote, reflected the gray
sky: one couldn't tell one from the other. As the rains continued, however, and the chances of once again seeing the young
woman on the beach dwindled, the letters began losing their
luster, their flamboyance. Yes, bit by bit, they no longer expressed that same sense of urgency, of imminence. They no
longer spoke of existing at 'revelation's very edge.' To the
contrary, the letters became increasingly retrospective and
read, more and more, like an inventory of meticulously recorded moments. Since, however, there were so very few moments to record, they'd dwell on the recollection of some
minute aspect: the shadow of the young woman's eyelashes,
for instance, or a freckle that seemed to float over the crease
of her thigh. Lea devoted an entire letter to how the young
woman stretched, and yet another to the way her fingers
would stab into the bewildering wealth of her hair, pulling
it — from the temples, backward — wire-taut.

"That flurry of letters lasted a bit more than a month.
Then, suddenly, it stopped. I had no idea whether or not

something 'had happened,' as they say, or whether the fascist authorities had decided not only to censor but to intercept our mail, as well. I was completing my last year of graduate studies at Padova at the time, and preparing my doctoral thesis in philology. The pressure on young Jewish intellectuals had now grown intolerable. It was only a matter of weeks before we, too, would have to go into hiding or be taken, incarcerated. No, none of us, any longer, knew 'what was happening.'

"It was nearly six weeks later that a letter — *the* letter, you might wish to call it — reached me. It was written in Lea's hand, and consisted of no fewer than fifteen dense, densely inscribed blue pages. It began without the usual solicitudes. It began, in fact, like a little novella unto itself, and, as I read it, I felt more and more as if I were being called upon to witness something I had no real right to hear, even overhear. That I had been invited, almost formally, into an area of such intimacy that I could only feel, once within it, a certain sense — I must admit — of impropriety.

"It began, as narratives will, with a long description. The two of them, my sister and brother, confined to their hotel room one day by the unending rains, decided nonetheless to brave the weather. At the end of the afternoon, they walked out and into the downpour. They'd taken one of those narrow little back streets in Juan-les-Pins, tightly packed with *épiceries* and *fleuristes* and all the pungent scents that arise from their fresh, perishable wares. Of all the scents, however, the strongest (one might even call it the highest note in a whole crescendo of scents) came from the *poissonnerie*. All salt, iodine, marine acids, it smothered even that of the plump bunches of pink carnations that were being sold, a bit everywhere, from little street stands. It was in front of one of those little stands, in effect, that they quite suddenly saw her. She was looking about, a bit lost — perplexed — with a raised umbrella in one hand and a pair of leashes in the other. Her two Scottie dogs were tugging at the leashes while, in the same hand, she was trying to keep her grasp on a straw shopping basket, filled — it turned out — with a half-kilo of pears. She didn't see them at first. She was still looking about, the two leashes wrapped taut about her long linen skirt, in the very same instant Lea and Amedeo came alongside. Out of sheer discretion — *politezza*, Lea called it — they would have kept on walking past. But just as they stepped directly in front of her, the young woman, the young woman from the beach, having just recognized them, reached out and — with the simplest of gestures — handed Amedeo the leashes, the twin leashes, to her paired Scotties. She did so without saying a word. Without offering the least reason, or pretext, or offhand apology. She gave no indication whatsoever to either of them, in fact, except for the faintest, most transparent of smiles.

"Both astonished and somewhat disarmed, they followed her, together with her dogs, from one boutique to another. She bought several sketchbooks in a *papeterie*, and then, after browsing through a number of pottery shops, finally found a faience fruit bowl that seemed to be exactly what she'd been looking for. She spoke to the shopkeepers in a somewhat 'small,' almost timid, even juvenile voice. It seemed to contrast markedly with the utter assurance of her gestures, which were infallibly forthright, unhesitating, unequivocal. Although her French was perfect, she pronounced her words with a distinct American accent that both my sister and brother found totally captivating. But she still hadn't addressed a single word to either of them, not even now, as they followed her to what they could only assume to be her hotel, or apartment, the three of them and the two dogs walking in total silence under the spread umbrellas through the heavy, unending downpour.

"The young woman led them to a somewhat anonymous, rose stucco *pavillon* located about two blocks from the sea. As she searched about in her handbag for her keys, Lea recalled, the rain pinged in sharp, stinging pellets against the glass, fan-shaped canopy overhead. They huddled there, the three of them, for a long moment, their bodies virtually pressed, one against the other, until the key was finally found and the front door swung open. The dogs, leashes and all, went rushing into the hallway, within. If the odors outside had been those of so much rain-splattered honeysuckle, inside they immediately gave way to that of turpentine. They'd entered into an artist's studio. Everywhere stood trestle tables, easels with unfinished canvases, tall stands with terra-cotta heads enveloped — turbaned, really — in damp muslin. Paintings stood stacked, one against the other, their faces to the wall, while 'arrangements' for still lifes lay scattered, a bit everywhere, throughout the spacious *atelier*.

"It was the laying out of a fresh 'arrangement' that they now witnessed, as the young woman unwrapped the fruit bowl she'd just purchased and filled it with one heavy pear after another. In no time whatsoever, she'd created a very simple, harmonious composition: the pears, ensconced in their bowl, seemed to burst from some invisible center, and — radiating outward — to lap, one over the other, like so many fat, tumescent petals.

" 'Like it?' she asked. Those were her very first words, in fact. But before either Lea or Amedeo could respond, she'd gone into her bathroom and, almost immediately, reappeared with a heavy black comb. She was combing her hair as she returned, walking barefoot now across the tiled floor.

" 'Here,' Lea said, 'please.' She took the comb into her own hand and began combing out the young woman's wet, luxuriant mass of curls, drawing them — but only for an instant — ruler straight. What with their dampness, they sprang back all the quicker. The young woman, now, had closed her eyes, and — as they both noted — was smiling.

" 'It's like such a long time ago,' the young woman said, her eyes still closed, her long lashes fanned tight against her cheeks and her lips, imperceptibly, spread.

" 'Just like then. It feels just like the time I couldn't even begin to remember,' she continued, her eyes still closed. 'Just like the time before everything got forgotten.'

"With her great, gray, luminous eyes clamped shut and her lips, now, very slightly separated, she seemed to be concentrating fixedly on some distant vanishing point, some inaccessible moment, some scene upon which the curtains, long ago, had been irrevocably drawn. Later, much later, Lea and Amedeo would learn exactly what the young woman meant by that 'time before everything got forgotten.' Learn of her *first* amnesia — not the one that occurred at the Hôtel Belle Rive two years ago — which, in fact, was only a recurrence — but the one upon which it was initially founded. About the morning in her earliest childhood when, wordless, breathless, paralyzed to the very tips of her toes, she'd watched her own mother — arms thrashing — drown in a sudden offshore undertow. Saw her drown no farther than a beachball's throw away. This, of course, she couldn't, wouldn't, remember. Her memory had gone blank, gone white, and from that moment forth she had to begin her young life entirely anew, if such a thing were possible. Had to give birth, or at least substance, to a second life.

" 'Like then, just like then,' the young woman said to no one now except, perhaps, to that phantom mother who was still drawing, pulling, tending to her wet curls. 'Just like then. Just like the very way I imagine it,' she continued, eyes still closed and her heart still fixed on that one inaccessible instant, that 'hole' into which her memory had vanished in the same instant as her mother's thrashing body.

" 'There,' she said, as Lea kissed her. 'There, like that. Just exactly like that,' she said as her teeth bit deep into her lower lip and her smile — in the very same moment — spread to its very edges.

"All night, that night, with the three of them lying in a single heap of sheets and blankets, the young woman (whose name they'd now learned was Milly) seemed locked in a trance as both Lea and Amedeo, first one, then the other, then both of them at the same time, released upon the young woman all the love that they'd never released upon each other. She was ravished — yes, ravished, it's the only word — delighted beyond measure, *transportée*. It was as if that night, for the very first time, she felt the emptiness she had always known suddenly fill. Suddenly close under the pressure of so many kisses, caresses, so much passionate, unabated attention.

"And so it began. For that was only the commencement of what was to become the happiest period in each of their lives. Their *âge d'or*, one might say."

There were tears in Giacòbbe Lampronti's eyes as I reached across the table (with all its cold, unfinished plates and serving dishes) and took the top of one of his hands in the palm of one of mine. "It was so very good of you to tell me all these things, Giacòbbe. So very kind."

"*Niente.* It's nothing, you know," he said. "Molly — because now you've taught me to call her that — Molly's story tells itself. For me, it begins with one instance of amnesia, really, and ends with another. Between the two, it's like some beautiful break in the clouds. It's like so much blueness. But there's more, much more, to tell you, if only there were time." Lampronti looked at his watch. He had to be at a meeting of his *académie* within the next half-hour and wouldn't be available again until after dinner. I sensed a certain hesitancy on his part to invite me either to a café or a restaurant, let alone his apartment. His apartment, I suspect, is well beneath the very elegant, richly cultivated surroundings he's been accustomed to. So I quite simply invited him here, to the living room of this two-room hotel suite I occupy. He didn't seem to mind, either. The stories of Molly — of Milly, that is — that we'd exchanged had brought about a kind of bond. A kind of intimacy existed now between the two of us. Yes, Milly, quite unwittingly, had linked our lives, Lampronti's and mine. At least for the duration of this single evening in Avignon, we'd become indispensable to one another.

I must admit, at this point, to a certain *coquetterie* on my part. While Lampronti attended his reunion, I busied myself by taking a long bath and then decking myself out in my limpest, most languorous dress. It was a pale jade affair, custom-cut in dripping satin. I matched the pale jade with a triple strand of clicking, bone-white abalone beads. For scent, I used no perfume whatsoever, only the lingering redolence of talc and bath salts with all their innate suggestiveness of steam, scrubbed limbs, and slick, glistening shoulders.

While I dressed, I couldn't stop thinking about Lampronti, about his beautiful manners and deep reserve. I thought, too, about his hands as I fastened (with my own) a pair of pear-shaped emerald clips onto my ears. I wondered whether he'd notice how close, how very close, the color of my eyes came to their cool, acidulous fires. Yes, I decided, Lampronti needed to be charmed. Needed to be drawn free from all those dark interiors his thoughts seemed to dwell on, pulled from all that draped mirror and ancestral shadow, from those tall, stately portraits (even Lea's and Amedeo's) that he harbored in the very depths of his heart. Yes, charmed, I thought, just as a ray of one of my emeralds quivered a bit in the dressing-room mirror, wavered in a single, loose, lash-like oscillation.

I telephoned room service. Having scarcely touched my lunch, I had a light dinner sent up to my room, along with a bottle of Dom Pérignon. But even now, I had little or no appetite. I enjoyed the champagne immensely, however, and smoked one cigarette after another. As always when I'm anxious, I adore smoking and sipping champagne. Both, by their very nature, are virtually weightless and seem to invite one into a world devoid of all substance, gravity, constraint. One gets a bit heady in the process and seems to rise along with so much blue fume, so many burst, yellow bubbles. One enters the effortless, the perfectly lithe.

I got up and opened the tall, louvered shutters that the chambermaid had closed, and leaned out into the early damp of the Provençal evening. "Milly, Milly," I whispered, as if to the night itself that had gathered, darkened now, just a few feet over the baked, lichen-struck roof tiles. Already, over Avignon, I could make out the first windswept stars, coming on.

"You've never been closer, Milly. Come closer yet," I whispered. "Come now," I implored, addressing as I did more the hollow shell of that word, that vocable, than the living person herself. Wanting, as I whispered, that the shell, at last, be filled; the hollow, ballasted.

Giacòbbe Lampronti arrived a bit earlier than I'd expected. He was wearing a dark tweed jacket now, and gray flannels, and his shoes — as if in a slight but significant concession — were a deep cordovan brown rather than the glossy black he'd worn previously. I appreciated the changes: they were so many signs in themselves of Lampronti's growing confidence, closeness, call it — if you will — intimacy. He brought along with him a well-worn briefcase, its lock and corners trimmed with so many delicate brass fixings. The fixings, by the perfect fit of their several interlocking parts, reminded me of some paleontological bone set. No sooner, in fact, had he sat down in an armchair, facing me, than he opened that very briefcase and drew from it several tightly ribboned packets. Each packet contained, perhaps, a score of letters.

"These," he said, "will tell you so much more than I can. Will tell you everything, if everything is what you wish to hear." He brought five packets out, altogether: Lea's accounted for two of them, and Amedeo's for three. The letters, or rather their envelopes, were frayed, even limp from so much handling; from, that is, all the times Giacòbbe had pulled their contents free to read and reread in so many endless acts of sheer devotedness. Over the next few hours I'd learn to differentiate between the sister's "voice" and the brother's: the former being intricate, elliptical, even baroque, and the latter terse, exclamatory. Over the next few hours, in fact, I'd come to grow attached to those two very disparate "voices," as if each were engaged in a musical duet with the other, such as between an oboe and a bassoon. Clearly, only both those "voices," those "instruments," could begin to capture that otherwise incaptive presence of the one who was then called "Mildred Pearl."

So, while I listened, Giacòbbe Lampronti would read one letter — or rather, one passage of a letter — after another. He knew every word of those letters, of course, by heart. He'd skip from one envelope to the next, from one vital sequence to another, while — at the same time — translating his sister's or brother's words from Italian into the impeccable French that he addressed me in.

I listened, utterly enthralled. Occasionally I'd pour

Giacòbbe Lampronti and myself a fresh glass of champagne; occasionally, too, while he read, I'd stand up and walk about, or lean against the iron balustrade of my tall living-room window, breathing in the now total night that hung — with all its stars — over Avignon. It looked like a medieval miniature. No wonder, I thought, Lampronti could speak of miracles. Under these skies, anything was possible. And, quite clearly, two summers ago, everything truly was. The three of them, Milly, Lea, Amedeo, had all fallen in love, one with the other. And this love, one could fairly say, was inextricable: altogether, they formed a wheel, "una ruota," as Amedeo called it, with their three beings, with their three bodies. Night after night, the notion of who gave, who received, dissolved into a single indissoluble movement. The wheel turned on so many perfectly attuned gestures: each appeal received its immediate response; each thirst, its deep quenching. In effect, the wheel was nothing more than a closed and continuous circuit of so many intricate, interlocking reciprocities.

"Flow, we flow. We've lost all sense of our edges, our identities. We enter and issue. We exude," as Amedeo wrote to Giacòbbe in the very first week of their intimacies.

And thus, it began. From the very start, they lived in utter emulation, one of the other. Both Lea and Amedeo wanted to become Milly, to be Milly, whereas Milly herself, as far as one could infer, wanted to be alternately one of them or the other. They exchanged everything. They'd wear one another's clothes (to the extent that Amedeo's shirts and jerseys would fit either of the two women, which they mostly did), or they'd go out shopping and buy three of a kind: buy three identical, sky-blue chamois jackets, for example, with as many ultramarine silk scarves to match. They'd bathe together in the same bath and afterward spray one another lavishly with the very same perfume. Yes, they wanted to smell, taste, look,

and — most of all — feel alike, think alike, fuse within the
ruota in which every individual attribute might at last be abolished in that living corolla, that heavy, three-petaled amalgam
where, finally, they'd even begun exchanging — as well as
their bodies — their very names. Yes, within the heat of that
high, refined passion of theirs, they'd begun calling the other
by their own name.

"*Lea,*" Lea would write. "*Milly adores being called Lea, just as I
adore being called Milly. We're really turning, you see, into one another's
mirrors. But how wet our mirrors are, how wild! You have no idea how
much I'd love to become Milly! How much I almost have!*"

Call it corolla, or mirror, or some kind of spiritual magnet,
they grew, month after month, increasingly indissociable. If
nights they'd make love until they'd fallen — voluptuously —
asleep, wrapped loosely in that wheel of wet hair, wet shoulders, and long, straddling limbs, day was a different affair.
Days, Milly painted. She painted, or — as a *gagne-pain* — she
modeled. Her time was divided almost equally between the
two. She thus managed to do exactly what she wished: to
paint, that is, and support herself in the process. What with
the emergence, however, of Lea and Amedeo in her life, her
days, especially the latter part of her days, especially toward
five o'clock of each afternoon of those days, were now devoted to an entirely new activity: aviation.

Yes, they'd begun teaching Milly how to fly. The rear of
the Caproncino's twin cockpits, with its dual control, had just
enough space for the two women to squeeze into. And
squeeze they did. I could well imagine them, all three covered
in tight headgear and goggles, taxiing past the fortress of Antibes, the twin wings of that slight, gracile aircraft trembling, it would seem, not so much from the vibrations of the
one engine, as the simple anticipation of the flight to come.
Still deep, still hauling water, it would reach the end of the

buoy-marked straightaway and, turning upwind, its engine at full throttle now, slip forward on its strutted pontoons, the pontoons themselves lifting gradually as the aircraft accelerated, slapping the hard, metallic flat of the water until — with several successive skips — it would rise free of the harbor, trailing as it went two neat, spuming threads of water, of jettisoned water-beads. From there, the "Flamingo" would bank clear of the coastline and, still gaining altitude, head south-southeast toward Corsica.

Nothing had ever made Milly so happy. The three of them, late each afternoon, ascending into that lighter element, into a blue sometimes powdered with sea mist, and, at others, a near limitless, near violet, near ethereal azure that Milly would compare to Fra Angelico's, entered into a euphoria of their own. Amedeo would spare nothing, either, in describing that "euphoria." For never had they been closer: closer to one another and — at the same time — closer to the possibility, at least, of some "sign," some "indication." For didn't they both feel (and perhaps Milly as well, for all we know) that they'd entered into something that they now called "redemptive space"? That, at a certain altitude, the wings of the aircraft might touch the wings of the godhead? Yes, and that touching, ever so slightly grazing, the struts of the one against the feathers of the other, they might be — who knows? — the recipients of "some message"?

One would have to understand the political as well as the spiritual climate of that particular time, Giacòbbe Lampronti insisted, to appreciate the sheer extravagance of their views. They were each living at history's very edge. ("But aren't we all," Lampronti quickly added.) And each of them felt that there was nothing now to turn to but the vertical, the still-untrammeled altitudes, at which lay — like so many dormant, utterly lambent particles — the recurrent notion of some form of messianic redemption. Yes, one would have to understand the entire climate of that spring and summer, of those circumstances, to appreciate — as well — the power of that notion. And, most especially, its power to intoxicate.

Imagine, then, how they responded one morning when Milly, awaking from a deep sleep, leaned over and, shoving the vast mane of her hair free from her eyes and forehead, announced that she was pregnant. She did so with a rather pert, clearly provocative smile on her face. She'd already foreseen their reaction. They were, of course, overwhelmed. Tears breaking through their laughter, and laughter breaking through their tears, they showered her in kisses. They picked her up, carried her like a queen from room to room, enthroned on their shoulders. They sang, chanted. They broke open their best bottles. Milly, of course, was equally overwhelmed, but — as befitting — in a quiet, enclosed, already introspective way. Clearly enough, they'd all been "blessed," as Amedeo put it, all three of them. By noon of the very same day, Lea was writing to Giacòbbe and, in elated terms, telling him of the joy that had befallen all of them. *"Even I, this morning, feel pregnant,"* she wrote. *"Even Amedeo, yes, even Amedeo feels a kind of swelling in his very innards, his very soul. Chosen, chosen is the only word, Giacòbbe. We feel chosen. Oh, how can we even begin to tell you how joyous, how grateful, we feel, today? And you, dear one, at that terrible distance, how can you even begin to comprehend? Come, come soon,* caro fratello, *come and join us. A light from heaven has fallen upon each of us. Yes, a light! A light!"*

From that morning on, their entire life changed. Then and there, they stopped flying altogether. It was too dangerous, they felt, what with Milly already entering her second month of pregnancy. They moved inland from Juan-les-Pins to a large farmhouse that Amedeo had located on the outskirts of

Grasse. The farm was not only surrounded but seemingly immersed in four, pampered, richly irrigated fields of heavily scented flowers. Roses and carnations dominated, but the variety (most of which were cultivated for the local perfume industry) was virtually limitless. Milly and Lea and Amedeo would live in the very heart of that massive garden, in the perpetual redolence of its buds and blossoms, for the next fourteen months. Raucously colored, the flowers would become, in fact, very much part of their days as, day after day, they'd decorate their farmhouse with squat little jugs full of anemones or tall, transparent vases — cylinders, really — piled high with so many fluffy, overhanging, white irises. Whatever bloomed at their door, bloomed a second time — but now as if magnified by the "blessed house" itself — on their tables and night tables, or — like blue lanterns — from the waxed walnut shelves of their high, dining-room buffet.

But best of all, the flowers, and most especially roses, would decorate "the Queen" herself. Lea and Amedeo would cover every part of Milly's naked body in wet petals. Yes, they'd virtually dress her in petals and garland her hair in bay leaves, studding the garlands with whatever buds happened to be in flower at that moment. "They'd literally breathe over her body, over the petals of her body," Giacòbbe recounted. "They'd whisper, as if praying, over that growing rotundity: the still barely perceptible swell that heaved — but oh so slightly — under its coverlet of roses or peonies or whatever. Yes, prayers, supplications. Such, in any case, is how I first saw them, the three of them, all together. How I first saw Mildred Pearl, with my sister and brother hovering over her, murmuring (in an almost monotonous, quasi-religious way) their adulation. It was, I must admit, utterly bizarre and, at the same time, perfectly hallucinating. I couldn't keep my eyes off the three of them. Off this intimate ritual that they'd invented for themselves. Milly, swathed in roses. Milly, Milly enshrined.

"I'd escaped Italy, you see, and arrived in France unannounced. I was traveling faster than any message I might send. So no one, actually, was expecting me. I knocked on the farmhouse door with one hand while holding, in the other, a single suitcase. But no one answered. So, what with the door being open, I simply walked in. From the dark vestibule, its coat hooks hung with braids of bone-white garlic, I called out. But still, no one answered. So I passed through the dining room and down a long corridor, following all the while a thin, insistent murmur that, scarcely audible, seemed to be emanating out of a room, upstairs. It was there, finally, at the top of the stairs, in an adjacent bedroom, that I found them. That I finally managed to trace the thread of that whisper to its very spool.

"This would be the one and only time I'd ever meet Mildred Pearl. I'd been informed of an available teaching position in the north of France, and wouldn't return to the Midi until the end, the very end. By then, it would be too late. That day in Grasse, however, in the farmhouse, walking in on the three of them, on the incantations of the two and the enshrinement of the third, I became a material witness of sorts to this outlandish cult. Yes, decked in flowers, Mildred Pearl, nearly grotesque in that tapestry of petals that sheathed almost every part of her naked body, held out her arm, her near-infantile hand. Petals were still falling as I took her slightly plump, fleshy fingertips and kissed them, one by one, with a reverence, I must admit, that astonished even myself.

"I stayed three days," Giacòbbe went on. "They were certainly the most unforgettable days of my life. I had no idea, no premonition, of course, that I'd never see any of them

again. I was so overjoyed at the time. As to Milly, to Molly
as we call her now," Giacòbbe said, with a smile that seemed
to arise out of some profound well of suppressed warmth, "as
to Molly, she was more than equal to everything I'd ever heard
about her. At last I could see how she'd become the object of
so much veneration. She was so guileless, so pure, so perfectly
receptive. More than that, her apparent placidity seemed to
draw, magnetize, even slightly insist, perhaps, on the nature
and extent of their attentiveness. She was, from head to toe,
totally icon.

"I, too, might have easily gone on to venerate her, to enter
that tight, luminous circle that believed in nothing any longer
but miracle. But messiah. But the possibility of some ultimate
redemption for a world that had already, in fact, entered the
irredeemable. I still remember the petals falling, falling from
her wrist, her forearm, from her breasts, as she sat up,
propped on one elbow to receive me, a kind of pagan Mary,
a mythical child-mother, yes: a she-god. Her smile, I remember, seemed to alight on one like the concentrated, still quivering beam of some distant stellar body. Yes, I, too, might
easily have gone on to venerate Mildred Pearl. Yes," Giacòbbe
Lampronti said with great wistfulness, "easily, quite easily, I
might have done so.

"Their child was born prematurely that fall, on November
thirtieth if I remember correctly, and they named him, after
the prophet, Eliseo. I never got to meet my own nephew, the
child really not only of Milly and Amedeo, but Lea as well.
For they'd *all* been pregnant with Eliseo in one sense or another. And now they were each his parent, and equally so.
Parent to this tiny, wizened miracle of theirs. This would-be
redemptor, wrapped tight in swaddling and blinking into the
bright candles that, like the whispers, encircled him. He had,
apparently, his mother's wide gray eyes and powerful

eyebrows. Within the six short months that he lived, he came to resemble his natural mother, in fact, in every way conceivable. My sister and brother worshipped him all the more for doing so.

"What happened after, happened very quickly. Happened, too, with great confusion. The entry papers that my sister and brother had once so anxiously awaited from the Spanish Republic finally arrived. The papers not only granted entry and safe conduct, but assigned both of them to a specific hospital in Madrid and indicated an exact date at which to appear for duty. They had to move quickly, now. As to the seaplane, the Caproncino, they could contribute it — for the duration of the war — to the coastal authorities stationed in Barcelona harbor, if they so wished. Again, an exact address was indicated.

"They had only three days, now, to make their arrangements. Milly had begun painting again and, at the same time, modeling for a major work by one of France's greatest portraitists. In fact, her modeling had provided all three — all four — of them with the small but necessary sums for their day-to-day living expenses. During the hours that she modeled, Lea would look after Eliseo. And, over the months, the two of them — Lea and Eliseo — had become quite inseparable. It was Milly herself, I believe, who suggested (in the midst of so much commotion) that Lea take Eliseo for the time she'd need (two weeks? three weeks?) to complete her modeling assignment. She'd then join them; become, like them, a nurse's assistant, wherever she might be needed. As a citizen of a nonbelligerent country, she wouldn't require entry papers, either. She'd be free to enter Spain whenever she wished.

"And that's exactly what happened. Or nearly. They all had to abandon their beloved farmhouse, buried in the deep, wind-scattered scent of so many blossoms. One can only imagine them, at that moment; imagine the grief that they must have felt. 'Imagine,' I say, because I'd never know otherwise, because I'd never again hear from either sister or brother. 'Imagine,' because the rest is assumption, is the piecing together of so many scattered, unverifiable elements. 'Imagine,' because there was simply nothing else I could do . . .

"So, on the day of their departure, their separation, Amedeo flew the 'Flamingo' solo as far as Barcelona. There, he handed the aircraft over to the authorities, contributing it, thus, to the Republic. Today, of course, it's certainly in the hands of the fascists, the *franquisti*, a sad fate for that fabulous toy of our childhood. As to Lea, she took the train with her precious charge wrapped securely in her unsleeping arms all the way from Nice to Barcelona, and then on again from Barcelona to Madrid. There, as planned, she met up with Amedeo. Once installed, she sought out a nursery, *una guardería*, for little Eliseo. She'd leave him there during her daily twelve-hour spell of duty at the hospital where she dealt with the wounded and the dying.

"As to Milly, she moved into the Hôtel Belle Rive, as you know, for the brief duration. From there, she was quite close to both the studio where she posed and the beach where she went, early each morning, for a dip. It was just after one of those dips, exactly as you were told, that she received the first telegram. I say 'first' because there were three, altogether. It came only a week after they'd all separated, and perhaps no more than ten days before Milly herself would have left France to join them. That first telegram (the only one she'd ever receive) came from the nursery in Madrid, informing her that her baby had been killed in the shelling of the city, the night before. That her baby had died, it specified, instantaneously.

"You know the rest, what happened immediately after. You probably heard it from the very same hotel manager as I did, two years earlier. As to the second telegram, the one she'd never receive (she'd already wandered out of the hotel lobby and, seemingly, into oblivion), it was I who sent it. I'd been informed by my parents that both Lea and Amedeo had perished on the very same night, in the very same shelling, as Eliseo himself. But Milly didn't know this, didn't need to know this. Because she had not only wandered out of the hotel lobby in Juan-les-Pins, but out of her own mind, her own memory, out of every conceivable trace of anything that might once have constituted a personal identity. Yes, she was lost to us, forever. Lost to us, that is, until today. Until your visit, your kindness (*la tua bontà*), until you came to express your love for this very same creature whom we've all loved, each in our own way: yes, you, Lea, Amedeo, myself. Each of us. Each in our own way."

I'd been pacing slowly about the room as Giacòbbe recounted the astonishing story of Molly, of Milly, of her brother-and-sister lovers, and — for me, the most astonishing of all — her child. Now, I stood directly behind Giacòbbe Lampronti, seated deep in his armchair. I placed a hand on each of his shoulders and caressed them gently, steadily, with something more than mere commiseration. "There was a third telegram, too," Giacòbbe said unexpectedly, facing straight ahead. "It came the day after mine, three days, that is, after Milly had left the Hôtel Belle Rive." As Giacòbbe talked, I continued caressing his shoulders. I felt, as I did, an access of affection pour through my fingers, my fingertips, then press — like driven pegs — into his muscles. He pretended not to notice. "That telegram, too, came from Madrid," he continued, "from the nursery there. It wasn't, I'm fairly certain, of much consequence. It asked Milly to come and personally identify, if she would, the little corpse. Since most of the infants in their custody were orphans, the telegram explained, it wasn't always easy to identify the victims with utter certainty. To know exactly which babies had perished, and which hadn't. Only the mothers could do this, could identify 'their own.' Could make, as the telegram read, 'the ultimate verification.' "

I was scarcely listening to Giacòbbe Lampronti now. I had run both my hands under his soft, lamb's-wool lapels, and was working my palms flat, hard, rhythmic across the muscles of his chest. As I did, he very gently took hold of my forearms. He ran the loop of his fingers up and down the length of my arms, from my wrists to the loose, overhanging sleeves of my satin dress, then down again. He did this over and over. "Please," I said, my head now leaning over his and my hair falling down on either side of his face and across his cheeks. "Please," I repeated.

"Millicent," he said, venturing to call me, for the very first time, by my first name.

"No," I whispered, shaking my head. "No, not Millicent. Milly, call me Milly."

"I can't," Lampronti replied.

"Milly," I insisted. "It's *my* name, too, you know."

"But it's hers. It's hers, first."

"Milly," I heard myself hiss. I'd unbuttoned his shirt now, and run my hands down over his abdomen, and just under it as well.

"Say it," I said.

He reached up, and behind, and took my head in each of his incredibly gentle hands.

"Say it," I said. I'd let my hand fall even farther now, and was reaching under, feeling the fullness beneath.

Then, suddenly, I realized that Lampronti was murmuring.

I leaned over his shoulder even farther and watched his lips, scarcely moist, rolling the same two syllables, one over the other, as if he were reciting some inexhaustible mantra.

"Milly," he was murmuring. "Milly, Milly, Milly . . ."

Now we were facing one another, holding one another. I could hear the two syllables tangle now, over and over, in my hair, catching on so many blonde strands before sliding into my ear, twisting wet through the wet whorl of my ear. "Milly," I kept hearing, kept wanting to hear.

"Milly, Milly," he kept repeating.

"Amedeo," I replied, holding him straight now against my flat belly, my high, contracted thighs. "Amedeo, Amedeo," I kept saying.

"No, no, you mustn't," he pleaded.

"My Amedeo, my dearest, most adorable Amedeo."

"Don't, don't, I beg of you," he kept saying.

Now, I'd pulled him down onto the bed and, together, the two of us undoing one another's clothes and underclothes with as much deftness, even delicacy, as speed, we surrendered to the weight and thrust and lightness of it all. "Amedeo," I kept saying, "yes, my Amedeo."

"Oh Milly."

"Yes, yes, my Amedeo, yes."

"Oh Milly, Milly, my Milly," he kept saying. Couldn't stop saying, well into the night.

Then, what happened happened. I wouldn't wish to linger on the events of the next few months — no, not even for an instant. But this journal, entering now into its very last pages, wouldn't be complete without some mention — no matter how summary — of the events that followed upon that single evening in Avignon. How one event led inexorably into the next. I must apologize, however, to any eventual reader who might someday hazard upon these last, remaining pages for my rather cursory treatment of that period. Perhaps, someday, I'll be able to expand upon what I've merely traced and suggested, herein. As for now (and for some time, I suspect), the less said — certainly — the better.

I returned to America, as I remember, feeling perfectly triumphant. Yes, "triumphant" is the only word adequate. I'd left Giacòbbe Lampronti in Avignon the very next morning after our *ébats*, and taken the "Flying Clipper" home from Marseilles. As luck would have it, I needed to wait only eight days for the next flight, and during that time I checked into a hotel by the sea in Cassis and busied myself writing the first scenes of a fresh scenario. I had everything I needed, now, for that scenario: a fabulous story, a suspense-filled plot operating on several interrelated time periods at once, and — along with a whole galaxy of supporting characters — a star, a single, fragile, glorious, inextinguishable star. Yes, I'd turn Molly Lamanna's whole story into a screenplay. And the screenplay — as soon as I possibly could — into a film. Better than that, I'd get Molly herself to feature in that film. Dark star, I'd get her to radiate out of her own obliterated past.

For Molly — it must be understood — was mine, now. Owning her memory, I felt assured, I owned her as well. I'd appropriated every bit of it out of thin air, out of rumor, and finally out of a chance encounter with that single surviving witness. Yes, her memory was mine, and mine to do with as I wished: to shape, twist, add or omit, dramatize as I saw fit. Flying back now, I remember, I felt pregnant with that memory. Felt pregnant with the life I could eventually give to that memory. Yes, yes, at last, I thought, pregnant with that very life that, until now, had so thoroughly escaped me.

Before landing on Long Island Sound, I remember, I de-

stroyed a long letter that Giacòbbe Lampronti had written to
Molly Lamanna, and asked me to deliver. I read it through
twice, maybe three times, then tore it into so many little bits.
No, Molly's memory, her lost past, was my property now,
and no one else's. I could see no good reason for including
Lampronti in what, after all, was a thoroughly private affair.

From La Guardia, I telephoned Sidney. I asked him to meet
my connecting flight at Glendale, the next morning. Dearest
Sidney, he was there, of course, bright and early, holding a
vast armful of white roses. Yes, yes, I told him, I'd had a
splendid trip. Yes, I'd accomplished everything, absolutely
everything I'd hoped to. No, I wouldn't be returning to our
house, but yes, we could see one another whenever he
wished. Yes, whenever, I reassured him, taking the white
roses into the crook of my arm. For dinners, I suggested, or
Studio receptions; even for weekends, if he so desired. We
could take the coast road northward for weekends like we used
to, I proposed. Yes, yes, that would be so lovely, Sidney
responded. So lovely. But now, was there anything I needed?
he asked. Anything whatsoever he could do for me? Simply
name it, he suggested. Yes, yes, there *is* something, in fact,
I answered. Anything, he offered. It's a question of a new
scenario, I explained. One that I'd very much like to see pro-
duced. Actually, it's rather vital, Sidney, no matter what the
costs, do you understand? Consider it done, he said, leading
me out to his black limousine that awaited us under the high
southern Californian sun. Consider it done, he repeated, as
the chauffeur opened the back door, and, as he did, the sun
swung free of its reflections, emblazoned — but only momentarily — on the door's slick, simonized surface.

On the drive out to Santa Monica and the ocean, now, I
asked Sidney whether Molly Lamanna was still under contract
to the Studio. And, if she were, would she be available —

say — in a month or two to star in the screenplay I was preparing. "She'd be so very perfect for the part," I explained.

"She's yours," Sidney replied without a moment's hesitation.
"She's entirely yours," he said with all the autocracy of those
who determine not only other people's careers, but virtually
their existences, as well. "Whenever you need her," he said.
"Simply give us a few weeks' notice and we can arrange whatever you wish. For that matter," Sidney added, "she's yours,
already. Consider Molly Lamanna already yours."

"Triumphant," indeed, was the only word adequate. Molly
would swell now with each day, each page of completed typescript, each overt revelation of her otherwise obliterated past.
Mine, she was mine now, as I reconstituted that past, and
with each scene, each "set," brought her — obscure, vaporous, still thoroughly enveloped — toward a gradual realiza-
tion. Yes, brought Milly to Molly, delivered her past onto the
empty, attendant table of the present.

It took me no more than five weeks to complete the prescribed, hundred-and-twenty-page typescript. It included
everything: everything I'd learned of Molly Lamanna's past
life. There was Lea and Amedeo, the three of them in their
chamois jackets, scarves flowing as they took flight over Antibes harbor. Yes, and of course the seaplane itself, the "Flamingo," so graceful on its long, slender pontoons, its twin
wings — with each take-off — trembling like laurel leaves in
a thin wind. Yes, the seaplane, clearly the symbol of their
impossible evasion, their mythic transcendence. For hadn't
they attempted to rise out of all contingency, all history, and
touch — at those altitudes — the face of the spirit itself?
Then there was Milly pregnant, Milly enshrined, Milly au-
reoled and sheathed in so many rose petals. Wouldn't all of
this awaken Molly to her own past? Wouldn't she realize, at
some precise moment, that the role she'd been given to enact

wasn't a fiction, wasn't a fiction at all, but — episode after episode — that of her very own personal history? That she was playing, in fact, herself?

And if none of the above awakened her to her own eclipsed existence, what about the flashback in which, as a tiny child, she witnesses her own mother's drowning? Or, twenty-three years later, when she learns of the death of her own baby in the shelling of Madrid, the same shelling that would take the lives of her brother-and-sister lovers? She'd awaken to her own past in acting it out, and — as she did — grow increasingly grateful, unendingly grateful, to the one who, quite literally, had delivered her. Of that, I was certain.

On the very morning I'd completed my screenplay, I made two telephone calls, each in its own way of the highest significance. I called Sidney first. I was, I remember, perfectly aglow.

"Have you given it a title yet?" he asked.

"Yes, yes, I have," I told him. "I'm naming it, in fact, after a certain color. But one that seems to escape any definition whatsoever. That escapes the spectrum itself, it's so indefinable. You might say it's a somewhat cold, metallic shade of cerulean blue. But it's not quite that, either. It's more like the color of air itself, if one could only name it. It's the color of what the ancients called 'ether' and *Vogue*, quite recently, in launching a new set of fashionable tones for the season, labeled 'Venus blue.' Yes, *Venus Blue*, that's the title I'm giving to my screenplay. That I'm giving to my film."

The second telephone call I made that morning was of a totally different nature. To make the call, I'd even changed clothes. I'd gotten into a loose, heavily pleated pair of white slacks and a blouse in burnished gold. I'd placed a fat glass ashtray, I remember, on the coffee table alongside me, and must have been wreathed in a gauze of gray, iridescent smoke as I dialed.

"That's very kind of you to think of me," a voice responded on the opposite end of the line. The voice itself was small, timid, almost childlike. "Very kind indeed," it repeated.

"The role is a good one," I assured her. "It's dramatic, moving, mysterious. It's perfectly fit for a young actress such as yourself."

"That's very thoughtful," she said with disarming simplicity.

"I'd like to see you, and discuss some of the finer points in the screenplay. Show you some of the things to look out for in a first reading."

"Whenever you wish, Mrs. Rappaport."

"You remember me, then, don't you?" I ventured.

"Why, of course I do. We met twice, I believe. Once at the Sherry Netherland Hotel in New York, it must have been about a year ago, and then, a second time, at some reception in Hollywood. That couldn't have been more than a few months ago, if I remember correctly."

I was stunned by her perfect recall; I, who'd always assumed that she was oblivious to the presence of virtually anybody about her.

"I remember your hair best of all, Mrs. Rappaport," she continued. "I remember your sleek hair, cut like a boy's, and your green eyes. I've always thought you might well be the most beautiful woman in Hollywood," she said.

Stunned, I said nothing.

"I've always regretted that time that you offered me a beautiful little beaded bag. Do you remember? It was in New York, yes, nearly a year ago. I was so rude in refusing it, I recall. So dreadfully rude."

We agreed to meet at noon the next day. "Yes, noon would be fine," Molly Lamanna said. "I probably won't be back until around ten. That will give me just enough time to freshen up." There was no doubt in my mind as to what she'd be doing that coming night, what altitudes she'd be playing at, and why she wouldn't "be back until around ten" the next morning.

After our conversation, I remember, I went walking along the beach. Molly's voice was still ringing within me, constituting, as I walked, an octave of its own. Of all the voices about me — the voice of the sea itself, its surf pounding hard in flat, impacted bursts of foam, along with that of the bathers shouting, tall on their toes in the rushing backwash — hers, Molly's, for all its smallness, delicacy, remoteness, resounded the deepest. How simple it was, how unaffected, how unexpectedly good. I, who'd chased this creature — this creature's lost memory — halfway across the surface of the earth for whatever threads, echoes, relics I might possibly gather, had simply picked up the telephone and called her. Nothing could have been easier, more obvious. Nor, I'd add, more profoundly enthralling.

That night, I scarcely slept. The mere anticipation of our meeting at noon the next day kept me turning, over and over, pressing — if such a thing were possible — my body against that voice, those words, that breath I could only imagine enveloped, either side, by a vast, unmanageable mane of irresolute curls. Oh, but if a voice could be pressed, press it I did, and throughout the night. Held it for the sake of its least whisper, its littlest word. For the warmth of its most imperceptible sigh. Yes, held it — that voice — to its very marrow.

Molly Lamanna had moved, fairly recently, into a lovely, Spanish-style apartment house called "The Andalusia." I was

well acquainted with that residence, with its gracious walk-
ways and courtyards, its blue ceramic, Moorish-style fountain
and its sets of brief, arbored staircases that vanished, labyrinthian, into so many invisible loggias, overhead. Yes, I knew
"The Andalusia" from the time Sidney and I used to visit
Myrna Loy in her apartment there, her rooms hung with so
many heavy, colorfully draped bird cages. It was easily one
of the most charming apartment houses in all Hollywood. In
fact, the next day, at almost noon, at nearly the appointed
time, that is, for my meeting with Molly Lamanna, I'd prac-
tically reached "The Andalusia," once again. I'd just come
down the steep incline on Sunset Boulevard, and was turning
into Havenhurst Drive no more than three blocks now from
that lovely residence, when it happened. When I heard it. I'd
been listening to the Dorsey Brothers, on my car radio, if I
remember correctly, when the program was interrupted for a
"special news flash." We had become accustomed to these sudden news flashes as the war intensified in Europe, and the
Japanese army spread, tentacular, across the Chinese main-
land. We'd even grown, I must admit, a bit blasé about these
incessant interruptions. Yes, tragedy now — at least on our
airwaves — had become quotidian.

So I was scarcely listening to the newscaster when he announced that an airplane, "piloted by that promising young
film actress, Miss Molly Lamanna, disappeared at sea sometime toward dawn, this very morning. The beautiful young
star," he continued, "sent out a distress signal just before vanishing approximately forty miles west-southwest of Catalina
Island. All radio contact has subsequently been lost with Miss
Lamanna's seaplane, a converted Curtiss R_3C racer. Several
hours after dawn, however, a Coast Guard search party located a pair of floating yellow pontoons. Everything indi-
cates," the reporter went on, "that these pontoons, both by

their color and their fabrication, belong to the missing aircraft. One can only fear the worst," he concluded, and then enumerated those very few films in which Molly Lamanna had starred.

I scarcely remember what happened after. I was numb, dumbfounded. It wasn't pain I experienced so much as a sudden but profound exhaustion, an ennui that's nothing more than the by-product of pain, its gray waste. I'd become as if anesthetized. I couldn't weep, I remember. I couldn't even bring myself to utter the first utterances of grief. I was somewhere beyond it, beyond bereavement itself. I could do nothing, in fact, all afternoon, but drive. Yes, drive. I kept driving, I recall, in no particular direction. To the contrary, I kept turning and turning, describing — in a dull, automatized way — a set of interlocking, overlapping squares throughout a fair section of West Hollywood. Somewhere at the very center of all those interlocking, overlapping squares lay — like an ultimate taboo, like some forbidden city — "The Andalusia" apartment house itself. I never more than approached it. I kept turning and turning, keeping it at a constant distance, drawn and — at the same time — terrified, repelled, not so much by the building itself as by that abrupt, profound, irreparable vacancy within it. By that bed, by those tables and chairs, by the now unwavering mirrors of those very rooms in which our rendezvous had just — eternally — been annulled.

At some point, I remember, there'd been a second news flash. An announcer declared that all hope of finding Molly Lamanna had been abandoned, and that the Coast Guard had subsequently called off its search. I went on driving, I recall, tracing at right angles, at never more than eleven, twelve blocks' distance, the peripheries of that void, of that sudden sepulcher. Curiously enough, it wasn't until twilight, when —

out of sheer exhaustion — I finally took Santa Monica Boulevard and headed home, that I burst into tears. Yes, I was driving on a straight line now, and could let it happen. Could let everything happen, since nothing any longer mattered. I can still recall, crossing Centinela Avenue, how my tears literally magnified the ocean that lay now, with all its sails and tiny, tufted whitecaps, before me, as traffic light after traffic light I returned to the very edge of that very basin of unbroken water in which Molly had just, that very morning, vanished. I was back, and she was gone.

There's little left, now, to add. There's nothing, certainly, of any consequence. About a week after Molly's death, if I remember correctly, I burned *Venus Blue*. I burned all three copies of the screenplay along with the original. Only Molly could play Milly, and now that she was gone, there'd be no substitutes. Of that, I was totally certain. If she'd lived, though, who knows? Would this role have restored her memory, her past? Would she have become, as they say, "entire"? Become, that is, like the rest of us? Would she, as I'd hoped, have grown dependent? Beholden for everything that I'd done? For giving birth, all afresh, to that life she'd lost? Oh, would she? Would she, bit by bit, have become, even surreptitiously, mine? Even unwittingly, unconsciously, yes, even unknown to herself, my beloved?

Oh, so many questions, tossed into the empty air. For Molly escaped us all. Even more, she escaped herself. Hadn't she vanished only hours before I would have presented her — intact — with an accounting of her entire obfuscated existence? But no. Molly always preceded herself. Through so many successive veils of amnesia, and finally through that heavier fabric — that deep, leaded curtain of death itself — she flew, kept flying into and past anything that might, in any way, define her. She was, and remains, utterly unqualifiable. She seems to slip, each time, through logic, language, through all the systems we've ever invented for the simple purpose of determining, with increasing rigor, our arbitrary realities. That I might reduce her, as Sidney once suggested, to a phrase, to "a single, perfectly observant, penetrating remark," was, and remains, now, utterly factitious. Molly's forever escaped.

I might add, at this point, that several months later, a speculator in Hollywood curios (a specialist, actually, in bizarre memorabilia) purchased one of the two pontoons that the Coast Guard had managed to salvage from Molly's vanished aircraft. The specialist had the panels of the pontoon welded apart and then machine-stamped into so many little badges, tokens, stickpins. Apparently, yellow hearts, yellow stars, even little yellow seaplanes, were punched out of the pontoon's already rusting flanks. They sold for outrageous sums to those who'd chase their idols, if they could, well beyond the bounds of the prescribed. A new cult, clearly enough, had emerged.

As for myself, I've said enough, I feel. I'd excuse myself, once again, to any eventual reader for the summary treatment I've given to Molly Lamanna's last months. How quickly they passed, and how slow, heavy, insufferable everything since has become. The journal ends, in a sense, having scarcely begun. How little, finally, I've said in these pages. How pitifully little. Oh, so much verbiage, so much impacted language, such densities for the sake of circumscribing a single exquisite escapee. For the sake of one, weightlessly ascendant soul. Molly, be well, my beloved. The thing you cherished most in this terrifying world of ours was — as you put it — "exits." Now you've found yours. Now you'll no longer need to return, each dawn, caught once again, by sheer gravity, into that network of fact, circumstance, inflexible definition. Now you're the air's, the air's currents. Now you're utterly your own.

Go, go, my Molly. And someday may I — *Deo volente* — go with you.

PART FIVE
(Stefan Hollander, 1989)

THAT, THEN, IS THE END. Or nearly. I'd finished reading Millicent Rappaport's journal at about nine in the morning, my head propped high, and my windows, at the Shangri-La, opened wide to the swish of palms and the distant, scarcely audible roll of a slow, insistent surf. After dressing, I slipped that single existent copy of the journal into a Jiffy bag and, as promised, mailed it registered, return-receipt-requested, to Mr. Luis deSaumerez at Consuelo Innes's address in San Pedro. I now felt, as I've mentioned, that my "mission" was accomplished. That I'd done what Millicent would have wished me to, and that my tiny responsibility in that near-mythical world of hers was, once and for all, discharged.

During the next few months, I must admit, my interest in Molly Lamanna and, by extension, Millicent Rappaport, gradually dwindled. Collectors are notoriously fickle fellows and I, certainly, am no exception. I had already been collecting whatever touched upon Molly's life and work for over a year now (and yes, I'd even managed to purchase one of those yellow stars that had been stamped out of the rusting salvage from Molly's last, tragic flight). But a collector's heart is a roaming one and, after a certain time, I'd begun to find Molly too abstract for my own particular tastes. Yes, too abstract, too removed, too unconsummated. Collectors, after a while, always want something "more," or something "less," or simply something "altogether different." There's a restlessness in collecting that's not unlike that of explorers, or investors, or of those that move, year in, year out, from one lover to the next in a continuous state of never-quite-satisfied expectation.

My new "lover" (to extend, or overextend, my metaphor somewhat) had become Deco period silverware, and most especially that of that great French silversmith, Jean Puiforcat. Gradually, and then — in a single moment — massively, I'd simply switched allegiances. Changed obsessions. I'd let my imagination, once again, be invaded by a new object, or set of objects, and had eliminated all others from any consideration whatsoever. Once again, I was, as they say, "captivated."

In fact, I'd been in Los Angeles (yes, Los Angeles, once again) bidding on a silver soup tureen with jade and glass fixtures, crafted by Puiforcat, when it happened. It was my secretary who telephoned from Tucson, telling me that my house had just been broken into. I scarcely reacted, as I recall. All my thoughts were already fixed — fixated — on that magnificent tureen with its matching ladle and underlying tray. I was bidding on it, in fact, no more than half an hour after my secretary's call. I bid very high. If I was outbidded, it wasn't from lack of resolve but simply that of resources. The "big boys" went higher.

So I returned to Tucson empty-handed and, I must admit, empty-hearted as well. I'd not only lost the prized object I'd dwelt on in idle moments over the past month, I'd been, in the meanwhile, burgled. I was pleasantly surprised, however, upon arriving home. Only a single windowpane had been broken (this, in itself, had set off the burglar alarm, which had functioned perfectly), and the rest of my house appeared totally intact. On first inspection, nothing, it seemed, had been touched; nothing taken. I was asked, however, by the sheriff's deputy to visit the substation just off Ina Road, and file, in due form, an accusation against the poor vagabond whom they'd arrested. He'd been nabbed just as he'd left my residence. After being searched, a single, insignificant piece of stolen property — a mirror — was found in his possession.

The deputy was puzzled. The vagabond might have chosen any number of costlier items scattered throughout the house. There were cameras and a considerable amount of video equipment to choose from, not to mention the keys to my second BMW, parked in the *ramada* alongside. There was even quite a bit of cash I'd left lying carelessly about. He wasn't interested, it would seem, in any of it. Instead, he must have rummaged — but in a concentrated, attentive way — throughout my entire collection of Molly Lamanna memorabilia. He vandalized nothing. To the contrary, he seems to have handled everything he touched with great care, even delicacy, until he came upon what he'd quite obviously been seeking. It was this that he took: that handcrafted, heart-shaped mirror into which, heavy-haired, gray-eyed, Molly Lamanna had once gazed in the single most memorable scene from her second feature movie. I'd bought it over a year ago from a dealer in Detroit, and — as I've already described — had it authenticated by Jasper May himself. Yes, the mirror, curiously enough, was the only bit of property that this curious tramp, this street person, had stolen, or attempted to. For, in the process, he'd set off the burglar alarm and, within minutes, three squad cars had surrounded my house. He hadn't had much of a chance, the poor fool.

The deputy handed me the mirror. "Would you be good enough to identify this? Is this your property, Dr. Hollander?"

"It is."

"Would you kindly sign this paper, then, certifying that

this particular object is yours, and that you'd be prepared to testify to such, at the appropriate time?"

As I was about to sign, three police sergeants, all Chicanos, burst into the small office, laughing. They were imitating — with great hilarity — a Spanish accent: one, that is, as spoken by a native-born Spaniard.

"Hey," the first one said, barely containing himself, "move your ath . . ."

"Thcrew you," the second responded.

"Thcrew me," the third one threatened, "and you'll find your ath in the thquad car." The three of them were laughing so loud, their mouths fully ajar, that I could distinctly detect — across the width of the room — the smell of beer, burnt onions, "red-hot" tamales.

"It's that fellow that broke into your property, Dr. Hollander," the deputy explained. "It's him that they're imitating, or trying to. He's a genuine Castilian Spaniard, or at least sounds that way to our own Mexican Americans." The deputy could scarcely suppress a small, somewhat officious smile of his own.

"Is there any chance I could take a look at him?" I asked, partly out of pure curiosity, but partly, too, out of an inclination that I couldn't, at that given moment, explain even to myself.

"Sure," he said, "nothing could be easier." He led me, his keys jingling, down a short corridor, to a small, one-cell prison.

"There he is," the deputy said, somewhat proudly. "There's your man."

And there, indeed, he was. It didn't take me more than an instant, either, to recognize him. He was seated on a cot, staring at the floor, his heavy hands crossed and hanging limply, exhaustedly, down. The hands, by being crossed, seemed to be keeping one another company in a world in which nothing else, apparently, would. When the prisoner looked up (it lasted only an instant) he was unmistakable. His rich, dark brows and his wide, immensely wide, gray eyes — gray as his mother's — were tilted, like hers, slightly downward, giving them a distinctly dolorous air. And, like hers, his face formed into an absolutely perfect oval, an oval that seemed to belong more to the visage of some forgotten ideology than to that of a particular individual. Yes, it was all — all of it — unmistakable.

"Do you know him?" the deputy asked, standing alongside. I shook my head.

"Do you have any idea of his name? His identity?"

"None," I lied, looking down. "None whatsoever." I kept staring down, down at this beaten figure, this street person in a decade of street people, who'd been done out of virtually every natural attribute: his health, his well-being, his very sanity, not to mention a fortune that could once have been calculated in eight figures. Worse, worst of all, he'd even been denied the simple statute of the living. Yes, acknowledged dead, legally dead, statistically dead, he'd gone on wandering among the living, disturbing no one's sleep, certainly, if not that of Consuelo Innes, his beloved, driven herself by dire need to prostitution. No, no one's sleep. Luis deSaumerez, you disturb no one's sleep in this comfortable land of ours. In this "plenty" that's no longer yours. This "plenty" that you've been so thoroughly dispossessed of by so-called public servants.

"Luis," I whispered, just out of the deputy's hearing. "Luis," I repeated.

But he didn't stir, didn't react, probably didn't even recognize any longer his name, which wasn't, I knew, even his. Eliseo, Eliseo was his name, his true name. And that poor infant, Luis deSaumerez, that poor orphan, I now suddenly realized, had died that terrible night in the shelling of Madrid, over a half-century earlier. Molly, if she'd gone on to Spain to identify that little corpse, would have seen that it wasn't hers, wasn't hers at all. Would have recovered Eliseo, would have recovered everything that she thought she'd lost in that single horrific telegram that came to her at Juan-les-Pins. That sent her into an irreparable amnesia. Yes, one infant's name had been erroneously attached to another infant's corpse, and Eliseo, after that night's shelling, had become Luis.

But the rest? What tropism, what deep, innate homing instinct had brought him first to America, searching without searching, hoping without hoping, for that mother who'd died so many years earlier? And Millicent? How had she tracked Luis — tracked Eliseo — to that dock in Tampa, that day; Millicent the incorrigible, the inexhaustible, who went on protecting, or attempting to protect, Molly, and Molly's interests — Molly's child — so many years, now, after her death.

Luis never stopped. He kept coming. He kept tracing his mother's cross-country itinerary, slower, certainly, much slower than hers (hers took only four, five months at the most), but knowing without knowing, sensing without sensing, moving irresistibly westward like an animal locked — magnetically — to a lea line that could lead him, mile after mile, year after year, only to his own lost origin. To the vanished source of his very own existence.

And thus, the mirror. Because even now, mad, I'm certain, by even the most elementary, clinical standards, and publicly a kind of monstrosity, an embarrassment to an advanced society in which "plenty" was supposedly within everyone's reach, Luis's, or rather Eliseo's brute, tropistic, irreflexive instinct had worked. Had functioned. Yes, he'd gone for the mirror. He'd come all the way from wherever he'd been, and, having my address, sought out my house, my collection. And he'd done this for the sake of seeing, if not his mother, if not his mother's image, at least the locus, the place, the heart-shaped reflection in which, half a century earlier, his mother's face, his beautiful mother's resplendent face, had once, even for an instant, swum into its own likeness and glowed. Or, at the very least, he could touch the very glass from which, like a magnificent wraith, she'd vanished.

Yes, Luis deSaumerez, or Eliseo Lampronti, or Eliseo Pearl, had come, certainly, to the right address. Yes, this would-be messiah in the eyes of his three parents (yes, *three*), who, half a century later, would be sucking the flesh off whatever fish bones he could find in the trash cans of seafood restaurants, had broken into exactly the right house. Had come as close as he'd ever get to seeing, if not his mother, his mother's one living replica, her still miraculously surviving image: himself.

"I'm not pressing charges," I told the deputy. He turned on his heel, and stared back. He was glaring. "In fact, I'd like to see the prisoner, here, released as quickly as possible."

In the deputy's office, I made out a check for Luis de-Saumerez's bail. The deputy didn't say a word. He pushed a paper toward me for a signature and then, just as wordlessly, withdrew it. I also asked that the mirror, securely wrapped in its brown paper wrapping, be given the prisoner upon release.

"It's important," I explained. "It's terribly important." The deputy remained wordless, immutable. Still standing, legs as-traddle and hands on his hips, he watched me leave his office and head down the hallway. I could feel his eyes on my back as I opened the door and walked out.

Outside, it was gray. I'd wish for the sake of my narrative that the sky had been blue — call it "Venus blue" — but rain clouds had moved in, and rain was imminent. The pollen count, inevitably, was up, and my secretary informed me over the telephone (I called as soon as I'd left the substation) that my waiting room was full of patients. She also told me that a catalogue from the Hôtel Drouot in Paris had just arrived. It was filled, I knew, with items from a coming auction on twentieth-century *orfèvrerie*. I was more than eager, I must admit, to look through it.

As I walked to my car, I heard, somewhere over the low cloud front that had moved in with the morning, the drone of a single-engine, propeller-powered airplane, traveling westward. No, it wasn't Molly's, of course, nor the ghost of Molly's. But it dragged along with it, as small airplanes often will (at least, it seems to me), not only a sound, but a message of its own. Yes, in the wake of its passage, it appeared to be carrying, like the vaporous pennant of some invisible sky-writer, the illegible phrase of some omen or portent, some blind divination. I'd heard the airplane emerge out of nowhere. And now, still invisible, still covered by the low-lying cloud bank, it vanished into nowhere as well. I followed it, from the parking lot, until it had grown, along with its message, entirely inaudible. Until it was well past my hearing.